GODS AND BEASTS

GODS
AND
BEASTS

Denise Mina

First published in Great Britain in 2012 by Orion Books,
an imprint of The Orion Publishing Group Ltd
Orion House, 5 Upper Saint Martin's Lane
London WC2H 9EA

An Hachette UK Company

1 3 5 7 9 10 8 6 4 2

A CIP catalogue record for this book is
available from the British Library.

ISBN (Hardback) 978 1 4091 4068 9
ISBN (Export Trade Paperback) 978 1 4091 4069 6
ISBN (Ebook) 978 1 4091 4070 2

Typeset by Input Data Services Ltd, Bridgwater, Somerset

Printed and bound by CPI Group (UK) Ltd, Croydon, CR0 4YY

The Orion Publishing Group's policy is to use papers that are natural,
renewable and recyclable products and made from wood grown in sustainable
forests. The logging and manufacturing processes are expected to
conform to the environmental regulations of the country of origin.

www.orionbooks.co.uk

For, Ben and Bella, and Freddy:
Two eyes and tadda!

Acknowledgements

There are too many people to thank and not enough hours in the day, but the following spring immediately to mind: Peter Robinson, Jon Wood and Jemima Forrester, Susan Lamb and Graeme Williams, whom God preserve, of Utrecht. From the outgoing administration, Jade, Sophie and Helen, many thanks and a kindly punch to the arm.

Eagle-eyed Margery Laird, whom I met in Barnes and Noble on the Upper East Side, for keeping schtum.

Richard Halligan for giving me Kenny McLachlan's autobiography *One Great Vision* . . .

Prof. Graeme Pearson for his time, advice and giving me a set-up on a plate.

Mr Willie Mottram for getting us to the flight from Edinburgh Airport when we went to Glasgow by mistake.

To all my family and friends for support and kindness and understanding.

'Nearly all men can stand adversity,
but if you want to test a man's character, give him power'

Abraham Lincoln

The sudden sound of frantic footfalls, and a woman's high voice, 'Joseph?' The boy loosened his arms and legs, pushed himself out from Martin, listened for it again. 'Joe!'

He clambered down from Martin's lap, stood facing the curtain as if afraid to pull it back. He looked tiny and helpless and close to tears, this engine, and Martin's hand rose towards him, needing him to come back. He dropped his hand quickly, remembering what a man craving the touch of a boy would look like, part of a generation brought up to suspect themselves.

He saw the boy shiver at the curtain, shoulders by his ears. On safari Martin had seen lions, hippos, even leopards, making kills, giving chase. He saw a hippo bite a lion's leg off. Exciting, surprising, humbling even, but nothing compared to what he had seen today because today had been utterly needless.

The curtain yanked back. A red Puffa jacket, long, like a bloody sleeping bag. The small boy didn't look up but stood, frozen, staring at the woman's legs. 'I'm sorry, Mummy.'

She fell to her knees, wrapped him up in her. She was hefty, thick around the hips – though the thick quilted coat wasn't helping that – with a dark, fine face. They stayed there for a long time until the nurse coughed impatiently.

The mother looked up at Martin and her raw-eyed sorrow gave way to horror. She pulled the boy out to look at him, spat furiously into her hand and rubbed at his face with her spittle. Martin looked at the back of his arm: he was covered in dried bloody freckles.

Smearing the blood into the boy's hair, she spat again, weeping and spitting. The nurse handed her a wet wipe. She scrubbed hard, shoving his head back on his neck and his eyes rolled in ecstasy at her touch.

She stood up. Her sorrowful face was familiar to Martin and he realised then that the dead grandfather was her father, and that she had loved him very much.

The curtain fell shut and they were gone and Martin was left alone and cold and numb.

People spoke to one another out of sight. Telephones rang. Time ground past around him.

A young medic came to see him. She shone a pen torch into his eyes, looked in his ears, asked him if he had been hit on the head. He hadn't. He was in shock, she told him. She left.

A nurse came with a pill and he took it. It felt a little like his stepmother's Xanax, but fast. After a while it made everything feel softer. It was nice.

A different nurse appeared, cupped his elbow, prompting him to stand up. Tenderly, watching Martin's feet and making encouraging noises, she led him down the corridor, around a corner and into a small bright room with white walls and a dead computer on a desk.

The blonde policewoman was there with a man. They stood up and introduced themselves: DS Morrow and DC Harris. They shook his hand.

They all sat down.

The policeman brought out a clipboard with photocopied sheets of questions. He was holding onto his bag as well as the board, though, and when he sat down the board slipped from his hand, sliding towards the floor. He was unduly alarmed, his fingertips scrabbled to catch it and he grabbed at the paper, ripping the blank top sheet out from the metal clip.

They all watched the board drop to floor, bounce on the corner and land face up: a filled out form below: Joseph Lyons, 9 Lallans— the policeman's hand fell over the address. He picked it up, pulled out the ripped top of the blank sheet. His lips were bloodless with embarrassment. Martin didn't understand why it was such a big deal.

The woman took charge. She asked Martin to tell her what happened in the post office in the Great Western Road. Why did he go in there?

He was sending gifts home for the holidays.

Martin should have gone home by now but he couldn't face it. He used the excuse of fictitious exams and a fictitious local girlfriend. He was going to her fictitious parents for Christmas lunch. They'd split up in January. His parents would never know he'd made her up.

He didn't tell the cops any of that, just that he was Martin Pavel, twenty-one years old, a geology student at Glasgow University. He had been in the post office with two parcels to send home for Christmas.

'Where is home?'

San Francisco.

She looked sceptical. 'In *America*?'

California.

'Did you grow up here, in Scotland?'

Martin shook his head.

'But you have a Scottish accent.'

Aye.

She looked angry about that. 'Where *are* you from?'

Here. As much as anywhere.

'But you didn't grow up here and your family aren't here ...'

The questions were too complicated, the answers too wordy and all he could think was he wanted the gunman to come here with his pistol and blow them away. He shook his head at the weight of it and the woman leaned forward, speaking softly to comfort him, when Martin knew he didn't deserve it.

'Look, never mind. Forget that just now. In the post office, before, who else was there?'

The grandfather was right in front of him, holding hands with the boy.

The man had white hair, a square face like the mother who came for the boy. He wore a red Berghaus jacket with black shoulders and a red scarf. He was tan, like a Sicilian peasant, and his clothes were as well pressed as a Parisian's, yet he spoke with a Glasgow accent.

Martin arrived at the back of the queue. He turned off his music and the boy smiled up at the grandfather and said, 'Sausage rolls?' and the grandfather nodded seriously and said, 'Of *course*, sausage rolls.'

Martin got stuck in that memory. Of course. *Of course*, sausage rolls. Internal goods, taking the matter of the sausage rolls very seriously.

'Did the old man seem nervous?'

No, because nervousness would denote uncertainty. He had none of that. He had given the boy to Martin with certainty, served the chaos, the gun-wielding barbarian with a firm, dignified clarity. Martin wished it had been him who'd done it and he knew it was wrong to feel that way. He started to cry.

'Take your time,' said the woman, trying to hurry him.

He was calm, the grandfather. Very calm. *Of course*, sausage rolls. The boy smiled and turned away, looking over at a 'Happy Christmas' banner that had slipped its moorings on one side and was flapping languidly in the breeze from a fan heater.

Beyond them, a big queue snaked through the retractable ribbon barrier to the counters. Five, maybe six people: a tall guy in expensive cycling gear, very fit, orange cycling bag and a black peaked helmet. Jumpy, impatient, watching the clock. Another man beyond him maybe, and a woman towards the front. Martin was only vaguely aware of the queue because he began playing with his phone. Checking emails, deleting junk. A woman arrived, stood behind him. He didn't see her but he knew her hair was yellow. He had watched it turn pink in the bloody mist.

There were three serving counters open in the post office, out of a possible four. Martin was often in there because it was on the way to the library, and he had observed the family that ran it. The man he took to be the father was always working: an Asian man in his fifties, a salting of the hair at his temples, polite and industrious; the post office was open on Sundays too. The daughter had a feminised version of her father's face, thinner chin, long black hair and glittery barrettes. She was too old for barrettes.

A younger man, a cousin maybe, he didn't look like the father and daughter but they behaved like family members, stood close to each other and conversed in single word asides.

'When did you become aware of the gunman?'

Martin sat up straight as he remembered a figure in his peripheral vision stepping in through the post office door. Black clothes, a heavy canvas bag. It stepped sideways, behind the free-standing shelves of stationery just inside the door; it slid behind displays of birthday cards, crappy fridge magnets, teddy bears with tartan sashes, cheap shit.

Martin checked his phone again.

The figure stepped back out. And the bag was no longer heavy. The man walked to the front, striding straight past the queue. Cutting the queue got everyone's attention, even before they noticed his pale grey mask, long before they noticed the curl of the AK-47 clip peeking past his thigh.

'In his right hand or left hand?'

He was holding it in his right hand, down by his right leg, away from the queue. It was a pistol.

'You said an AK-47 . . .'

Yeah, but an AK-47 pistol.

'What's the difference, for someone who doesn't know much about guns?'

Pistol: shorter barrel, of course.

He wore a tightly fitted hunter's hood that covered his mouth and neck and head but not his eyes.

'With two holes for the eyes?'

No. It had one continuous hole. An oval. It was a hunter's hood. The cops didn't understand so Martin had to explain: it was made of fitted felt not knitted wool, tailored to fit around the chin and mouth, stop the prey smelling the hunter's breath. Martin had seen them when he was hunting in Canada.

The gunman walked to the front of the queue. The balaclava looked comfortable. And the eyes inside looked comfortable. That's what really struck Martin: this man was in control of his entire world but he wasn't anxious or doubting or searching for guidance. He wasn't attending a psychiatrist and weeping like a girl. He was comfortable.

'What do you mean by comfortable?'

Martin remembered those eyes. The man wasn't anxious. Not at all. The eyes were shining as he lifted the gun to his face. Deep blue eyes framed with white lashes.

The cyclist screamed. No one looked at him. They were hypnotised by the gunman. He raised his chin so his lips came to the brim of the eye hole and shouted, 'GET DOWN ON THE FUCKING GROUND!'

'What did he sound like?'

Greenock–Ayr-ish accent, lower working class. Spent a bit of time in Birmingham, England, maybe.

'Ayr-ish?'

Wide, open-mouthed vowels from the West Coast and the mellifluous lilt of a Birmingham accent. Also, he had a kind of roughness to his voice, as if he'd smoked a lot the night before, as if he'd hurt his throat shouting over music at a night club.

'What happened then?'

Everyone got down on the floor. They scrabbled to the ground as if it was a race. They lay as flat as they could, noses pressed to the dirty wet floor, all of them. Except the grandfather. He stayed on his feet.

'How do you know that?'

Martin was nose down on the floor when he saw the boy next to him, curled up walnut-tight, knees under his chest, fists over his mouth. The grandfather had shifted two steps away, so it looked as if the boy was with Martin.

He heard the grandfather mutter, 'You?' like a question.

The gunman breathed, '*You.*'

A pause. The grandfather waited for the gunman to turn away and then he whispered to Martin, '*He's yours.*'

Thinking back, Martin didn't know if the grandfather was talking to him or the boy but, suddenly, he was part of their story.

'Who was part of what story?'

Martin, he was part of their story.

'Do you mean you felt detached before?'

No, but he had obligations to them because he was part of their story now. The policewoman looked a blank. *Story*, he explained, we are in a story now. She looked sceptical.

'No, we're not. This is real.'

He opened his mouth and shut it again. It was too much to explain, being Scottish from California, barbarians and being in a story. She frowned, annoyed at him. 'He said "he's yours" and what then?'

The old man stood, facing the gunman, fists tight at his side. Martin could only see up to his chest.

'Did you know the grandfather?'

Martin said he didn't.

'Are you sure?'

Martin thought about it, his life before that moment. Grey streaks of time, lawyers, walks, heat and hills, palm trees, rats, and oranges and arguments. And then he remembered the grandfather, catching his eye in the queue, their eyes meeting, click, a blink, click, second look. Nothing. No hint of recognition.

Martin was sure he didn't know him. He would have remembered the man. He was very tan and neat but very Scottish and Martin would have asked him why.

'He said "he's yours" and then?'

And then quiet, a deep, horrible quiet, until the gunman spoke again: 'Fucking get out here, then.'

'He said it to the grandfather?'

Yeah.

'What did he mean by that?'

He meant come out here. He meant stand by me, feel the glorious heat of me. He meant come here and help me and then I'll kill you.

'And what did the old man do?'

Martin told them what he had seen: *fucking get out here*. The old man's loafer heels lifted off the ground in response, as if he was saluting: a soldier chosen for a glorious mission. The heels of the leather loafers were metal-tipped for long wear, made a loud tick-tack when they hit the floor.

One loafer stepped high, across the cyclist who was sobbing into the ground, over the people and the bags sprawled on the floor. Martin's eyes followed the feet until they stood a foot away from the black trainers at the counter. The gunman handed the canvas bag to the grandfather and the old man held it open for him.

'He willingly helped the guy?'

Martin didn't answer. Of course he helped him. She hadn't been there. Martin wouldn't have believed it if he hadn't witnessed it himself.

'Where were you then?'

The question flicked him back to the sound of the boy panting face down into the wet smears from the street. For no reason, Martin lifted his arm over the kid's back and pulled him over and in, until their foreheads were pressed tight together. The boy looked at him with emotionless brown eyes. Martin looked back and they blinked at each other, anchored, hearing the world beyond but seeing nothing. Martin was an only child and a lonely child. Lying on the dusty floor, looking at the boy, he had never felt closer to anyone. The gunman had done that for them.

Behind them, in a far-off place, the gunman ordered the counter staff to get out here, not you, you stay. People moved. Doors opened. Doors shut. The world was reordered at his command.

A voice behind the counter, muffled by the thickened safety glass.

'Move it,' said the gunman.

And then he must have hit the glass because thunder shook the room and everyone on the floor jerked with fright.

'Don't fucking bother, it's *still* cut off.'

Martin was sure about the wording. The policewoman asked him to repeat it and he did – *it's still cut off*. The man got angry about it. 'Aye, *still*, don't try and fucking trick me!' He got angrier and angrier and then he shouted, 'You! Get over there and smack her.'

A pause.

Then the sound of the old man's feet tick-tacking down the shop. The weight in the feet shifted, soles grinding against the dirty floor, and the heavy sound of a slap followed by a woman's shocked yelp. He was making them attack each other and Martin felt his enjoyment of that.

The boy's eyes shut, just once, a slow blink, taking ownership of his grandfather's hand.

'BRING IT OUT.' Doors open, feet moving. The drag of a bag over the gritty floor.

Then both sets of feet, clip-clop loafers, squelchy soles on the robber's sneakers, moved toward the exit. Martin's breath quickened at the memory and what was coming next.

The door clicked open, a shrieking hinge, and the cold draught from the street hurtled across the floor, picking up dust and flinging it in his hair. He blinked hard to break eye contact with the boy, and rolled his head to the door to see if they had gone.

But they were still inside, quite far away down the shop now and Martin could see them clearly. Between them and him, the blonde woman lay on her stomach, face turned to Martin, tears seeping through her tightly shut eyes.

The two men faced each other in front of the open door.

'How tall was the gunman compared with the grandfather?'

He was tall, maybe six foot one or two. He was wearing a black sweatshirt with no logo on it and dark jeans and black trainers. Cheap, battered clothes, but his pose was elegant, like a rakish cowboy. The policewoman asked him to explain and Martin stood up to show her: the gunman stood with his pelvis forward, the butt of the gun resting on his right hip bone, barrel pointing skyward, holding it with one hand. Martin stood and looked up at the wall in the nondescript room, enjoying mimicking him, felt the wave of his spine and knew how relaxed and certain he would need to be to stand like this. He looked up to where the old man would have been and felt, for just a sliver of time, that he could see him there. Then she spoke again and spoiled it:

'Why was he standing like that?'

Martin sat back down. He gathered himself, lost the dumb-assed grin. It's the weight, he explained. In those guns all the weight is at the front so you tip them when you hold them one-handed. Martin stopped. He'd gotten carried away and his accent was sliding across the Atlantic, swooshing up over towering waves, skimming the black-blue valleys, homing to nowhere. He stopped and was lost.

The woman prompted him. 'Who had the bag? Who had the bag at this point?'

The gunman had it in his other hand, he had the holdall with whatever they had taken. It didn't look heavy or especially full. It was a pittance, really. Martin didn't think it was about the money.

The grandfather was holding the door open.

Martin felt suddenly exhausted as he remembered the old man's stance: upright, shoulders back, as dignified as an Upper East Side doorman with fifty years' service. But his chin was bobbing on his chest because he was crying. Martin felt that he knew what was going to happen and he just stood there, crying.

The barrel of the pistol lowered to point at his chest.

The sound of the first shot hit Martin's ear and fire flashed in the barrel. He was shocked by how loud it was. He had never heard a gun go off without ear protectors. Too loud to hear, not a bang but a painfully loud *phut* slapping his inner ear.

Fire in the chamber, and *phut phut phutphutphut phutphutphut-phut*, ten rounds, cartridges flying everywhere, glittering brass cartwheeling joyfully through the air.

Martin saw exit wound after exit wound exploding out of the old man's back, red mist puffing out of him, landing on cards and turning the sobbing blonde's hair pretty princess pink.

Suddenly, the glass wall onto the street shattered milky white. Then quiet.

The old man's jaw dropped open. His body listed to the side, shoulders twisting to face the door, as if he was showing the people in the shop the cratered flesh of his back. Then it sort of slid, the torso, slid off the legs towards the door and the legs and pelvis fell forwards.

Martin lost his breath at the memory but a tiny hand, like a fleshy spider, flattened on his cheek: the boy had reached through the space under his neck. It pulled Martin's face back around, ordering him to look. *I am still here. Now we are in a story together.*

Grateful, Martin was met by the boy's brown eyes and they stayed there.

The saviour hand stayed on his cheek for a long time, until the police arrived and screamed at them to get up.

2

It was already dark. DC Tamsin Leonard and DC Wilder were driving back into the city when they got the call: an Audi G7, the drug dealers' last-season car of choice, was last seen on camera 217, passing junction 2 of the M77. It was wanted in connection with an ongoing investigation. They were to stop it and check the driver's phone for a call received at 16.53 and take a note of the number.

It was an errand and it fell to them because everyone else had just left for an armed robbery in a post office. Errands often fell to them.

Wilder hung up and glared at Leonard, raising an indignant hand at the traffic in front of them as if she was responsible for the rush hour. They'd have to navigate the nose-to-tail north-bound carriageway before they even got onto the southbound road, but that wasn't why Wilder was pissed off. Wilder was just always pissed off.

They were often paired together, Wilder and Leonard. Both were marginalised from the other DCs on their shift; Wilder because he was charmless, Leonard because she was female, English, older, and watched cricket, not football. She wasn't bothered, she was happy on the margins, but it had started to matter: redundancies were coming and being on the edge of the pack made them both vulnerable. They resented being paired now, as if the unpopularity of the other amplified their own failings. Both felt they were marked for the bullet.

Leonard got stuck on the Kinning Park slip road and Wilder tossed her a tut.

She ignored it. 'D'you think I should put the lights on?' She was actually looking for guidance, not just kissing up to him.

'What do you *think?*'

Rather than give him the fight he was after, Leonard turned on the lights and siren. It was a mistake. Startled out of their commuter trance, the cars in front slowed down, nudging to the side, trying get out of the way.

Radiating opprobrium, Wilder raised a hand at the delay. Leonard said nothing but carefully negotiated the mess of the off-ramp and eased through the roundabout to the southbound lane.

She'd be glad to get away from Wilder today. It wasn't as if she had no worries. Her wife's second round of fertility treatment had been one week ago and they were waiting to see if the embryo had implanted. It was cripplingly expensive and they had miscarried before. Against regulations, Tamsin kept her personal mobile in her pocket on silent. Whatever else she was doing in her day, part of her mind was on the skin of her right hip, dreading the tickle of bad news. She didn't talk about it at work. No one else talked about procreation or their sexuality, she didn't see why she should have to.

Wilder huffed as she got stuck behind a lorry that was awkwardly trying to exit the fast lane. She should have left the siren off.

Very gradually the traffic began to clear and they hurried up the road. As they approached the estimated position of the car Leonard turned off the sound so that she didn't give the driver a chance to leave the road before they spotted him.

They came to a long straight climb of motorway with a rear view of the entire city, and spotted the Audi straight ahead.

The big boxy car was halfway up the hill in the fast lane, taking it steady, keeping its place. The discretion of the driving was nullified by the make and size of the vehicle; it stood out like a boot in a row of flip-flops. The cars were so popular among drug dealers that some officers automatically stopped every Audi G7 they saw. This one had a custom paint job, telltale blackout windows and the optional chrome trim that marked it as top spec.

The cars between them and the Audi melted into the slow lane and Leonard pulled in behind it, flashing her lights.

He knew they were here for him. He made panicked little swerves left, small speedy jolts forwards, trying to think of a move, of a way out, but there wasn't one.

Leonard flicked her indicator, signalling to him to pull over. The cars next to them cleared a two-car space and, moving in tandem, they nudged into the slow lane. She flashed her indicator lights again, meaning for him to stop on the hard shoulder but she hadn't noticed that they had come up to a slip road and he took that instead.

Wilder panicked as the Audi pulled away. 'He's getting off—'

But Leonard saw that the Audi had slowed down, was trying to comply but didn't know where to stop. 'No, he just misunderstood, I think . . .'

The off-ramp was uphill. After the summit it dipped straight into a filter lane. The Audi took it at ten miles an hour, aware, perhaps, that he'd given an alarming impression, hoping to reverse that. Another possibility was that he wanted to seem compliant, make them drop their guard, and was driving slowly because he was reaching down for a knife, a gun, was phoning for back-up.

They couldn't even see into the back seat: the height of the Audi meant that the rear LCD lights blinded them to possible henchmen.

At the give-way lines the Audi stopped, the driver's window lowered and he leaned out just enough for Leonard to see his face in the side mirror.

He was surprisingly young, wore a pale blue beany hat and large glasses. He showed her an up-raised hand, not knowing what to do. He looked small but it was hard to get a sense of scale because the car was so big.

'Shit,' said Wilder. 'Shit, shit, shit! It's Barrowfields, they said the call came from someone in Barrowfields . . .'

Leonard began to sweat: the investigation into the Barrowfields crew started as a minor inquiry: small time dealers who were targeting inappropriately young kids. Then their sixteen-year-old informant was found sitting at a bus stop with her neck broken. Local rumour took them to the door of a fat bodybuilder called Benny Mullen. Cursory surveillance showed that Mullen ran a gang of very bad men blatantly distributing crumpled poly bags full of cocaine and heroin and guns. When they looked at him in depth they found that international agencies had been following Mullen avidly for six years. No one in the area would speak, they had stopped even answering the door to the police. A contact in the housing office told them that sixty per cent of the residents had applied for transfers. This driver had been called from that crew.

'There could be a car load of them—'

Wilder's panic made Leonard artificially calm. 'Well, we'll see . . .' She lowered her own window and gestured over the roof of the car, telling the Audi driver to pull in and stop.

The Audi did exactly as she had requested.

They were at the top of a road leading to a dead business park. Beyond a row of concrete bollards all the street lights were brand new, the roads perfect, but in place of buildings were fields of knee-deep brown grass, swaying gently in the soft evening wind. Hiroshima one year on.

The Audi's engine went off, the handbrake and hazard lights came on, shining razor-sharp through the dark.

Leonard flicked on her own hazards, the *tink tink tink* like cheap glass breaking. Wilder opened his door, triggering the yellow cabin light.

'I'll do the talking,' he warned and got out.

They weaved in front of their bonnet so that Wilder was on

the driver's side. Leonard could see his shadow at the opposite door, checking the back for an army of gunmen.

She looked in at the driver.

He was alone. He was dressed in jeans and a pale blue tracksuit top, zipped right up to his chin, the pull dangling like a pendant. He turned and smiled at her, bad teeth, thin face, hat pulled down over his eyebrows, so low that his eyelashes cupped the rim when he looked up. Not attractive, not even healthy. He had thick glasses, unfashionable glasses and a slight turn in his right eye. When he grinned at her Tamsin wanted to smile back.

Leonard indicated at him to lower the window on her side and he did it, watching her, aware of Wilder behind him, eyes flicking back.

'Could you open the back door, please, sir?' said Leonard.

He returned her smile almost gratefully and reached for the button. Leonard opened the back door and was hit by the delicious smell of new leather. The back seat was empty but she couldn't resist reaching in and touching the buttery seat.

Wilder demanded his attention, asking his name and address, jotting them down in his notebook: Hugh Boyle, 9 Abernathy Street, The Milton.

Hugh tittered at his own address, looked to Wilder to join in, but he didn't.

'Not nice,' he muttered, probably meaning the Milton but sounding as if he was reproaching Wilder for not laughing along.

Wilder left a pause as he wrote and looked up at Hugh. 'Is this your car, sir?'

'Aye.' Hugh stroked the leather steering wheel proudly and Leonard heard the powered hush of skin on skin. Boyle was not sweating, Leonard noticed. His fingers were dry.

It was an expensive car even for a drug dealer but Boyle wasn't behaving like someone hardened enough to be that far up the food chain. He was making eye contact, had made a self-deprecating joke as if he was slightly embarrassed at being pulled over. A hardened crim wouldn't care. A hardened crim would have been on the hands-free to their lawyer before they left the motorway.

Wilder tapped his notebook with his pencil. 'Were you using your phone back there, sir?'

'While I was driving?' said Hugh. 'No . . .' Genuinely baffled at the accusation, he didn't recognise it as a classic trick to get an unwarranted search of his phone. Wilder left a momentary pause for him to object, but he didn't.

'Could I see your phone, sir?'

Reluctantly, Hugh reached into his tracksuit pocket and took out a BlackBerry. He handed it over to Wilder. Wilder took it and stepped back, sliding out of Hugh Boyle's line of vision as he checked it, leaving him and Leonard alone.

Boyle smiled over at Leonard. 'Ye all right?'

She didn't smile but nodded, being respectful back.

Wilder was jotting something in his notebook: they had the number.

'Ye having a busy night?'

'Not bad,' said Leonard.

He smiled and tried again to make conversation: 'Is this you on all night, then?'

'No,' she said, and left it there. Criminal knowledge 101: Boyle didn't know the times of their shift change. Ten-year-old Glasgow vandals knew that.

Wilder stepped back to the window, handed the phone back to Boyle, thanking him briskly. 'Would you step out of the car for me please, sir?'

Stiffening suddenly, Boyle clutched the steering wheel with both hands and stared straight ahead. In profile, Leonard saw his bottom lip twitch a smile. Wilder didn't seem to notice, but Leonard had a strong feeling that something bad would happen if Boyle did get out of the car. Something very bad.

'Out of the car, sir.' Wilder pulled the door open, stepping back to make room for him.

Still Boyle stayed where he was. After a resigned sigh, he swivelled in his seat, dropping his feet to the ground. He was taller than Wilder, six foot one or two, but lanky. Leonard looked to his pockets and waistband for signs of a gun, a knife. Nothing.

Wilder directed him to walk ahead, to the squad car. Boyle took one reluctant step and then another.

Hurrying around to join them, Leonard found Wilder holding the back door open for Boyle to climb in, shutting it after him. Wilder and Leonard got into the front and shut their doors.

She hoped Wilder had a plan, other than a bit of professional bullying, because very clearly there was something going on with Hugh Boyle and she had no idea what it was.

Sitting in the driver's seat, not looking back, Wilder quizzed Hugh about the car: Where did he get it? When did he get it? What made him choose that garage? A pal recommended it, said Hugh. Which pal? Hugh couldn't remember.

Wilder continued with the meandering questions: Where had Boyle been this afternoon?

'Dunno. Kinda, out and about, know?'

'Out and about *where?*'

He shrugged. 'Seeing some pals and that. In the town.'

'Whereabouts in the town?'

Leonard watched him in the rear-view, saw him remember exactly where he had been and then change it.

'Just driving around. Looking in the shops and that.'

'Which shops?'

He didn't hesitate about the shops. 'Cruise, Boss, Baker, Lacoste . . .' He seemed to soothe himself with the recitation. 'Armani, JD Sports . . .'

Leonard asked, 'What route did you take?'

'I drove.'

'No.' Leonard turned to look at him. 'When you were walking around the shops, which shop did you start in and where did you go next?'

'Started in . . . um, Cruise?' His confusion gave way to an infectious grin.

Leonard tried not to smile back. 'And what did you look at?'

'Shoes?' He cringed then, smiling and cringing at the same time and the two of them grinned at how bad his lie was.

'Did you buy any shoes?' she smirked.

Boyle blushed. 'Um.' He examined his feet. 'Doesn't look like I did, no.'

She stopped herself smiling: it was unprofessional. 'And where did you go then?'

'Ah . . . eh.' He tried to read her face, as if he had forgotten his lines and wanted a prompt. 'Maybe to Boss?'

'*Maybe* to Boss?'

His eyebrows rose in confusion. 'Did I?'

'Why are you asking me, Hugh?'

'Don't know why I'm asking yees.' He tittered, 'Why are yous asking me?'

Wilder wrote something in his notebook. 'Where else did you go, sir?'

'Not sure,' he whispered. 'Just wandering about and that . . .' Hugh looked out of the window at the dark and his eyes rose up the steep grassy bank to the motorway, to the chain of coned headlights passing on the rim.

'You went to all those shops,' said Wilder, 'but you didn't buy anything?'

'Not really.' Suddenly afraid, Hugh lurched forwards. 'Why are ye asking me all this?'

Wilder turned his head slowly until his nose was an inch from Hugh's. '*Sit back in your seat.*'

Boyle did so but Leonard noticed that he sat back slow, controlled, calm.

Wilder wrote silently in his notebook as the rhythmic *tink tink* of the hazard lights rattled around the cabin.

Leonard turned to look at him again. She had wondered suddenly if there could be an innocent explanation: he was a spoiled boy from a good family who'd been given a big car and had moved to the Milton, but she could see that he wasn't. His nails were bitten down to the quick, his hands scarred and dry.

'Have you ever been stopped by the police before, Hugh?'

He shook his head.

'Got a trade?'

'Joiner.' His hands confirmed it.

'That's a big car for a joiner,' said Wilder, leaving it open for him to make an excuse: my dad's got a business, my uncle gave it to me, the usual, untraceable sources.

Boyle leaned forward, looking at the car boot. 'I just want out. If I fuck up they'll never trust me again.'

Abruptly, Wilder flipped his notebook shut and opened his door. 'Could you use your keys to pop the boot for me, sir?'

Unaware that Leonard was watching him in the side mirror, Boyle's mouth twitched a smile.

Wilder climbed out of the car and opened the passenger door. 'Out, sir.'

Boyle stepped out. Leonard got out too and they all three assembled at the boot of Hugh's car. The something-very-bad was about to happen, she knew it and tried to catch Wilder's eye. Her sense of panic grew as she realised that Wilder wouldn't heed a warning from her.

Wilder flicked a finger at it. 'Open it, please.'

Boyle reached forward and touched the mechanism on the boot. The door lifted slowly.

It was empty. There was nothing there.

Leonard looked at Boyle, saw a pleading expression on his face and followed his eye to a chrome handle in the floor of the boot. Wilder had seen him looking too. 'Lift that please, sir.'

Boyle reached a hand forward and froze. He dropped it to his side. All he had to do was refuse. They didn't have a warrant, had no right to look in there if he said no.

Car lights passed on the brim of the hill, the wind hissed through the long grass and for a moment no one said anything.

Leonard looked to Wilder and tipped her head towards their squad car. They had the Barrowfields phone number. Their shift was coming to an end. Wilder saw her, she knew he did, and yet he didn't move.

Suddenly, Boyle stepped forward and slipped his finger under the handle, lifting the floor panel. A big IKEA bag sat in the boot, squashed flat as a fossil, full of twenty pound notes. Grubby, crumpled, held together with red elastic bands, a tumultuous pit of greasy cash.

Boyle spoke so quietly it was hard to hear him. 'Do me a favour. I'm scared shitless of these guys. I just want out. My mum's ill, I'm all she's got. I mean, that boot's empty as far as I'm concerned . . .'

Then he slipped away, slinking guiltily to their squad car, got in and slammed the door shut, leaving them alone.

They stood shoulder to shoulder as the dark deepened around them. Wilder stared into the boot and licked the corner of his mouth. 'That's about two hundred thousand.'

'Wrong,' Leonard found herself whispering, 'wrong.'

'Yeah.' Wilder still staring and panting a little. 'Yeah, OK, it's more than that—'

'No: Wilder, *Boyle's* wrong. I feel there's something *wrong*.'

Wilder looked at her. 'We don't need him to be right. Who could he tell? Even if he does, it's his word against ours.'

'Don't know. He's smirking.'

'He's nervous.'

'Is he?'

Wilder was looking at the money. 'He wants out.'

'Look at the size of the car, Wilder. He says it's his.'

'It's Audi A3s now, G7's last year's car. He could just have been given it. They sell them on for small change to avoid proceeds of crime.'

A breeze picked up, chilling the sweat on her top lip. She followed Wilder's eye to the cash. Cars hurried blindly home on the motorway high above them.

'He needs our help. These people are trapped by this gang, you know that.'

Leonard looked at the money. She could have misread him.

'They're going to lay me off, Leonard. I've got kids and a mortgage. There's nothing else out there . . .'

3

It was ten fifteen as Kenny Gallagher looked down on the room from the speakers' table. Coarse-looking wives in sequined evening dresses, fat arms reddened on the underside, enjoying a joyless, counterfeit Christmas dinner served in a dowdy hotel banqueting hall. The retractable wall was concertinaed shut behind them because tickets hadn't sold that well. There was a time, not long ago, when he could have sold this hall out twice over. There was a time, a blink ago it seemed, when he was going all the way. But they didn't like Kenny any more. It hurt him deeply to admit it. He felt it as a pain behind his eye, as pin-stabs in his gut, as an impenetrable fog of adolescent self-pity.

Kenny Gallagher had spoken at international conventions, in front of audiences of thousands composed of everyone from business leaders to trades unionists, and he had commanded their fond attention. Wives asked after his family, wanted their picture taken with him, husbands shook his hand. And now these, his own people, could hardly look at him over a tiny morsel of malicious gossip.

It had all been glorious once. Sixteen years ago, on a cold, bright morning, Kenny Gallagher stood at the head of a three-thousand-strong march. He remembered it in stills: a bright banner, hand painted. Himself: young, sincere, as yet unknown. A photographer walking ahead – Move in tight for me, boys, make it look busy. Back then they stood together at the brim of the hill, unified. Kenneth wasn't even important enough to carry the banner. A private-school boy, just out of university, looking for a place to belong, a management trainee who took the side of the workers.

They marched as far as Bath Street before the battle began. Flanked on either side by the graceful townhouses of wealthy Georgian sugar and tobacco traders, the front line squinted into a low sun like Soviet war heroes, defying the line of police officers ahead. They had no marching permit because they were a new union, unregistered, and it was an unpopular cause – better wages for well-paid workers – but they were young and idealistic and saw it as something else: a defiant statement of entitlement from those with nothing. The press were marshalled against their cause, ridiculing, and their old union had disowned them. But they were young enough to believe in absolutes, for the illusion of consensus to be intact.

A police officer, whom the later inquiry would find was acting on his own initiative, raised his nightstick over the head of a young man and Gallagher stepped out to defend him and took the blow full on the cheekbone. He was stunned, didn't feel the split of skin or the warm blood, but reached out to the officer. 'We just want to be heard,' he was quoted as saying, though he didn't remember saying it and it didn't sound like him. The officer saw the hand coming towards him, misunderstood and lashed out again. Kenny was photographed: bloodied, dignified, hands out in entreaty, and it changed his life.

Now he looked down at the fat diners spooning the last mouthfuls of Christmas pudding into themselves. These were the same people who used to stare at him in the street. They used to harbour small admiring smiles. Women would blush at the sight of him, ask about his dead brother, his mother, his wife. Men would ask him about bands, about golf, about cars. They wanted to claim him for their own. Not now. The hurt felt familiar, like an echo of something else.

The dinner had been organised to raise awareness and money. Gallagher didn't know anyone with the illness, but it was genetic and a disproportionate number of his constituents had it. Whenever it was mentioned in the pre-dinner speeches everyone frowned. Gallagher frowned. People nodded.

Fifty quid per seat and twenty-five went on costs. If the audience really cared they'd just hand the charity fifty quid, but they were here to network and show off at the auction. Everyone mugged sincere concern when the charity's aims were mentioned. They were all fibbing. Those nodding their heads adamantly, looking to their neighbours for confirmation, particularly so. Gallagher knew from experience that adamance and indignation were signs of a fib. But those fibs were necessary. They might hand over fifty quid once, but they'd come back for a dinner year after year. It was all about compromise.

'He's not a doctor's *son*,' was all his stepfather said when he first saw him pictured on the front page of the newspaper. In hindsight, Kenny felt as if Malcolm sensed the threat in him. Malcolm had been his father since Kenneth was three and had lost an election himself as an independent. Kenny had never lost an election because he had what Malcolm could never have: he had warmth, was trustworthy and he could see both sides, he could compromise.

That moment, when he first saw himself in the newspaper, was a more vivid memory than the blow to his cheek, or the march, or even his first election win. It was a more visceral memory than the birth of his children. He recalled it often, to keep himself going day to day, ennobling the mundane.

It was the morning after the Battle of Bath Street. Gallagher was in a café with some of the strike committee – strong tea and bacon rolls with vinegary ketchup – and someone came in with the morning papers.

'We've won.' She dropped them triumphantly on the table. She was a machinist, older, thick ankles.

Same picture in all the papers: Gallagher, his body a dynamic diagonal, and a sheet of blood from the impact blow, red red blood as if they had colourized it, dripping onto the front of his white sweatshirt. The article was about him, not the movement: 'DOCTOR'S SON MAKES PEACE WITH POLICE – "WE JUST WANT TO BE HEARD."'

She was right, the machinist, the image won them the dispute.

Gallagher remembered seeing that photo for the first time, the tang of vinegar and the sticky damp rising from his rained-on jacket, the hardness of the bench beneath him. He saw it and felt the world shift. He had done a good thing. In that café, in a fug of vinegar and damp, he felt a mantle of shame lift from him. No longer the disappointing child, no longer a burden on his grieving mother, no longer less than Malcolm.

He fingered the scar on his cheekbone. It was an old scar now, becoming less and less visible every year and the conviction born that day seemed a long way off this evening.

He looked down at the evening suit he had picked carefully with his wife, Annie. Not an evening suit, just a dark suit, with hints of an evening suit, but not a formal evening suit. Annie said he couldn't buy an evening suit, it would look as if he'd lost sight of his support. Now they were turning away from him. Annie was wrong, he should just have bought the evening suit.

Annie was sitting in the middle of the room with the other partners of those on the top table; he could see the back of her head. She was listening to the man next to her, a young man. Even Annie, she was turning to ash in his hands. He never thought that would happen.

Kenny wanted Annie before he even saw her. He was on a balcony, standing with Lizzy, his girlfriend at the time, at a reception for Donald Dewar. Together they watched the room moving around a woman who turned out to be Annie. She walked and the men's eyes trailed discreetly, the women envy-twisting after her. 'Fucking hell,' said Lizzy, 'who let her in?' Lizzy was his ex-girlfriend by the time Annie emerged from the crowd. Annie wouldn't have looked at him but for the Battle of Bath Street picture, he knew that. She was class-prejudiced, born and raised by a couple who met at the Maryhill Branch of the Communist Party. His stepfather gawped at the bin man's daughter, couldn't speak when they first met because he couldn't speak without speaking down and Annie would have none of that. She was proud and strong and knew her politics. She'd wanted a career herself at one time. But now her stomach was scarred from three pregnancies and her face was getting hard. In bitter moments he saw that she was no longer that authentic self. She had become a bourgeoise housewife, proud of her new kitchen, wanting stuff, always wanting stuff.

Down on the floor of the banqueting hall Kenny's attention was drawn to a heavy-built shadow slicing past tables, cutting between pushed-out chairs, heading straight for Annie. He was wearing an evening suit, an expensive one, but the way he carried his weight, all high in the shoulders, made it look as if he was about to fight. His head was shaved as well, which didn't help. He interrupted Annie's conversation with a hand on her bare shoulder and, before she even knew who it was, she smiled and turned her face up as if she was going to kiss him.

Her lips mouthed his name, 'Danny,' and she stood to kiss his cheek.

Danny McGrath's meaty hand slid down her bare upper arm, cupping her elbow as if he was holding her tit and then, as if he knew he was being watched, he dropped his hand, turned to the top table and saw Kenny. He waved.

Kenny waved back and Danny came over, standing under the raised top table, fingers on the edge, looking up like a peasant pleading a petition. 'All right, Kenny, how's yourself?'

'Great, Danny, how are you, yourself?'

'No bad, man, no bad at all.'

'Having a good night?'

'Brilliant. What a brilliant night. You?'

Kenny nodded. 'Absolutely brilliant. Isn't it nice to see so many people out supporting the event?'

'It is brilliant. Absolutely brilliant. Hope you've brought a wad of cash for the auction?'

'Wife won't let me.' Kenny did that smile he did, the helpless one, and bit his lip.

Danny did the smile people always did back. 'Well, I'm dropping a wodge tonight.'

Danny was a local gangster, successful, wealthy. He came to Kenny's first campaign fundraiser and made himself known, complimented Kenny on standing up for the workers though he wasn't one himself. 'Like your style,' he'd said with a curl of his lip and a sideways glance. They were the same age. It was a useful introduction: afterwards Brendan Lyons sent Kenny to talk to Danny about a boy who was getting into trouble. Danny released the boy from a debt, as a personal favour to Kenny. He had kept in touch without ever trying to implicate Kenny in anything. Off the record, admitting it just to himself, Kenny liked Danny.

'New suit?' asked Kenny.

'Aye.' Danny rubbed his chest with his hands as if he'd just found the suit on him. 'I'm not used to these dos.' He touched his silk bow tie. 'Think I over-dressed a bit.'

'I'm kind of surprised to see you here,' smiled Kenny. 'Thought you were more of a football-causes man.'

'Aye, usually.' Danny looked uncomfortable. 'Tired of the wee pond, know? Full o' wee fish.'

Kenny felt grateful to him for saying it: that was precisely his problem. 'I know, Danny. I know *exactly* what you mean.'

'Nipping at your heels.'

'Exactly. I know exactly.'

They nodded away from each other for a moment and Danny broke it up. 'See ye later.' And he walked off, heading back to his own table.

'See you later,' Kenny parroted to his back.

The coffee came round, shallow cups, the right colour but with no taste, coming to the top table first, as had all the courses. The speakers began to sip and wake up, chatting faster now, adrenalin kicking in at the proximity of their turn. The Master of Ceremonies, an authoritative man who worked as a funeral director and was used to ushering upset people around, told them the order in which they would speak.

He put Gallagher second to last.

Last up would be a heavily made-up woman whose sister had died of the disease. Peter had briefed Kenny about her: she'd been on a local teatime TV show, talking about her sister's last few days. Caused a stir. She'd be trawling through that again, giving it Christmas-without-her, leaving them in tears.

'Thanks,' said Gallagher. 'Great.'

He smiled down at his coffee. Gallagher should have been last. He was the only professional speaker on the platform. He was never out of the papers or off the telly. He had been voted the Greatest Living Scot in two polls running. Sisters die, it was a tragedy, but it did happen to lots of people. His own brother had died in a car crash and he got over it. Maybe he could mention that.

He looked into the room for Annie, hoping to make her look at him but she was still listening to the young man. Gallagher wondered if they were talking about him.

He lifted his coffee cup to cover his face and emptied it. The woman whose sister had died was sitting next to him. She had been trying to chat. He'd rebuffed her with monosyllabic responses but now it was nearing the end and he knew that she was given the honour of being last, he spoke to her.

'I heard you were tremendous on TV.'

She turned to him, her face alight. 'Oh, it's very kind of you to say that.' She touched her hair. 'I was so nervous before I went on and that Stephen Jardin – what a nice man – he made me feel so comfortable, as if I was in my own home. It all just came out.

31

Afterwards I had to watch the video to see what I said, I didn't even remember it.'

Pausing to think of herself as seen, she blinked and slowly ran her tongue between her top lip and her teeth, a languorous swipe, left to right.

He imagined her sitting in a cramped sitting room stuffed with ornaments and celebrity magazines, watching herself on TV. He wondered if she felt outside herself, if, afterwards, she accidentally thought of herself in the third person. He leaned in: 'I hate seeing myself on TV.'

She giggled, 'I know! It's not how you see yourself at all, is it? Like when you hear a recording of your voice and you're like, oh my God, who's *that*?' She giggled again, flirting with him, touching her chest. 'And it adds the pounds, God, I looked so fat.'

Gallagher responded blandly, 'You mustn't worry about that, you look great.'

She laughed too hard and blushed a little. She had misunderstood and thought he was flirting with her. More rumours were exactly what he didn't need so he toned it down: 'I'm sure your sister would be very proud of all the good work you're doing. My own brother died young, you know.'

She stopped laughing suddenly and made a serious face, a sad, adamant face. 'Sad.' She said it as if her facial expression needed annotation. But then she brightened abruptly. 'Anyway, it's lovely to meet you. My mum loves you. Our Sandra, her that died, she used to say she loved your hair when it was like that . . .' She flattened a hand unintelligibly to one side of her head.

'Oh, yes,' he said.

She leaned into whisper, 'My pal fancies ye.' She snorted. 'She'll be mortified at me saying that.'

'Oh, yes,' he said again.

The Master of Ceremonies rose to the lectern and the speeches began.

They went as well as could be expected, which was not well at all. The audience were fractious, a bit tipsy and there was no consensus about what they wanted. The speakers all read the atmosphere as hostility, lost their courage and got stuck to their notes. They read word after word, trudging to the end of the last page while the floor started muttering among themselves. Committee members were thanked without conjoined applause, jokes were met with apathy. Then the next speaker stood up, shuffling along the narrow platform to take their place and do their reading.

It was Gallagher's turn. The audience might not know what they wanted, but he did: they wanted someone to take charge. He stood up and shucked his jacket, loosened his tie and made his way to the mike. Holding the lectern, a hand on either side, he took the time to look around the room and meet their eyes. Then he leaned in and told them that he knew what it was to lose a family member: the sense of aching loss, the awful void of a life unlived. He told them that family and community were all that mattered because that's where things got done. He used all his oratorical tricks, the pauses, the emphasis, the punchy phrase that implicated the audience in some great common purpose. But their responses were Pavlovian, they clapped when he prompted them to, they smiled, because they didn't love him any more. But he still loved them.

Looking down at the upturned faces, asking him to make them feel something, Gallagher felt a spark of uncontrolled rage.

'And *you* . . .' he paused, looked around the room, reining in his loathing, 'are the people who can make a difference. You *are* making a difference.' He'd tried to make the second emphasis match the first, but he didn't feel it. 'Just by being here tonight. Thank you very much.'

He stepped back from the lectern to a decent round of applause, smiled at the final speaker, handing on the baton. The applause was dying down as a man at the back of the room stood up and shouted:

'THOMAS McFALL!'

The room swung to face the heckler. Some titters. A whoop of indignation.

They wanted an answer. They wouldn't love him again until they got one. The argument wasn't even with Kenny, it was with his stepfather, Malcolm. Thomas McFall was Malcolm's most recent rival. The two aging stags were having a pointless rut over a golf club in which Malcolm blocked McFall's membership several times. It should have ended in cross words, or an old-man scuffle at a bar. Instead, McFall upped the ante to an extraordinary degree by going for Kenny in the press. But it didn't really matter why McFall made the allegations now, or whether he contacted the *Globe* newspaper, or they him. What mattered was that the public wanted an answer. This was what public life had become: a perpetual game of knock-down-ginger when you weren't allowed to object to the bell being rung.

Furious, Gallagher stopped and looked for the voice. There he was, at the back of the room, face glazed with drink, overhead lights glinting off his glasses, waiting for an answer. Two women at the heckler's table saw the room staring at them and tried to distance themselves by pantomiming outrage.

Gallagher's fury rose in his throat. He stepped back to the mike and his lips brushed it, filling the room with an electric crackle.

'Thomas McFall,' he hissed venomously, 'is a traitor to his class.'

The audience loved it. They cheered and applauded. They loved him. They stood, lifted their hands over their heads to show their solidarity with him. Raising their open faces, drink-dewed and elated, they saluted Kenny Gallagher's adamance.

Except Annie.

Deep in the dark heart of his audience, his wife's eyes burned up at him, smarting like a pricked conscience.

4

DS Alex Morrow and DC Harris walked briskly out of the back corridor into the A&E waiting room. She needed to know about the grandfather, Brendan Lyons. After talking to his daughter, to the witnesses, to the first-on-scene officers, she felt he could have been anyone: he was nice, he was kind, he was buying stamps. Morrow wanted to see what he had in his pockets, the minutiae that make a life, and all of that was in the morgue. As they crossed the warm waiting room hunger and tiredness hit them and slowed their pace.

She glanced down at Harris's briefcase. 'You doing market research on the side?'

Harris rolled his eyes and blushed. 'Oh, ma'am, I'm so sorry.'

She'd been hurrying him and had hardly given him time to file the Joseph Lyons information sheet before getting Pavel in. He must have thought he could just cut a corner, but it turned into a disaster when he dropped it. It had a witness address on it and now Pavel might have seen it. They didn't know Pavel was clean; it was shabby and unprofessional. She was surprised at Harris, he was usually so dependable.

'Never do that again.'

'I won't.' Harris frowned, as if he too was baffled by his lapse. He brightened at the sight of a food vending machine. 'I bet I could eat now.'

'Yeah?' said Morrow, thinking maybe she could too. 'Think I've shaken it off as well.'

She shouldn't have said it, she was reminding them both why they hadn't been able to eat before.

Sticky, bloody mist had settled on every surface by the time they walked into the post office. To move in the space was to feel contaminated by the metallic tang of blood. Brendan Lyons was omnipresent. When Morrow looked up to give her eyes a break she saw puncture marks in the polystyrene ceiling tiles and realised that they were shards of bone.

Her eyes had begun to run as she stood there, controlling her breathing and looking at it. More bizarrely, her nipples tightened and soaked the pads in her bra with breast milk. She had to use next door's toilet to sort herself out and phoned home at the same time, giving in to the compulsion to multitask.

Now she watched Harris feed some coins into the machine. They stood, shoulder to shoulder, solemn, trying not to remember, and watched as the metal spiral twisted away from the queue of crisps. A big bag of salt and vinegar tumbled over a cliff and into the trough below.

'Well,' Harris raised his eyebrows at her, 'that went well,' and they smiled at how serious they must have seemed.

Harris pulled his crisps out. 'You get something,' he said, feeding coins in for her.

'Oh,' she flinched at the image of the ceiling, 'I still don't know ...'

'No,' he said firmly, 'get something. You need something.'

She didn't want to eat but he was right, she should. She was breastfeeding twins and her body wasn't hers to mess with. On anyone else she would have found that impertinent but Harris had kids himself, he knew the score.

'Money's in now anyway,' he said. 'Take pot luck: just jab some buttons.'

Morrow covered her eyes with a hand, peeking between the fingers and pressed A6. The spiral holding the cheese and onion crisps jolted to life and Harris gave a surprised little grunt, knowing it was Morrow's snack of first choice. She turned and looked at him through her hand and he grinned at her stupid joke.

They opened the crisps and ate, staring into the waiting room. Three, four minutes would be long enough to eat, she calculated. Four minutes to find the morgue, get in, meet people. Eight minutes to look at Lyons' personal effects, drink it in, find what there was to know about him. Back to the car, station, home. Straight home? Maybe Harris could drop her. She had the two a.m. to six a.m. shift with the boys, possibly no sleep at all if the night was restless, and then back to work. The Barrowfields investigation was turning into a curse. If they got Benny Mullen she'd be showered in glory. If they got some underlings she could justify the spend. If they got nothing she'd have her card stamped. The latter was looking most likely.

She caught sight of herself in the floor-length window, eating crisps, faster and faster until the bag was done and her cheeks ridiculously full. Harris's reflection was looking back at the waiting room, chewing calmly, tasting, even swallowing before he put more in his mouth.

She followed his eye. Pub closing time was still two hours away but the casualty department was busy: waiting parents reading newspapers, a group of three young men in football strips, one sobbing over a bloody shin, his companions masking their embarrassment with artificial jollity.

The Christmas decorations were confined to the bulletproof-glass nurses' station: strings of thin blue tinsel, paper snowmen stuck to the inside of the window with Blu-Tack bullet holes on their foreheads.

Harris looked at her and frowned. 'Pavel's tats,' he said, gesturing to his neck. 'Wasn't exactly pictures of dolphins, was it?'

Morrow nodded as she thought back to their last interview. Everyone had tattoos now, it didn't mean Pavel wasn't a bank manager, but his were extensive, on his hand, his neck, and not pretty either: dots snaked up his arm, lines of numbers, odd words out of context. 'Beast' she'd read on his neck. They were all different shades of black. It looked as if he was deliberately marring himself.

'Like prison tattoos but done by a professional. Think he's a nutcase?'

Harris nodded. 'And that bloody accent.'

Pavel's accent had bothered her too, sliding from place to place. She felt so indignant it actually made her reflect on her reaction. Morrow had a chip on her shoulder, she knew that, but Pavel's forensic knowledge of accents made her feel more than mocked: it felt as if he was being evasive, almost academically inauthentic.

'Maybe all Pavel tells us is that even weirdos use the post office at Christmas.'

'D'you think?' She folded her empty crisp packet, and muttered to herself, 'His teeth look American.'

'Mm,' he had a mouthful, 'right enough. That's odd: tats and teeth don't match.'

Pavel had ludicrously straight, white teeth. Morrow had wondered if they were dentures until she saw his gums.

However odd and unsympathetic Pavel was, he had given them important information. The robbery looked like a random crime, very hard to solve, but from what Pavel had told them the gunman knew the alarm system was off: *Don't fucking bother, it's still cut off.*

The alarm system had malfunctioned that morning. The manager knew it was a burnt circuit board because of a sulphurous smell hanging in the corridor when he arrived to open up. It had happened before. According to their insurance they should have shut down the shop but it was the week before Christmas, the busiest week of the year. The manager didn't tell the other workers, not that he didn't trust them – they were his daughter and his wife's cousin – but he didn't want to frighten them and, anyway, it was due to be fixed in the early afternoon: the manufacturers had been notified. Mid-morning they would deliver the new circuit board to a mechanic who would come straight in and fix it. The gunman had three possible sources of information: the manufacturer, the mechanic or the PO manager.

She chewed her faceful of crisps, wishing she had a drink, or more saliva, and worked down the list: the manufacturers had everything to lose by leaking information. The post office wouldn't be insured for the lost money, so they'd lost out. Her money was on the mechanic: if he had contact with the gunman it might be traceable.

She looked out at the dark night beyond the glass doors. It was windy and the light from the waiting room caught silver needles of sideways rain. A sheet of newspaper flew across the dark ambulance bay outside, landing in a wide puddle, sticking to the surface of the water.

'Come on, Harris, let's go.'

She didn't wait for Harris to zip his coat but led the way out of the door, shutting her face to the rain and the cold.

The Southern General Hospital was a city state under construction. Cranes slumped over a half-built multi-storey car park. In the distance, beyond the A&E helipad, a massive concrete lift shaft stood alone behind a fence pasted with posters proclaiming a new children's hospital.

The modest Victorian sprawl of the old hospital was still there but the closure of the next-door dockyards had left it on four square miles of cheap, windswept land. Facilities from better appointed hospitals were being moved here. Heavy building equipment had compromised the ground, creating broad puddles of unknowable depth. Morrow and Harris snaked around them, picking their steps from road to pavement, across muddy paths cut deep through patches of grass.

The signposts for the morgue led nowhere, but Morrow had spent two months at the maternity unit four blocks on and was minutely familiar with the hospital grounds. She had already guessed that the mortuary was in the unmarked, flat-roofed building.

She walked around to a door next to a loading bay and pressed a button. Stepping back, she looked straight into a small convex eye, seeing herself smiling back, distorted. She made a mental note to smile less, be less playful at her work. It was undermining her authority.

A voice asked her who she was. She told them, took out her wallet and held up her warrant card.

The door fell open.

This corridor was more welcoming than the A&E department, despite the bright smell of disinfectant. A young Asian man in a black woolly jersey and a security badge hovered nearby, watching them.

'That's not the entrance,' he said pleasantly.

'Sorry,' said Morrow, remembering not to smile, 'the signposts just sort of run out.'

'Best not to have a big sign, you know? Because we're right next door to the surgery department.' He gave an apologetic smile. 'Can I see your ID again, guys?'

Morrow and Harris showed off their cards and the guard's eyes flicked from their photos to their faces, checking points of confluence. It was unusually thorough. He leaned backwards and shouted over his shoulder, 'Hey, Johno! Polis here.'

A middle-aged man with a teenager's lolloping walk came out of an office and shook their hands, introduced himself as John the Mortuary Supervisor. He told them what they already knew: the grandfather had been shot so much his body fell apart. He drew his hand across his belly, and nodded at them.

'Do you want to see him?'

'God, no,' said Morrow too quickly. 'No, we'll get the photos in the morning.'

'Sorry,' said John, blushing as if he'd suggested they might like to.

'No, we just wanted to see his effects.'

'Sure.' He stepped over to a large steel door. 'It's all in here.'

He used a swipe card hanging from his neck to open the door, stepped in and flicked on brutal lights. A long metal table sat in front of a series of steel filing cabinets. It was a big room, made pleasantly cool by all the metal surfaces.

John the Supervisor pulled a drawer open, carefully lifting out a clear plastic bag. Holding it underneath to keep it flat, he set the blood-smeared bag on the table.

'Sorry,' he said, blushing again, 'it's filthy, I know, but they won't let us—'

'No, I know,' interrupted Morrow.

'For trace evidence and that.'

'Aye, that's right. Don't worry.'

John laid a flat plastic sheet on the table and teased the red zip lock on the bag back, peeling the mouth of the bag open. He stepped away.

Morrow took latex gloves out of a box and snapped them on.

Despite the chill in the room she could still smell the blood. It took her back to the post office and stabbings at parties, anonymous slashings and murderous couples, snapshots of other times, back to the fast-flowing vein of human nastiness she'd witnessed over the past ten years. Somewhere deep inside her she glimpsed again a deep reservoir of black despair. She was a little shocked to find it there, unchanged.

She reached into the evidence bag. A bloody bus pass in a blue plastic pouch. The old man's face was slightly blurred in the picture but pleasant nonetheless. He looked straight at her, eyes twinkling, his lips parted as if he might smile. Morrow put the bus pass down carefully on the plastic sheet.

A union membership card, profession down as 'driver'.

'Says driver,' she muttered.

Harris watched her reach back into the bag as if he was witnessing an operation. 'Confirms what the daughter said: drove the bus for a special needs social club. Retired.'

'How long ago?'

'A year. Did occasional fill-ins but no regular job.'

Some coins: a fifty and two coppers.

A plastic toy robot, cheap and small, one arm broken off. It looked like a cracker toy.

Handy Andy tissues, the top of them sodden with blood, swollen like a rose blooming out of the packet.

John was embarrassed again. 'Sorry. They say to put everything in. I've put a packet of silica gel in it but it hasn't had much of an effect yet . . .' He pointed at a little cushion nestling in the bloody corner of the personal effects bag. Full of chemicals and crusty with an old man's blood: *Do not eat.*

'Ah, you're right enough, John, don't worry.'

The final item in the bag was a wallet. It was slim, made of soft brown leather which had moulded into a slight crescent where it cupped the old man's buttock. The outline of bank cards was discernible through the cover, pressed into dark ripples on the surface. Smearing the blood off, she saw the word *Mallorca*. The dark pattern was a map of the island. She flipped it open with a fingertip. One bank card for a joint account with his wife. A blood-sodden tenner, a concession rail ticket from Kelvindale train station, some till receipts from a chemist and a folded repeat prescription form. She opened it. Brendan Lyons had been taking statins and a mild laxative.

Morrow put all of the items back in the bag. John the Supervisor stepped on the pedal of a yellow bin, flipping the lid as she peeled off her bloody gloves.

'His wife's here, IDing him,' he told her quietly.

They looked away from each other, none of them wanting to think about the wife or the family that would have to deal with this in the week before Christmas.

She dropped the bloody gloves into the darkness of the bin.

'OK,' she said, too tired to feel compassion but rolling through the motions. 'I want her to know we're here. We'll wait until she comes out and introduce ourselves.'

'Sure.' John rezipped the evidence bag and lifted it off the table, put it back in the drawer. 'I'll go and see if Mrs Lyons has finished.' He led them out, across the corridor to a small room and left them.

The bad news room at the morgue was crammed with social cues; a box of tissues on the table, one sticking out, ready and waiting. A water cooler, an armchair and a small couch, both upholstered in wipe-clean fabric. On the wall: a calming print of a field in summer, blinds on the corridor window, muted light. Morrow wondered at the lives haunted by the soft murmur of a stray detail in here: the car has not been traced. Cause of death was blood loss. Neighbours called when they heard him screaming.

Harris and Morrow waited for a few minutes, looking at the settee but not sitting down, keeping their coats on.

'So, d'ye get something for Brian?' said Harris.

Morrow shook her head. 'Nah, we're not getting each other anything this year. Spending it on the weans and the christening.' They weren't religious but both enjoyed the punctuation of ceremonies.

'Me and the wife're doing it the other way,' muttered Harris quietly.

Morrow caught his eye, clocked the cheeky twinkle. 'Don't—'

'Weans can whistle for it. Wife's getting me a boat and I'm getting her a facelift . . .'

She gave a despairing wail of 'Oh, ya bugger.' The nightclub joke became sillier and funnier because they were in a morgue, because it was before Christmas, it was late and Lyons' grieving widow was around the corner and they must not be found laughing. They snorted and struggled.

Morrow recalled the crime scene to straighten her face just in time as John the Supervisor came back with a woman in tow. Harris still had his face turned away.

Rita Lyons was tanned, her hair dyed russet and styled in a

mane. She looked chic in pale blue linen shirt and slacks, wore them flatteringly loose. A single gold chain sat on her sun-wrinkled décolletage. She stayed at the door and took in the room, defying all the cues to crumble, taking deep breaths.

'Mrs Lyons, I'm DS Morrow. I'm very sorry for your loss. I'll be heading the investigation. I just wanted to introduce myself to you. Can we get you home?'

'No,' Rita took another deep breath, 'I've got a taxi . . .'

'OK.' Morrow tried to read the woman, to see whether she was hostile or grief-stricken. She couldn't quite work it out. 'Well, whatever you want. We can wait with you.'

Rita Lyons took a stalled breath and then looked at Morrow. 'Do you need to talk to me now?'

There was no hostility there, but not much love either. 'You've probably had enough today,' said Morrow. 'We'll come and see you tomorrow.'

Rita crossed her arms and stared hard at her. 'You'll get the man that did this. You will, won't you?'

Morrow hated that question and they all asked it. 'We'll do our best.'

Angry at the evasion, Rita glared at Harris for back-up. He stepped nearer to Morrow, clarifying his loyalties.

'I'll ring . . .' Rita had an old-fashioned mobile and selected 'recently called', choosing the first number. It was answered immediately.

'That's me now, Donald,' she said. 'Just where you dropped me.'

She hung up and dropped the phone back in her bag, chewed her lower lip for a moment and said, 'I met Brendan when we were both thirty-five. I'd never met anyone like him. He was a deeply, deeply moral man.'

Morrow nodded. It was an odd thing to say. 'He was a good man?'

'Really good.' Rita's eyes looked suddenly hollow and distant. 'But practical, not sentimental, and he made a difference.' Her head dropped forward and perfect, pearl-shaped tears dripped to the floor.

'You know,' said Morrow, 'he said hello to the gunman and then held the bag with the money in it?'

Rita frowned at her. 'You saying he *helped* that man?'

'Maybe. Can you think of any reason he'd recognise him?'

She shook her head. 'Did he threaten him? I don't know.'

Morrow shrugged. 'Could he have known him from some-where? What sort of work did Brendan do?'

'He was retired. He had been a bus driver. Why would he help him just because he recognised him?'

'Well, they seem to have greeted each other, as if they knew each other . . .' The soft murmur of a stray detail.

Rita looked at the floor, her eyes widening as she traced the path Morrow had already traced for that moment: that Brendan knew his killer, helped him, that maybe he knew the man was going to kill him.

'Was Brendan religious?' said Morrow, thinking that he might have met the villain in the course of church work.

Rita spluttered indignantly: 'Good God, no, Bren was a life-long communist.'

'Oh, when you said he was a good man . . .'

'He was a different sort of "good man".'

'Right, I see. Maybe he could he have met the man at a com-munist meeting?'

'No.'

Morrow looked sceptical and Rita explained, 'Because he didn't go to meetings any more. He's not been active in the party, not for a long time.'

'Was he ever in trouble with the police?'

'Never. Even when we were young, he was politically active, went on a lot of marches in the eighties, supported the miners, even then he was never in trouble and the police were hoovering people up . . .' She looked at Morrow. 'Sorry. No offence.'

'None taken.' But Morrow disliked her for saying it. 'Did he know any criminals?'

'None.' Rita was adamant.

'No one living near you or related to you . . . ?'

'Certainly not.' Her mouth twisted at the corners with mild disgust. 'We wouldn't have anything to do with people like *that*.'

Morrow's half-brother, Danny McGrath, was a gangster. Most people in Glasgow knew someone, lived by someone, had a relative or a daughter with an inappropriate boyfriend. But Rita Lyons was unequivocal. It made Morrow feel sure she was lying.

The two women looked at each other, not kindly either.

Rita broke it off. 'My taxi will be outside.'

Morrow regretted the indulgence of that look. She knew she'd need Rita as an ally. 'We'll walk with you.'

She was suddenly angry and tearful. 'No—'

Morrow reached over to touch her forearm. 'It's my job to ask awkward questions.'

But Rita slipped Morrow's touch and looked at her outstretched hand disdainfully. 'Woman,' she whispered at it, 'my man just died. I won't make allowances for *you*.'

Then she turned and walked away towards the exit. Morrow and Harris followed her out.

On the wet and windy roadside, downstream of a puddle, Rita took out a packet of duty free cigarettes and a plastic holder. Morrow watched her trembling fingers fit them together and light it. She wondered at the authority of the woman. Rita Lyons was a working class woman, didn't seem to come from or have money, yet she was more than just proud: Rita was regal.

'I'll come to see you again tomorrow,' she said, 'We need to work out if Brendan knew the gunman and if so, where from.'

Rita gave a slow, composed nod, deigning her assent, but she raised the cigarette to her mouth and the orange glowing tip of her cigarette trembled in the dark. A red Ford car drew down the road towards them and they turned to watch it careening carefully around the puddles.

It pulled up in front of them. Morrow nodded at Harris to make a note of the registration.

The door opened and a squat, bald man got out, ran around to the passenger side and reverently opened the door for Rita. He watched her face as she got in, hoping for eye contact. Rita didn't grace him with it. He walked back around to his own door and Morrow saw that his eyes were swollen from crying.

'Excuse me?' she called.

The driver looked back and his face hardened. 'Aye?'

'What's your name?'

'Donald McGlyn. You the polis?'

'Aye.' Morrow noticed a red dot flare in the back of the cab. It was Rita's cigarette. She knew how taxi drivers were about their cabs: Donald must have thought the world of her to let her smoke.

'Donald, can we come and talk to you if we need to?'

'Anything, anything for Bren,' he said, swallowing hard. 'Abbi Cabs in Anniesland. I'm there after lunch.' His tears got the better of him and he waved goodbye and got back in his cab.

'Get that licence?' muttered Morrow.

Harris nodded and slapped his notepad shut.

They watched the Ford drive through the blueprint of a city, forging carefully through puddles, slow tsunamiing the pavements.

'Check him out first thing in the morning.' She looked at her watch: eleven forty. 'Christ, we're back on in seven hours.'

'Six,' corrected Harris, 'including travel time.'

Morrow watched the red tail-lights disappear into a grey veil of rain. She felt the bitter wind rise from the river, needle-sting rain on her cheeks, but she warmed as she said the blessed phrase, 'I'm going home.'

5

Morrow leaned into the bedroom door and whispered, 'Brian?'

Deep in a dark velvet sleep, Brian lay across the bed as if he had fallen from a tall building: one arm flat across his body, a leg to the side and the duvet half over his face.

'Brian?'

His breathing faltered and then resumed, belly deep, delicious. Alex walked over to the bed and sat down, brushed the duvet from his face. She smiled down at him. Salty sleep had dried in circles at the corners of his eyes. His face was slack, she could see the skin of his cheek folding over by his ear. They were getting older.

'I need to go to my work, Brian.'

Brian strained to open an eye. ''M up.'

But he lay immobile.

'Thomas's just had a feed and Danny'll be waking up in a minute.' She stood up and straightened her work suit. 'His feed's warmed and on the side. Can you call about the christening this morning? Are ye getting up, Brian?'

He opened the eye again, showing more than the white this time, and looked up at her. ''M up.'

She smiled. 'Want me to put on the light?'

'Hmm. You going to ask Danny today?'

'Auch, dunno.' She flicked the light switch as she left the room and heard him groan and throw off the duvet.

Tiptoeing downstairs, she picked up her briefcase at the bottom and pulled on her coat, smiling to herself as she opened the door to the crisp cold day.

48

Chill morning washed over her face and she closed her eyes for a luxurious moment, soothing the burn in them. She shut the door and heard behind her a baby's yawl coming from all the way at the top of the house, a soft sound carried on a secret frequency.

In the car she turned on the engine, the heater, the radio and then sat for a moment, waiting for the condensation to clear, grinning at the shadow of the house through the screen. She often felt tearful with gratitude as she sat and waited in the morning, for having a soft bed to crave and a peaceful home to come back to. The news came on, reminding her of the reserve of black despair she had glimpsed the night before. She knew all of that was waiting for her, but in front of her was the house and in it were her boys.

It was different this time. Before her young son Gerald died of meningitis she took his health for granted, complained about sleeplessness, moaned about his eating. This time she was grateful for all of it. The stasis wouldn't last. The boys would get bigger, the workplace resentments and worries would come back, but for now, just for now, Morrow savoured her state of grace.

The screen cleared slowly and, still smiling, she reversed out of the steep driveway, turned and took the road to town.

As she drove she thought about Brendan Lyons, continuing thoughts that had half formed as she fell asleep.

Lyons' behaviour didn't make sense. How could he know that man? *You.* Lyons was dapper, everyone said he was dapper. He might be secretly gay, have had a liaison with the gunman. He might know the gunman through the special needs bus, through the local community, through an old family connection.

She pulled up in the empty car park behind London Street station and turned off the radio, eager to get in and get on.

The booking bar was busy for seven in the morning.

It was the sore end of a night shift and Morrow found the desk sergeant barking questions at a tiny, muscle-bound man. The man looked coked-up, standing with his shoulders hunched like a bull about to charge. The desk was spattered with spit and the two officers holding him back were red faced, panting as if they'd been shouting.

When they saw Morrow coming in the door, the officers' demeanour changed. They stood taller, professional, and the desk sergeant nodded a thank you at her for reminding them that they weren't thugs too. The muscleman felt a change in atmosphere and looked over to the catalyst.

'A WOMAN!' he shouted, without inflection or ire, a hollered observation.

The cops holding him burst out laughing, realising suddenly that he was a nutter, just a nutter, and they were better than him. The muscleman seemed to realise too that he had lost his audience's engagement, that he was a chaotic fool, outnumbered and in a tight spot. Defeated, his shoulders slumped.

As Morrow took the door to the lobby, the door swung closed behind her and she heard him shout again, 'DON'T PHONE MY MUM!'

Through the lobby and into her office, she found her desk full of preliminary reports.

The back shift had been working hard. Brendan Lyons had been a member of the Communist Party from 1967–83. He was an office holder for fifteen years. He left a year and a half after losing his position. More importantly, he had life insurance. His family were due a payout of seventy thousand pounds. The cop who had written the report anticipated her questions: Lyons had no traceable debts. The Lyons didn't own their house but rented it from the council. Lyons wasn't known to be a gambler. There was no obvious reason for him to orchestrate his own murder so that his family could get a payout. But not all debts were legit or documented. He might have been into a loan shark. It wasn't hard for illegal debts to get out of hand.

She shut her eyes and thought it through: if Brendan offered to help the gunman, arranged to be there and get murdered, he wouldn't have brought the grandson. Unless Pavel was in on it too. Unless Pavel was supposed to get the kid out of there and didn't.

She forced her eyes open and pulled the next report over.

Reports of two old cases where an AK-47 had been used; one a family dispute on a scheme, the other four years old, gang-related and the weapons had been recovered in both instances.

The search they'd done on robberies with guns was just as patchy: a few cases with replica guns, irrelevant; old ones, again irrelevant.

There was only one that sounded worth pursuing: a lone gunman wearing 'some sort of grey balaclava' had walked into a modest flat in Battlefield, menaced the householder, Anita Costello, and her fourteen-year-old daughter, Francesca. The police were called by neighbours when a shot was fired at the ceiling. He absconded before the first unit got there. The mother had a lot of previous for small offences: possession, breach of the peace, supplying alcohol to minors, all of which added together to create the unmistakeable impression of a minor dealer who may have had money in her house when the gunman arrived. She didn't have it when the police got there. Pinned to the back of the report of the robbery was an incident report from two months later: Anita Costello had been murdered in a park by persons unknown. Morrow made a note: *Francesca Costello.* They should speak to her if they could find her.

She dug under the files to the list of witnesses and opened it, looking specifically for Martin Pavel's file: Pavel had lied. He was not registered as a geology student at Glasgow University. He was also a member of a number of political groups: 8G, FEPA, the ULF. Morrow didn't know any of them but they sounded paramilitary and might have access to guns.

It seemed too much of a coincidence: Lyons and Pavel being heavily involved in politics.

She checked the signature on the paperwork and opened her

door, stepping over to the incident room. DC McCarthy was sitting at his desk, chewing his cheek and glaring at a computer screen. McCarthy was a fantastically ill-looking man, thin with poor skin, no lips. His weediness was almost a disguise; Morrow had seen him shoulder burly suspects to the ground. He had a weakness for vintage motorbikes but she suspected it was because the leather trousers and jacket were padded and made him look normal.

'McCarthy?' He looked up at her and she held up the report. 'You do this on that witness Pavel?'

'Aye.'

'Come here.' She went back into her office and sat down.

McCarthy came in and shut the door behind him. A little trepidatious, he read her face to see if he was in trouble.

'Nothing wrong,' she said, waving to a chair in the corner. 'Bring that, sit down.'

He did so and when he turned around she saw he had a smirk on his face.

'What's funny?'

He shrugged a shoulder. 'Nothing. What can I tell you about this?' He paused before adding, 'Ma'am?'

Too familiar. She saw this all the time now, this warmth. They had felt the fearful anger go out of her and weren't intimidated any more. She stared at McCarthy, exhausted and wondering if it mattered, if it would be worth shouting at people, or developing a habit of scowling all day. It took her quite a long time to process the thoughts, to feel resentful, and decided to reserve judgement. By the time she had finished she found McCarthy blinking uncomfortably and holding onto the side of his chair.

'Right,' she said, feeling that maybe that had done it. 'What are these organisations about?'

He looked at the sheet: '8G is a campaigning organisation, it links organisations in other countries with this one so they can lobby.'

'Lobby for what?'

'Against poverty.'

She frowned. A lot of these organisations seemed pointless exercises in sanctimosity to her. 'Not exactly sticking their necks out . . . What's this one?'

'FEPA is "Further Education Parliament Action". They lobby MPs to divert any extra money in the education budgets into further education funds for needy students.'

'Nearly fell asleep when you were saying that.'

'I know, boring. Even the website's crap, it looks like a one-man band. There's pictures of events in the gallery and they're all of the same guy shaking hands with people.'

'But Pavel joined them?'

'Yeah.'

'McCarthy, how did you get this information?'

'He's got the links on his Facebook page.'

'You friended him and he accepted?'

'Yeah. I joined FEPA first though.'

She didn't like police involvement in anything political. However it went they always looked bad.

McCarthy knew what she was thinking. 'It's OK, I used a fake name.'

'Yeah, still. Don't do it again.'

'OK.' Not sure if he was in trouble McCarthy pointed to the next page. 'But, ma'am, look at the pictures on his Facebook page.'

Attached to the rundown on Pavel was a printout of his Facebook photos: Pavel in skiing clothes on a snowy mountainside; Pavel looking quite sad in a crowd of youths, American, judging from their clothes and hair styles. He was handsome but gawky, would grow into his looks. His was wearing a T-shirt in among the Americans, and only his left hand was tattooed at that point, the neck still clear. Towards the bottom, Pavel in yellow safety glasses, more tattoos. Then Pavel smiling, holding a rifle, holding a pistol, holding a submachine gun. In the submachine gun picture he'd had half his neck tattooed: a big black slogan on his collar, creeping up his neck, too high to hide under a shirt. Morrow didn't like the look of tattoos very much but facial tattoos seemed especially self-defacing.

'That "ULF",' she said, 'is that a unionist organisation?'

'No, it's the "Unity of Life Foundation".'

'What is it, abortion? Anti-abortion?'

'The website doesn't say anything about abortion. It's not that clear. They've got a lot of money though, the website's stonking: high quality videos, downloads, meetings all over the world. They seem to be a religious organisation. Talk about virtue a lot. It says,' he leaned forward and read the sheet upside down, 'they're a "think-tank, developing alternative solutions to social problems".'

'That could mean anything.' She thought about it. She hoped it was religious. Religion was easier to investigate than politics. 'Anyone in any of them got previous?'

'Not sure who's in them. Pavel's clean anyway.'

'Is that really his name?'

It hadn't occurred to him. 'I'll check.'

She looked at the papers again. 'If they're religious get me some membership records.' But McCarthy'd be going off in an hour, so he wouldn't be able to follow it up quickly. 'Forget it. I'll hand it over to someone.'

He waited, looking at her for further instructions. 'You look knackered, ma'am.'

She broke into a smile but stopped herself. 'Get out,' she said, so he did.

Tamsin Leonard sat in the dark in her car, ignoring the windscreen wipers screeching indignantly at a break in the rain. She had seven minutes to get in, shove her stuff in her locker, sign in and get to the briefing room but she wanted to catch sight of

Wilder before she reported for duty, to see how he looked. She hadn't slept for thinking about him.

The back entrance busied as the hour approached: cars pulled up and parked, her shift-mates hurried out of their cars and into the station. Two of them cycled in. They greeted one another as they wheeled their bikes through the entrance to the car park. She felt sad watching them, distant from that sense of belonging now. She had always felt sidelined, hadn't expected to miss that so acutely.

Just then she saw the bonnet of Wilder's blue Corsa nudging out of the entrance to the car park. Leonard sat forward, trying to see his face, but he was looking away, checking for oncoming cars and she couldn't see his expression. But he was leaving the car park which was odd because their shift was due to start in six minutes. Perhaps he'd found the car park full. He drove out and around the back of the station to the wasteland. It was broken ground but safe; cameras were trained on it because the station was next door.

Leonard started her engine and pulled slowly down the street after him. She'd park next to him, act casual when they met, get the measure of his mood.

At the end of the street she looked over to the waste ground and found it empty. She glanced left and saw Wilder's tail-lights at the corner, circling back around to the main road. He'd know she was following him if she took it too.

She parked on the empty stretch of ground and got out of her car, looked around at the cameras out of habit, checking they were working, that it was safe.

It hit her with a jolt: nowhere was safe, not any more. She had three bags-for-life sitting in her boot with a total of one hundred and sixty-three grand in them. If it was nicked she couldn't report it. She was completely alone.

Soft rain caressed her face in the dark as she listened to the rumble of the distant traffic. She felt like a lost child and she wanted to call home, call Camilla and tell her what she had done.

But she didn't.

She got back into her car and restarted the engine, took the corner and parked up nearer the other cars, climbed out and locked it.

Then she walked up the ramp to the back door, aware all the time that she had reached into Hugh Boyle's boot with her own hand, that she had reached in thinking she was taking a bag of security. She saw now that it was a fearful thing she had done, that she had gained one thing but lost more.

The back bar was quiet as she signed in, the doors to the cell block open. Someone was snoring in there, their gentle snuffles echoing between the concrete walls. She went through to the bustle of the locker room, helloed a couple of the guys as she took out her keys and opened her door, shoved her jacket and handbag in. She had a mirror glued onto the back of the door and retouched her mascara, feeling absurdly self-conscious.

Through the lobby, she punched the entry code into the CID wing and went straight into the briefing room. Resisting the urge to hide at the back or side of the room, she sat right at the front, where she usually did. She didn't dare look around for him but felt sure that Wilder wasn't there yet.

DS Morrow came in, flanked by Harris who was carrying a slim file. The shift took their seats with exaggerated respect. It was only partly sarcastic. Morrow was a good DS, not heavy-handed, not embedded with the management. They felt that she was focused on getting the job done, that they were all in it together. Leonard was drawn to Morrow but wary of showing it: she didn't want the shift to think they had a special bond because they shared the ladies' loo.

Harris left the folder for Morrow on the table and came over to sit next to Leonard, nodded a hello to her as Morrow glanced back at the door pointedly. Routher jumped up and closed it as a quiet fell over the shift. They weren't expecting anyone else. Wilder must already be in there.

Morrow gave them the rundown: the case in Barrowfields was coming together nicely – they got a mobile number yesterday that would help in tracing a dealer's movements. She nodded appreciatively at Leonard, referring to the Audi stop the night before. Leonard watched her eyes, waiting for her to glance at Wilder, but Morrow moved on.

They needed two pair for the Barrowfield questioning today, she said, one to dig around the neighbours, another to sit in a van and film Benny Mullen's door. Hands shot up for that, because it was sedentary. Leonard's hand stayed in her lap. She was afraid of being teamed with Wilder and having to sit with him all day.

Morrow allocated the Barrowfield jobs – Gobby and Evskine in the van, a couple of the new guys to work the neighbours – and turned to the briefing on the case they all wanted to hear about, the post office raid. She set the briefing as a series of questions:

First: the granddad was a good-living man from a good-living family. Why did he leave his grandson with a weird-looking stranger and help the gunman?

Second: the weird-looking stranger had lied about his circumstances and they had to find out why. Morrow would head that up, it might have political implications and was sensitive.

Someone at the back of the room snorted: DS Morrow wasn't known for her sensitivity. Morrow looked up, a warning delivered with an acknowledging smirk.

Third: the gunman knew that the alarm system was broken in the post office. How did he know? They needed someone to visit the alarm system mechanic who'd been waiting for the part to arrive before he set off to fix it: what was his history? Was he reliable?

Morrow pointed to Leonard and then, finger hovering over

their heads as if she was choosing from a box of chocolates, pointed to the back. 'Aye,' she said, 'you and her.'

Leonard looked around and found Routher looking back at her. She scanned the room. Wilder was missing. Morrow caught her eye.

'Your usual neighbour got sick this morning,' she said. 'He had to go home.' And she went back to her notes.

Next: the gunman had an AK-47, one witness said it was a pistol, had anyone ever seen an AK-47 pistol? They mostly came from Ireland. Paramilitaries liked them because it didn't take much training to use them and the guns could be buried for months without losing function. Most of them were a goodwill gift from Gaddafi. Morrow told them to keep an ear open for Republican or Loyalist associations, or any mention of Northern Ireland.

Leonard stopped listening and got lost in her own worries: where the fuck was Wilder? Why come in and then go home? If he'd reported her Morrow wouldn't be giving her jobs. Last night, as she drove home from the station with the bags in her boot, she'd argued with herself: Wilder must have been in that situation before, he'd been on the force a lot longer than her. She'd been looking to him for reassurance this morning. She could phone him but an out-of-hours call would put them together, make it a provable conspiracy. She had planned to throw the money away and call him a liar if he got caught or reported her.

Harris passed her a photocopied photograph of an AK-47 pistol. It was shorter than a rifle but had the same curled clip for bullets, the same short grip. Guns were rare in Glasgow. They weren't really used for fighting, more for business, for threatening or committing gang assassinations.

Panicking, Leonard considered chucking the bags of money away right now, right after roll call. She could drop them in the river. It felt cowardly, though, an unsatisfying resolution. She looked at Morrow, frowning at her papers. Maybe Leonard could tell her about the money, clear her conscience and take the consequences but she couldn't do that without putting Wilder in it.

Morrow looked up, a small smile playing on her face.

'Now, I'll finish on a high note: our old boy, DS Bannerman, has been promoted within PSU and we're going to use our vending slosh to buy him a bottle of whisky.' A disgruntled murmur ran through the room. No one liked Bannerman, he was a bully and had been whipped out of their division after individual DCs reported him on an anonymous phone line. Morrow only found out afterwards that Harris had orchestrated the calls to get rid of him and she'd been furious about it. Now she slashed the room with a finger point: 'This job is not about being *popular*. It's about being decent. Bannerman wasn't bent. He wasn't *wrong*.'

Morrow had silenced but not convinced them. She dropped her hand. 'Come on, Bannerman's aggravating, but he's not a class traitor.'

The laugh took a moment to gather momentum, a slow rumble as they put the newspaper headlines together and saw that Morrow was making a joke. She rarely joked at briefings, never joked about politics. The room erupted, laughing loud and long, banging the table.

Leonard felt the realisation like a kick in the neck: what they had in common wasn't a pension, or a uniform, or a cert from the college. She sat at the front of the room, the suffocating laughter rolling over her head. Morrow was appealing to their sense of decency, they were all this side of decent. Only now she wasn't.

6

When Martin Pavel's alarm clock gave a longed-for beep he slapped it quiet and got up. He was dressed already, had woken up at five twenty-two but made himself lie back down and rest, waiting. Doctor Leonowsky had said it herself: Martin's overly developed self-discipline might also be used for good purpose. Running was a good purpose.

He swung his legs over the edge of the bed and thought back to yesterday morning. Yesterday at eight a.m. he had slapped the alarm quiet and slept on for an extra hour. His biggest worry was posting the gifts home and resisting his parents' attempts to be with him for the holidays. There were threats: if he wouldn't come to them, they could come to him, but he had said no. He was glad they weren't here now, all four of them straining to be civilised, wondering what the hell was wrong with him, silently pricing everything in the house.

During the two hours and thirty-eight minutes lying in the dark waiting for the alarm to go off, what he mostly thought about was the gunman. He was less shocked now. He had a bit of perspective. He knew, for example, that the gunman was not radiating light. He was probably not as tall as Martin had supposed, either. Lying there he realised that beneath the stalker's mask the man could have been sweating or frightened; sometimes people smiled when they were nervous. Martin had supposed him wonderful for this simple reason: he was doing what Martin was always trying not to do, he was causing harm and it looked glorious.

Martin smiled to himself as he walked downstairs. He sat on

a dainty love seat at the very far end of the hall and pulled on his running shoes, thinking about causing harm, about letting go, not being accountable, not being liable.

He stood up: fuck it, he wasn't doing the Great Western Road today. He'd just make up his route as he went along, get some hills in, even if it meant inflaming his shin splints or doing less or more than it said on his running app. Just lose control and enjoy it. He put in his earphones. His finger hovered over the running programme but he went straight to iPod and picked 'shuffle'.

He looked up and, through the glass on the distant front door, saw the orange street lights pierce the black morning. Stopping by the chiffonier, he opened a shallow drawer meant for gloves, took out a heart monitor and strapped it on his bicep. His water bottle was back in the kitchen but his heart rate was already rising in anticipation, the need to run a pressing imperative. He ought to do stretches, avoid injury, but this morning he was experimenting with chaos.

He threw the door open into the black and stepped out into the gusty rain, touching his pocket to check for his house keys just as the door swung shut and *click-clock-clacked* behind him.

Martin ran.

Sprinting up Cleveden Hill, past the Victorian mansions, along heavy hedges, his thighs and calves straining, his buttocks tightening at the fierce gradient. He ran into the rain, felt it smear across his face as he sped into it. Stiff at first, he warmed up, the adrenalin kicked in, then a meagre trickle of endorphins. He ran in a low leap, a Muybridge horse, both feet off the ground on the flat. He ran, not from but to, into something new and hopeful. He ran in perfectly equal steps, his heartbeat steady, his eyes narrowed.

Reaching a roundabout he saw a break in the sparse traffic, and ran over. Suddenly he felt the black, worn sneakers right behind him, toes to his heels, and he sped up until his steps were ragged and uneven, fleeing, bounding along with his weight unsteady, fast and reckless.

For a mile and half he sprinted through fear, listening to anything that came on his earphones, *Agnus Dei* as agreeable as club mixes, not needing the beat to pace him today.

The music faded, the road became a blur and he was suddenly conscious of his breath burning his lungs and the stab in his heels.

He looked up to find himself deep in the heart of Kelvindale and saw suddenly the Google map overview of the area. Nine, Lallans Road. Lallans Road was a thumb on a small hand of streets curling around the canal. Just down there. He slowed to a jog and looked around for it.

Shitty little houses. Gardens worked by the homeowners themselves, little patches of industrious autonomy. Slowing, he ran past a row of shops.

A corner store was open, advertising hot coffee and newspapers. He tried to speed up again but his teeth were dry and aching with the cold, and his throat had started to throb. He thought he might vomit. He stopped at an intersection, panting, rubbing at the twinge in his hamstrings, looking around, though he knew no cars were coming in either direction.

Dropping forward at the waist Martin admitted that he was fucking himself up. Dr Leonowsky told him: hurting yourself is an articulation of self-disgust. It helps no one, prevents nothing. This wasn't a glorious loss of control, he was fooling himself, it was self-harm.

Flinching at the pain in his heels he walked back to the newsagent. It was only now that he felt the numbness in his toes and the weight of sweat dragging his T-shirt down. He checked his heart monitor: 165 bpm. Too much. 165 bpm for sixty-three per cent of the run. Bad, reckless, his heels were on fire.

He waited outside the shop, forming a self-care plan: he would catch his breath and buy a bottle of water. He would walk home.

When he got home he'd eat: eggs and OJ, bread even. He would have a shower, not a scaldingly hot one, just moderate, and then he'd get back into bed and he'd watch TV.

The shop door triggered a buzzer and Martin walked into a wall of warmth coming from a three bar fire. A radio behind the counter played old songs and recounted traffic news for the local area. A man came out of the back shop, his face wrinkled from a lifetime of smiling at strangers.

Still panting, Martin asked for a bottle of water. He handed over the five pound note he kept folded in his jogger pocket. It was damp. The man was handing him a cold one and his change when the door to the street opened and she walked in.

Joseph's mother. She wasn't angry now. She had no smudged make-up on now, looked soft, her dark hair was unbrushed and thick. She wore an old woman's beige raincoat unbuttoned, as if she'd just run out of the house, and her eyes were puffy. She looked straight at him and her eyes were Joseph's eyes.

Martin couldn't look away.

'Yees know each other?' asked the shopkeeper, looking from one to the other.

Martin didn't know what to say. Joseph's mother answered for them both: 'Yes. Ten Marlboro Lights and a blackcurrant Fruit Shoot, please.'

The shopkeeper busied himself finding things. 'Where's the wee man today?'

She kept her eyes on the counter. 'He's indoors.'

'Not at nursery today?'

'No.' She glanced at Martin. 'Got a wee cold.'

'Well, you're right to keep him off. Don't want to give the other wee ones the cold, do ye?'

She didn't want to talk. She put the money on the counter, picked up the cigarettes and the drink and turned away to the door.

'I'll come out with ye,' said Martin, coming around the counter.

She had her back to him but glanced at the floor to her side, as if to say that was all right.

Outside the sun was easing up. A bus rumbled past, passengers dissolved into misty blobs of colour behind windows running with condensation.

'I thought you might live around here,' she said bluntly. 'Near the post office.'

'But I don't,' said Martin, puzzled. 'I'm two miles down that way.'

She looked down the road, suspicious. 'Did you come here looking for us?'

'No. I'm just out running.'

She didn't know whether to believe him or not. 'Seems a bit weird.'

'Very weird. I've never even been in that shop before.' His shins and heels were burning, ligaments peeling away from the bone like wallpaper from a wet wall. Martin was glad of the distracting pain because he didn't want to seem too intense. 'I must look like a stalker or something.' He winced at his shins. 'Shit. I've hurt my legs.'

He was hoping she'd invite him home, but she didn't. She motioned instead to a green railing further up the road. It was a swing set and a low slide in a small bit of municipal park. 'There's a bench in there. I could smoke . . .'

She walked ahead, still unsure of him, glancing back as he hobbled after her.

She pushed the creaking metal gate open and swiped rain off the seat with the edge of her hand, then took out a tissue and dried two seats as best she could. She sat down and lit a cigarette. Martin sat next to her and watched her blow a stream of white smoke into the smattering of rain.

'Sorry,' she blinked hard, 'I can hardly look at you without thinking of my dad's blood all on you.'

'Yeah, aye.' He had his breath now and could concentrate on

64

the feeling in his ankle. It was bad, a stabbing in his heel and up the back. He should have stretched out beforehand, he'd gone crazy fast on hills. If he didn't start moving soon he'd have to get a taxi home. 'I woke up at five and I've been staring at the ceiling ever since.' He thought about telling her how he understood her father being so drawn to that man, but he knew it would sound creepy and he couldn't think of anything else to say.

Her eyes rimmed red as she took a draw. 'He's a lovely man, my dad.'

'You close?'

'Very. We live together, me, my parents, my granny, Joe. They're good to me.'

'You're a single mom?'

She laughed at the phrase, muttered it to herself.

'Why's that funny?'

She shrugged, 'Dunno,' and sucked her cigarette. 'Auch, no I do actually.' She spoke quickly, suddenly animated. '"Single mothers", such a fucking crock of— it presupposes an ideal family construction of a heterosexual couple living alone with their children and, you know, historically, that's not even the norm. It's a retrospective construction.' She shrugged one shoulder, an apology for talking so fast, for sounding so pompous.

Martin looked at her. He liked that she sounded pompous, that she could talk about abstracts. He nodded at her and she half-smiled and carried on.

'I mean,' she said, 'that whole "single mother" thing has kind of shaming connotations. Like you've lost something. Joe's dad's not even in the picture. I live with my parents and my granny.' She tried to look at him but her nose wrinkled at one side.

'I didn't mean to offend you.'

She looked away and tiny raindrops confettied her hair. 'You didn't. I know I should be grateful that you looked after Joe but I really can hardly look at you.'

'Well,' he said, 'I think gratitude's overrated anyway.'

She smiled at that, but a sudden tear made a break for it down her cheek. She swatted it and looked at his sneakers. 'You're a runner?'

'Yeah. I usually run the Great Western in the morning but today I just wanted a hill and ended up here. I've had an injury...' He gestured to his leg. He didn't want to say he'd been running it off, all the drama of yesterday – it sounded melodramatic and self-important. Her father had died, after all.

'I run too,' she told his feet. 'I did the five k last month.'

'Right?' Martin looked at her thighs. He wouldn't want to run with all that extra weight on him. 'Well done.'

'What's that?' She pointed to his left hand. 'The dots?'

'Oh.' He held his little finger up, where the tattoo began. ''S Russian. In Russia the criminals all tell their stories in tattoos—'

'You a criminal?'

'No! I'm not a criminal.' It sounded odd, the way he said it. It even sounded odd to him.

She smiled awkwardly. 'You mean you haven't been caught?'

Martin was as clear as he could be: 'I'm not a criminal. I don't commit crimes. I just . . . it's like the idea of having your biography on your body, so you can't deny it. It keeps you true to yourself.'

There was a pause then; he'd have said something but didn't know how to make it any clearer, or if there was anything else he could add.

'OK.' She looked at his hand again. 'What does the circle mean then?'

'Well, this,' he pointed to the black circle on the fattest knuckle of his little finger, 'if the dot is on the outside of the circle it means "I am an orphan". It means "In this life I rely on no one but myself".'

'But you've got a dot inside.'

He found her smiling at that.

66

'Good,' she said simply. 'That's good. And these other ones snaking up your arm?'

'It's a narrative. Life is a narrative.' They were looking at each other, Martin taking in her brown, Joseph eyes. 'When you ask "what should I do?", the answer is "what stories do I find myself part of?"'

She considered it. 'Suppose you're part of our story now,' she said casually.

He looked at her properly now, not just at Joseph through her, but actually seeing her. Her hair was thick but her brown eyes wide and fine. Like her father, she had high cheekbones and a small mouth with articulate, twitching lips. He had tried to explain about the narrative to lots of people and it usually took a long time and ended in disappointment.

'Please don't think I'm going to look after you,' she said, 'because I've got my hands full.'

'I'm not looking for anything—'

'I've got a lot of obligations already. Especially now.' She exhaled her cigarette smoke. 'And then these other dots coming away from it, are they stories you're a part of too?'

Dr Leonowsky said that depression was either caused by, or the cause of, a lack of endorphins. Martin had understood this only academically until Joseph's not-especially-attractive, over-weight, smoking, single mom, said that. When she said that Martin understood exactly what Dr Leonowsky meant, because he felt endorphins shower from his pituitary, a warm orange shower flooding his neck and shoulders, his chest and belly, to his knees and fingers and even his calves. The insistent stab in his heels ebbed away. He pulled his sleeve up to his elbow to show her the snake of dots trailing across his forearm.

She nodded, mock disapproving. 'You get about, don't ye?'

They laughed together, both sad, both grieving, but still laughing.

'Not conquests, are they?'

'Oh, no,' he assured her, 'not at all.'

She looked his face up and down. 'No. You seem a bit intense for casual joy. How many's there, anyway?'

'Thirty-three.'

'A lot.'

'Yeah.' He was proud of that. It was a lot. A lot of controlling and changing. He felt sick at the level of control that had been required to achieve that: changing the course of rivers, holding back landslides, moving the sun. He wanted to cut his arm off.

She didn't notice: 'I can't remember if I've looked thirty-three people in the eye since Joe was born. And my dad had a rough time recently. And my gran's a bit wandered. Swallows you up, all that day to day . . .' She raised a shoulder and it stayed there, stuck in a regretful shrug.

He wanted to stop thinking about himself. 'You're young to be a mom.'

'Aye, I'm twenty-two.'

'I'm twenty-one. Twenty-two next month.' But it felt longer since his birthday, a lifetime ago since he had felt hunted.

She looked at his arms. 'What do your folks say about the tats?'

He burred his lips. 'They think I'm nuts.'

She laughed at that, took it as a colloquial expression, but what Martin actually meant was that they'd tried to have him hospitalised.

'I always wanted to have a kid. My dad, he was a communist, he thought I should run the electricity board or a steelworks or something.'

Martin saw the grandfather holding the bag open for the gunman, slap the postmaster's daughter, smiling, casting off his grandson for a bag of money. '*He* was a communist?'

'God, he never shut up about politics.' Her eyes flicked nervously behind him to the road. 'Don't say I said that.'

'Who to?'

'No, I know, just, wouldn't want him . . .' Martin watched her remember that her father would never hear anything again. Her face crumbled, flushed pink. The cigarette fell from her hand, hissed and died on the damp ground. She covered her face with her open hands and seemed to shrink into her shoulders.

'Hey.' He slid along the bench, put his arm around her shoulder and squeezed. 'Hey,' he said again, unable to think of anything comforting that wasn't crass or insulting.

Ashamed, she kept her face covered and rolled down over her knees, her back convulsing as she sobbed, hands rising to her dark hair, clutching her head as if it might burst. And she whispered to herself between sobs, 'No. No, no, nononono.'

Martin held her shoulder, awkward, found he was tearful too, but he recognised that she was experiencing a loss that would define the rest of her life, and he was just shocked and sorry for himself. It didn't exactly have equivalent moral value. He kind of hated himself for it.

The rain fell on her back, colouring the beige to a muddy grey. His arm was really stretched over to her shoulder. He wanted to let go and considered rubbing her back but thought it might seem intimate, sexual or something, and he didn't want to creep her out. So he held on, though he was bent over to the side and the skin on his hip prickled hot where it was pressed hard against her thigh.

He was holding on too long. He was acting weird. He let go of her shoulder and carefully lifted his hand high as he brought it back so as not to touch her.

He leaned forward to meet her face and took one of her hands in both of his. 'Hey.'

She looked past him, her face wet and red as a newborn. She shook her head, thumbed back to Lallans Road. 'My mum and Joe and Gran, you know?'

'Yeah.'

'I can't cry there.'

'It's OK.'

She sat up and sighed, pulled a paper tissue from the coat pocket, wiped her face and struggled for breath. 'God, I wished I'd listened to him more, you know? All his politics and that. He was a clever man. Good. Ham-fisted, big gestures and that, but he really meant all that stuff and I just rolled my eyes at him.'

'And he was a communist.'

'Tempered, not Stalinist.' She waved a hand, slumped as if it was too much to tell. 'The Rights of Man, all that. If he was a stranger I'd have listened. He did bang on, though.' She sniffed hard. 'You're a nice guy.'

'Nah.'

'Aye,' she said with the certainty of sausage rolls, 'you're a good guy.'

'I don't know – it's complicated . . .'

She looked at his mouth. '*Camp*licated? Where is it you're from?'

He was from nowhere and she was from *here*. She had *here* stamped all over her: these streets, that shop, this sky. She'd know people here from childhood, would have played in this swing park before she started school, even, and he was from nowhere.

'I moved a lot. My accent changes all the time. It's not deliberate.'

'You're trying to fit in.'

It sounded OK, the way she said it but he was still embarrassed. 'Suppose.'

She smiled down at his arm. 'But you've covered yourself in mental tattoos, which sets you apart.'

He looked down at his hand and smiled at that. It seemed funny now, that contradiction. Not important, not sinister or anything. It felt OK.

'You're smart,' he said and meant it.

They couldn't look at each other then. Martin didn't know what else to say. He glanced down towards 9 Lallans Road and then remembered he wasn't supposed to know where it was. He looked up. Rain fell from a low, grey sky. 'How's he doing?'

It was a non sequitur but she knew what he was talking about. 'He slept for five hours as soon as we got him home. He woke up at three and he's just nodded off there now. My mum's in a bad way. I should get back.'

She stood up and he copied her, turning back, and saw their dry shadows on the rainy bench. She bent down and picked up her cigarette end, muttering to herself, 'Someone's dog might eat it.'

She dropped it in the bin. They walked back out to the street. Damp inside and outside, Martin felt his body temperature drop and knew he was in danger of seizing up. He should start running now, warm himself slowly but he walked with her, back along to the newsagent's door.

'That's where we live, straight down there, with the post box outside.'

Lallans Road was only five houses long, ending in a short wall and a dip down to what he knew from Google maps was the canal. He could see number nine, a neat little house behind the postbox, warm yellow light from the windows, pierced by the pastel shaded blink of fairy lights.

'Well, I hope he's OK.' He couldn't say more without sounding creepy, so he began to back away, untangling his earphones.

She took a step after him, as though she wanted him to stay.

'Yeah,' she said, watching him fiddle through the knot of wires, 'me too.'

'Hey, Joe's Mom, what's your name?'

'Rosie Lyons.'

'I'm Martin.' He didn't say Pavel, he didn't want her to Google him.

She held out her hand. He took it and they shook very formally, like diplomats in an official photo.

Martin looked back to the house. It fitted into the row of five houses, a neat little paragraph on a perfectly justified page. They had order and community, four generations living in one small house. Martin felt convinced suddenly that he should get away from them if they were to stay safe.

Not knowing what to do now, he put his earphones in and gave her a wave, as if she was a long way away. She smiled at that. He turned and began to run through the burn in his heels.

He ran without looking back, thinking in images: a small house, a small park, a small shop and the Google maps overview, pinch in, pinch in, pinch in to a damp bench and two people crying and being kind to each other.

He was half a mile away before he remembered to turn on his music again.

7

Kenneth Gallagher sat at a kitchen scattered with the wreckage of a hurried breakfast: Sugar Puffs floating in milk like drowned bees, a half-eaten slice of toast with chocolate spread. Annie let the kids eat a lot of sugary rubbish and it was making them fat, especially Andy, their youngest. It was embarrassing. She was having to buy trousers that were two years too old for him, and hem them. His GP stepfather, Malcolm, scanned the kids like an airport security guard when he saw them, noting how fat they were, mentioning it always. Malcolm himself was whip-thin. Kenny's mother didn't dare get fat. Kenny wanted to talk to Annie about it but was afraid to touch on anything contentious this morning; he had woken up with an awful sense of foreboding, as if he were already mourning events yet to happen. They had left on the school run before he came down. Annie would be back in ten minutes.

A faint sour smell from the bin begged his attention. The bin men came today. Looking after the house was Annie's only job, but she took no pride in it. She used to mop the kitchen every day, hoover the hall, but not any more. She wanted him to get a cleaner. He said he thought working-class women were supposed to be house-proud and she said she was striking for better conditions. She said it as if it was a joke against herself though, in front of the kids, and never brought it up again.

The house was oppressively quiet. He wished the postman would come, the phone would ring, that something would happen. An old familiar horror crept over him. He swung around and looked out of the window, tried to imagine someone looking in at him, a neighbour, a hostile reporter, a stalker, but there was no one out there. He was alone.

Panicked, he turned to thinking about fucking, conflating memories and fantasies in a confused jumble of snippets: splayed women, fat women, young women, three men in one woman, four men, father and son, mother and daughter, fucking harder, nastier, people watching, people fucking and watching. It wasn't working. He was rushing into the thoughts, the colours were dim and he couldn't make anything coherent out of it, it wasn't calming him down. Seven minutes until Annie got home.

He sat rigid in his chair, thinking he was going to start crying, for Christ's sake, when his eye fell on the newspaper. Kenny Gallagher was on the front page of the *Globe*.

His lungs filled with sweet, fresh air. His back unfurled and there, at the kitchen table, he felt as if he was rematerialising.

'CLASS TRAITOR!' quoted the headline.

Casually, Gallagher flicked the paper around so it was facing him and then sat back, looking away from it, picking an orange from the bowl on the table. With his thumbnail he scored an incision in the skin and a small spray of citrus oil stung his lips. He peeled back the fleshy skin, rolling the soft pith down with his fingertips and shoved his thumb into the hole, splitting the orb in half. He pulled a segment off, bit it in two and allowed his eyes to stray to the paper.

Last night's dinner. His phrase. A fresh quote from McFall repeating the accusation: Gallagher had been having an affair with Jill Bowman. Worse, on the tenth of October they had been to Inverness for a meeting and Jill's accommodation and travel were paid for with parliamentary expenses.

Paid for with Parliamentary expenses. Jill worked for the party, she had every right to have her expenses paid. If expenses weren't paid then politics would only be open to the middle classes. The professionalisation of politics. The exclusion of working-class people from the process.

Inverness on the tenth of October. He flicked on his phone and checked his calendar. The Inverness meeting was on the eighth. They hadn't even got the dates right. On the tenth he had been at that housing thing, a grim round-table with a lot of ugly angry people wanting houses for disabled kids. Twenty or so people there.

Gallagher looked away from the paper, diffident as it begged his attention. He ate the orange slowly, segment after segment.

A text chimed on his phone. He pulled it out of his pocket, sat it on the table and read: *Bstrds. Anyfin I cn do, let uz no. McG*

Danny McGrath. He couldn't spell and always wrote from an unknown number. Danny had been a gangster, he seemed to be going legit, but he knew how it felt to be the despised big fish, to expend all that effort only for the very people you'd brought up to turn on you. Danny knew the value of loyalty. Kenneth knew its value too: he deleted the message immediately.

He looked at the paper again. McFall didn't understand the implications of what he was saying. He wouldn't know about the Westminster expenses scandal. Someone was working him.

He read the story byline: Gordon Buchan. Gallagher might have fucking known. Buchan was a year below him at school, a smug little shit who had introduced himself to Gallagher several times: 'I was a year below you at school,' he said each time, eyes narrowed in a mocking smile as if he was questioning Gallagher's integrity. Kenny had made no secret of his private school background. It was part of his appeal to the electorate. And hadn't the outgoing President of the Communist Party of Great Britain (Marxist–Leninist) himself said of Kenny Gallagher that it was a great man who fought for the rights of class, not his own? Buchan tried to shame him every time, and Gallagher responded by pretending to forget him every time. That probably upset Buchan enough for him to follow up McFall's story when he heard about it, to coax and coach him to make the slur catastrophic: did Gallagher take Bowman with him when he travelled? Who did McFall think would have paid for that? Would it be fair to assume that Jill got expenses? Wanker.

Social exclusion from the political process: that was a good point. He should jot a note of that, tell Pete, refer to himself and his privileged background, make it self-deferential. He could incorporate it in a speech later, not in reference to this, just set it up before the issue went live. Then refer back to it, make the whole thing look like part of an ongoing discussion.

Now quite calm, he opened the paper. Page five (should have been page three): McFall pictured grinning, wearing a pink Pringle sweater, toasting the lens with a flute of cheap champagne. He was standing in the driveway of his yellow-brick Lennoxtown mansion. The Carpet King of Kirki. Kenny would have found it funny if it wasn't levelled at him. McFall's house was made of yellow brick, the path was made of yellow brick and behind him was his three-car garage, doors yawning to show off the cars. Next to that picture was another, of Kenny sitting in the Parliament chamber, looking tired and crumpled and shifty.

Gallagher sat back. Bad lighting in there, natural light drained everyone. No one could look good in that light. He wondered who at the paper had editorial control, who chose it, who took it. It was taken from the public gallery, was it? From the TV camera? A still from footage?

He felt very calm.

He should call Peter, his secretary, decide on a course of action. He should call the paper, demand a right of reply. That point about exclusion, he could write a piece about expenses and participation in the political process, mention his private school years again, take the high ground. Pete might say it would make him look as if he was siding with the expenses fraudsters in Westminster. He should talk to Pete.

The sound of a car drawing up outside brought him back to himself. Annie. Car door slamming shut, car beeping locked.

Metal scratching metal as Annie's front door key sought the lock. Gallagher crossed his legs so that she would see his foot under the table from the door and know he was there.

The door opened and she stepped into the hall, dropped her bag, her coat. Gallagher gently swung his foot, beckoning to her but Annie stood still, watching him, he felt, but she didn't come into the kitchen. She jogged upstairs instead.

He called out, sounding annoyed, 'Annie?'

No answer. Rolling his eyes, he stood and went upstairs, not touching the banister, aware that his hands were tacky from the orange. 'Annie? Annie, where are you?'

She was in the bathroom at the top of the stairs, sitting on the toilet with the door open, skirt gathered around her waist, thighs bare and dimpled.

He was shocked, he'd never seen her on the loo. Annie didn't even want him there when she gave birth. Something fundamental had shifted.

'Oh, that's nice,' he said. 'Couldn't you shut the door?'

She glared at him. 'Have ye seen the newspaper?'

He looked down at her. She wasn't who she used to be. And it wasn't all new either, these were massive flaws that she had hidden from him, her sense of entitlement, her craven need for money, her burgeoning bourgeois pride.

She wasn't proud now, though. She looked him up and down and her lips tightened in disgust. 'Wee Kenny asked me if you've a girlfriend again. Boys at school have been asking him. Have ye?'

She held his eye, her disdain cutting through him until she started to piss, splashing loud into the water.

Rolling his shoulders back to make himself breathe in, Gallagher stepped into the bathroom and turned on the tap to wash the stickiness off his hands.

Little Kenneth was only twelve but already a shit-stirrer. He raised his eyebrows, mock innocent, and could be relied on to say whatever he shouldn't: 'Why is Granny Helen coughing like that?' when Annie's mother stank of cigarettes and had yellow fingers; 'Mummy, why is Daddy's accent different when he talks to Grandpa Malcolm than when he talks to you?'

'*I asked you a question.*' She hadn't raised her voice but he cringed at the sibilant hiss.

As he wiped his mouth to take the sting from his lips, he glanced at the mirror, saw Annie with her legs apart, rubbing herself dry with toilet paper. She met his eye in the mirror, her face contemptuous. 'You promised me.'

He was reaching for the hand towel when he felt the blow to his back, sending him crashing head first into the wall. As he fell his glance flicked past the mirror and he saw Annie, face obscured by the black black hair, airborne, moving like a wrestler on American TV. It was her shoulder that had hit him between the shoulder blades, her lips tight, teeth exposed like a fighting dog.

Gallagher went down, his head smashing off the edge of the sink with a glancing blow.

Trapped between the foot of the sink and the wall, pinned on his side with Annie on top of him, he struggled but couldn't get out. She had her weight on him, slapping wildly at his back, his head, his ears, scrabbling on the tiled floor, her legs shackled by the knickers around her ankles.

He grabbed for her wrists but missed, shouted, 'STOP!' the way you were supposed to if attacked, loud as he could. But Annie kept flailing ineffectual blows, her tears spilling onto his neck and face, panting disconnected syllables – sick— fuck— bas— shit.

Abruptly, the fight went out of her. She lay still, not looking at him, panting. Then she slid off him and got up, pushing the heel of her hand into the softness of his belly as if he was a thing, a rug, a bathmat. She stood then, looking dispassionately at herself in the mirror over the sink. Without glancing at him she bent, grabbed the knickers at her ankles, yanked them up and left the bathroom.

Kenny rolled onto his back, listening for her. He heard the door on the fitted wardrobe slide open.

Annie had hit him before, a primitive slap, overcome with shock or outrage, blinded by love and the need for him, but never like that, never with her knickers around her ankles.

She could have marked his face. Kenny scrambled up and looked in the mirror. No bruises. No throbbing that meant bruises would come up later, thankfully. He found a scratch of blood above his ear but it was under his hairline. He took a bit of toilet paper and dabbed at the wound, pressing hard to force more blood out, make it look dramatic.

She passed the bathroom door, hurrying downstairs and he followed her down. He stopped at the doorway to the kitchen, holding the tissue to his head so she would see what she had done.

'Annie, the papers are stirring all this up. It's Buchan again, check the byline. D'you think McFall could come up with that himself? I wasn't even in Inverness on the tenth. McFall reads the *Sun*, for Christ sake.'

She ignored him, picking up the breakfast things, dropping them carelessly in the sink.

'I was *here* on the tenth. Ask yourself *why now*. That's what you should be wondering about, Annie, not whether I broke a promise but *why now*.'

She froze, turned stiffly towards him, still not looking at him, and spoke as if she had prepared this speech: 'Kenny.' She looked very attractive, though her chin was wobbling and tears ran down her cheeks. 'When I first met you I had a job. I had ambition and self-respect and a degree. I had everything going for me.' Her voice cracked. 'You've belittled me. You've reduced me to the daft bint that does your cleaning and washes your clothes.'

'Annie, you're my *wife*.' He meant to elevate her out of the role she was sketching for herself, but it occurred to him that it might sound as if they were saying the same thing. 'Would I lie to your face?'

He had done that before, to be honest, and they both knew that, but they'd argued that one to a standstill and each was afraid to get into it again.

Annie stood very still and shut her eyes. 'Can you honestly believe that I don't know what a come-stain looks like?'

He was shocked to hear her use that coarse word. It took him a moment to appreciate what she had actually accused him of.

'Are you serious? When? When d'you think you saw that?' It must have been months ago, the last time he hadn't had the chance at a shower afterwards. Made sense of her change of mood, the coldness, the widening space in the bed, the jokes about strike action. It must have been months ago, so he said, 'This week? When? Yesterday? Let's see them, then.'

'I washed them.'

'Why did you wash them?'

'They were in the wash.'

'Do you honestly think I'd do that? Just throw them in the laundry for you to wash? Do you think I'm that sort of man?'

She was crying now, ashamed, and tried to leave the kitchen but he blocked her. 'Just . . . piss off to work, Kenny.'

'Annie,' he dipped at the knee to catch her eye, '*think*. Why now? The election's coming up. We're a threat to them now, for the first time ever. I warned you it would get dirty. It's no coincidence. They're afraid of us. It's Buchan, chasing this story, keeping it going. He's jealous. Think about it: when did McFall ever bother about expenses? "The Carpet King of Kirki"?'

He had hoped to make her smile with that but she didn't. He watched her think about it, doubt herself. The come stains were her one solid piece of evidence and he had her questioning that now. She was suddenly unsure and he went for it:

'They're afraid. I warned you. I said they'd use tricks like this, didn't I?'

Annie dropped her chin and pleaded. 'Just tell me the truth, Kenny. Just for once. Please?' she whispered. 'Just, please – as a friend – tell me the truth. Please?'

They were having completely different conversations.

Kenny was brighter than Annie. It was a fiction between them that she was brighter, because she had made her way up with no advantage, that he only got a better degree than her because of his private school background, but that wasn't true. Now she didn't even seem able to follow a simple train of thought. And she'd pissed in front of him. A woman couldn't piss in front of a man and expect him to respect her.

'Annie,' he stepped back and sounded stern, 'listen to me: *it's what the papers do.* They *ruin* people's lives for profit.'

She smirked and wiped her face with an open palm, smearing tears so that her cheeks glistened. 'The bastard capitalist press?'

'They ruin people's lives, Annie, and this is how they do it.'

'Who does?' She sniffed hard, tipping her head back and he saw the shadow of how beautiful she once was. 'The fucking *press*?'

He was annoyed at her swearing. 'The press in this country have a *grossly* disproportionate power. In the last year alone five—'

'DON'T BRING THAT TONE INTO OUR HOUSE!'

He stood still. Her voice was so loud it reverberated in his ear. There was a wildness about her, an expression wavering between fury and misery and he couldn't read her.

'DON'T BRING THAT HUSTINGS TONE INTO MY HOUSE.' As she shouted she shut her eyes tight, chopped a hand at him as if she might hit him again.

He backed away in case she did. She sounded unhinged, ir-rational, so he changed his manner and tried again. 'What I'm saying is this: it's the press. They're lying to discredit me. To discredit *you*. Humiliate you.'

'Humiliate me?' She was crying again, looked puzzled and frightened. 'Do you think they should be allowed to tell lies, to humiliate me?'

He didn't know where this was going, so he shrugged. 'No.'

'No.' She was crying and laughing. It looked disgusting. 'They *shouldn't* be allowed to lie and humiliate me.' 'Cause lying's wrong and if people just lie, and lying becomes normal, then the person who is telling the truth looks mental, don't they?'

She was calling him a liar, in their family kitchen, but Kenny decided to rise above all that and squinted as if he didn't get it. 'What? Are you saying they're trying to make me look mad?'

'Tell me the truth.'

'I *am* telling you the truth.'

Through her tears, she laughed, possibly at herself. 'God,' she shook her head, 'you're such a shallow, middle-class prick.'

She had never called him middle class, ever. She wasn't sorry either. She stood before him, every belligerent constituent he'd faced, every whining one of them. He felt the anger rise in him, a hot rage Annie couldn't possibly understand because she never had a place at the table to give up, to be here and fight here and work for the good of people who despised him for not belonging.

'Yeah. You know what?' Matter-of-fact. 'You know what, Kenny? You shouldn't let them. You should take a heroic stand against the press. Sue. It'll be great: one honest man against the combined forces of the capitalist press—'

'No—'

'Oh, yeah, yeah, no, come on.' She was shouting, laughing, furious, half mad. 'Sue. *Prove* to everyone that you're not a liar.'

'Annie, grow up—'

'Are footballers and press barons the only people with the right to a reputation? Why's there no legal aid for defamation? Can't ordinary people have a reputation? Ordinary families? There's a campaign you could get your righteous teeth into.'

Smart, he thought, using his own rhetoric against him. He had taught her something after all. 'You don't know what you're talking about. These are massive multinational companies. We don't have the resources to go up against them.'

She crossed her arms. 'Put this house up for it. It's worth half a million. Be worth it to me.'

They looked at each other, she snarling, he calm and reasoned, until he broke it off. 'Be realistic, Annie, even that won't be enough. We could lose everything. Think of the kids, we can't be reckless—'

'Oh, no, Kenny.' She looked hard at him. 'It's not reckless because we can prove it's not true. We'll win. We'll win because you're not a liar and you're not treating me like an idiot. You didn't marry me or have children with me to enhance your working-class credentials, parading me around your parents' golf club friends like a circus freak while shagging every rough-arse bitch that crossed your path.'

'Annie—'

'So, we'll sue. We'll win. We'll get Jill Bowman to give evidence that it's crap. We'll get McFall to admit he was made to say those things. And you were here on the tenth. We can prove that.'

She watched him, waiting, looking at his lips, willing him to speak. He didn't.

'Let's phone Jill now. Make sure she's on-message.' Her hand hovered over his mobile on the table. 'Is her number in here?'

He stood very still. 'Her number's not in my phone.'

'Oh.' She withdrew her hand. 'Not in your phone? Oh, that's odd. You have everyone in the office's number, but not Jill's?'

'She really wasn't there that much.' He gestured to the mobile. 'You're welcome to look if you don't believe me.'

Annie looked at the phone. 'I don't need to. I know it's not. It's in "recently deleted". I looked last night while you were getting ready to go out.'

He was thinking through his shower, trousers on the bed, phone in the pocket, when she said, 'It doesn't need to be you that calls her. I'll call her for you . . .'

He understood then that Annie was planning to leave him.

Kenny Gallagher felt his breastbone crack. Annie was going

to leave him and take the kids. She was going to leave him alone. The press would hear that she had left him. It would be confirmation of the rumours. Women, lots of women would flock forward and talk in snippets, fat women, young women, three men, watching men, fucking men, in hotels and bedrooms with photos of grannies on sideboards, with children's toys on the floor, in taxis and bars after hours.

He'd be ruined. He was a family man, a trustworthy man, a good man. And all that he had fought for, all his work would be lost, and he would be a middle-aged man alone in a lonely room and Malcolm would see him for the shadow he was.

Annie was going to leave him. McFall would phone her to commiserate, buy her mother cigarettes. He'd come over, pour wine, he'd fuck her to spite Malcolm. McFall was going to fuck Annie.

His mobile rang out suddenly.

Annie reached over and picked it up. She said 'Hello' in a normal voice and asked who it was. When she turned back to him her eyes were hooded. '*Daily News*.'

He took the phone.

'Hello, Kenny? It's Paddy Meehan at the *Daily News*. I wondered if you had time for a word about Tam McFall?'

He looked at Annie, her dead eyes watching.

'Sure, Paddy, what can I do for you?'

'Great.' Meehan sounded surprised that he was willing. 'McFall claims that you've been having an affair with Jill Bowman, is that true?'

'Look, Paddy, I have been very clear about this: I *do* know Jill Bowman. She has done some work in my office on a temporary contract. But *any* suggestion that our relationship has been anything but professional is nonsense. Party workers have the right to have their expenses paid. If we don't do that all working-class people will automatically be excluded from the political process. Social exclusion. That's what this story is about, Paddy. Think about it: you're from an ordinary family yourself. When you were young could you have afforded seventy quid for the train fare and overnight accommodation?'

'No, you know what, Kenny, you're right, I couldn't have. I'm very sympathetic to your position as you know but, honestly, I hadn't thought about that. Are everyone's expenses paid for, usually?'

'Of course they are, Paddy. The Labour Party is the party of social justice. We don't exclude people from the process because of their bank account.'

A cold, hypnotised smile seeped across Annie's face.

'So, Jill Bowman's expenses *were* paid?'

'Well, Paddy, here's the thing: I can prove that I wasn't even in Inverness on the tenth—'

'TELL HER, KENNY.' Annie spoke so loudly that Kenny was afraid Meehan would hear her.

'Is that Annie in the background, Kenny?'

'**TELL HER**.'

'Is that Annie? Can I speak to her?'

Kenny held a warning hand up to Annie, telling her to shut up.

Annie screamed, '***TELL HER!*** She might hit him and if she did Meehan would hear and it would be all over the papers.

Panicked, Kenny pressed the mouthpiece into his broken chest. '*What?*'

'Tell her you're not a liar. Tell her you're going to stand up for yourself.' Annie smirked. 'Go on. Tell her you're going to sue them.'

'Hello? Kenny? Hello?' Meehan was squawking into his chest. 'Can you hear me?'

He lifted the receiver to his mouth again. 'Paddy, can I call you back?'

'Sure,' said Meehan, sounding uncertain. 'Any special time that suits you?'

Annie blinked, disgusted, and turned away.

As her gaze left him Kenny felt his chest crumple, his ribs crush his lungs, pressing the heavy air out of him.

'Paddy! Are you still there?'

'Yeah?'

'Paddy. I'm going to sue.'

Annie turned back to him.

'I'm suing them.'

He watched as Annie's face softened to the beautiful girl she once was.

'I wasn't in Inverness that night. This is an attempt to discredit me before the election. I've been advised that I shouldn't say any more at this time but, eh, a press conference will be organised and we'll contact you with the details. OK?'

Meehan was hanging on his every word. Annie couldn't take her eyes from him, but they weren't dead or angry now, they were brimming, with hope, with respect, with love.

'OK,' said Meehan. 'OK, Kenny, thanks. You'll let me know where and when?'

'Pete'll call you when a time has been arranged.'

'Fantastic.'

8

Tamsin Leonard sat down across the desk from Alex Morrow and found she couldn't look at her boss. She had papers with her, set them on the desk to disguise her mood and tried to read the first page.

'The first organisation Pavel's in, 8G, has a large membership page on its website—'

'Why are you doing that?'

DS Morrow was sitting back, looking at Leonard's hands. She seemed annoyed.

'What, ma'am?'

'That.' Morrow flicked her thumbnail against her forefinger frantically. 'What's that about?'

Leonard stopped it and put her hand on her lap. 'Sorry.'

Morrow stared through her for a moment and nodded at the papers. 'Tell me.'

'8G has a large membership published on its web page. It's nine years old. Comparing Martin Pavel with the members who come after him on the membership page and declaring the fact that they joined in other sites, he's been in it for about three years.'

'So it's not a new thing?'

'No. Membership just involves signing up, it's more of a petition than anything.'

'What are they about then?'

'Paper campaigns during the G8 conference. Sending mass emails to the governments of member countries.'

Tamsin looked up. Morrow was listening with her head tipped. She nodded at the papers again.

'FEPA is, again, a pacifist organisation—'

'Yeah, they do some dreary education thing . . .'

'Yeah.' Tamsin smiled up, caught Morrow's eye. She blushed, shamed at the honest connection, made her eyes drop back to the desk. 'They're fine. He's a member but again, they don't seem to do any fund-raising or anything, just online support through pestering emails to local government. That sort of thing.'

'And the ULF?'

'Unity of Life Foundation.' Leonard wriggled in her chair as she warmed to her task. 'Couldn't find anything apart from their website. But take the "foundation" aspect out and suddenly loads of stuff comes up' – she pushed the sheets towards Morrow – 'evangelical organisations, pro-life organisations, an insurance company . . .'

'Where are they based?'

She checked her notes. 'The church is based in Surrey. The pro-lifers are American.'

'They shoot people, don't they? American pro-lifers. Do we know anything about Brendan Lyons' position on abortion?'

Leonard didn't know if she was being rhetorical. 'I don't know anything about that. Was he political?'

'Member of the Communist Party. What's their position on abortion?'

'I'll check it out.'

'Sounds like they'd be pro-choice. See if Brendan Lyons was involved in any campaigns or anything like that. Focus on current ones.'

Relieved to get out, Leonard stood up. 'Thank you, ma'am.'

'Yeah, Leonard? What's going on with you?'

Leonard froze. This was it. This was the time to own up.

It would be a relief to say it out loud, let the hot words spill out of her and fill the room. But Camilla would find out. She might miscarry. And she'd be turning Wilder in, and his life was shit already. It was too high a price to pay for that small relief.

'I'm ... I feel a bit sick,' she said, gathering her papers together. 'Queasy.'

She made her way to the door, to the corridor, out of that bubble of time where telling the truth was a possibility. At the door she glanced back and found DS Morrow watching her.

'Wilder was sick this morning. Maybe you two have caught a bug.'

Leonard nodded and shut the door behind her.

Tamsin drove slowly down a road of brand new brick warehouses, long red buildings with doors punched in at regular intervals. Next to each door was a three foot high number, white on red, denoting the unit address. Many had 'To Let' stuck over defunct business signs: a print shop, a baker.

DC Routher looked out of the window, quietly counting down the numbers like an excited child. He was young, had a spot on his chin, short brown hair as if his mother had told the barber what to do, and Leonard caught him smiling whenever she saw him out of the corner of her eye. She sensed that he was enjoying being driven, especially by someone ten years older than him with five years less service, but she didn't think about it too much. Her mind was taken up with Wilder.

Maybe Wilder was genuinely unwell, or having a crisis of conscience. Or he was drunk. Maybe he went home to take delivery of all the crap he'd bought on the internet last night – the cars, the traceable goods – and they'd get caught.

She thought about being caught, about Camilla being furious. Camilla was as pragmatic as a frontierswoman: if Tamsin was sent to prison there would be no question of her waiting for her.

'Twenty-one.' Routher grinned up at a red brick warehouse with a sign in almost illegibly elaborate Celtic lettering – 'TSF Electrical Engineers'.

Leonard parked in one of the many empty spaces.

Moving with perfect synchronicity, Routher and Leonard

unclipped their seat belts, slid the buckles over their shoulders, opened the doors and stepped one foot out onto the tarmac.

Suddenly, Leonard froze: her personal mobile was ringing in her trouser pocket, a dread vibration on her thigh.

Routher was out, standing by the open door, but sensed the change in her and bent down to look into the car. 'What?'

'My phone.' Her voice was high, breathless as she reached into her pocket and took out her personal phone.

'Bad girl!' Routher waggled a finger. 'Against the regs, having your phone with you on a call.'

But they were the same grade and she didn't have to take shit from him. 'I'll be with you in a sec.'

He looked disappointed that she didn't want to play with him, and shut the door. Then he stood with his back to the car window as she looked at the phone.

It was a text but it wasn't from Camilla. It came from an unknown caller and was a photograph, too small and dark to make out.

She opened it, pinched it wide and watched as it resolved. Blurry dark strips down each side and a silver rectangle bridging them at the top. Leonard's eyes strained to read the grain. Abruptly the picture blossomed into focus.

Leonard blinked.

She opened the car door, put one foot out, wide, leaned over and vomited neatly on the ground. She waited, a string of saliva dangling from her bottom lip, waiting to see if there would be more. No. No more. She lifted her foot back into the car and shut the door carefully.

This was why Wilder went home. This.

She looked back at the picture. She was the dark strip on the left of the picture and Wilder was her twin. The silver rectangle between them was the rear-view mirror from the squad car. They were standing in front of Hugh Boyle's car boot, holding bags. Even in the poor definition of a phone photo taken in the dark she could see the wideness of Wilder's eyes, the blank, stunned hang of her jaw. The picture had been sent from an unknown number.

A tap on the windscreen made her jump. It was Routher, eyebrows high. 'All right?'

She nodded. Made a sick gesture with her hand. Raised a rigid finger. Give me a minute. He nodded and looked away.

She'd been sick, it fitted in with Wilder being sick, with her saying she felt sick to Morrow. It still looked OK from the outside. She looked back at her shiny new phone.

Three weeks ago Leonard sat on a toilet in a pub and her phone slid from her back pocket into the toilet pan. This phone was new, this number was new and only eight or ten people had it; she hadn't even registered it at work yet. Wilder was one of the eight.

A snapshot memory of Wilder's face as he reached into the boot and touched the cash, the sharp white lights from the Audi uplighting his face. She considered, briefly, Wilder being lured somewhere this morning, being murdered, his phone being stolen and someone sending the text photo to her. That was too elaborate. She considered Wilder having a second phone, trying to blackmail her for her half of the money. But the picture had been taken from inside the squad car, while they were out of the squad car. Hugh Boyle had taken the picture.

Outside, Routher shifted his weight. Leonard pushed the phone back into her pocket, realising too late that Camilla hadn't miscarried and she should have been relieved. She climbed out of the car.

'You OK?'

'Got a bug. Felt sick all morning.'

Routher nodded. 'You want to go back to the station?'

'No, we're here now. Let's do it.' She led the way to the warehouse entrance.

'Sure you're OK?' he asked. 'What was the phone call about?'

'Nothing. Text junk ...'

Conscious of the need to seem present and alert, she pointed up to the roof of the warehouse. 'Three vandal-proof cameras.' She was stating the obvious, she might as well point up and say 'clouds'.

'Yes, and that's not a real burglar alarm box.' Routher smiled, as if joining in a game. 'The red light inside the grating is from a camera.'

Now they were playing a game and Tamsin didn't know how to get out of it. She fell quiet.

Routher pressed the buzzer, smiling at her, prompting her to take a turn. There was more to him than she had thought. The realisation made her suspicious.

A sing-song voice came from the speaker: 'TSF electrical engineering, how may I help you today?'

'Strathclyde Police,' said Leonard. 'Russell Crossan is expecting us.'

'Just a moment.'

She sounded young on the speaker, but after she had cross-checked the appointment, made them hold up their IDs for her to examine in the camera and let them in, they found a doughy middle-aged woman in girlish clothes and make-up.

She asked to see their cards again when they got through the door.

The company were making a big show of impregnability, they knew they were in the frame, Leonard thought, but the cameras on the front of the building were expensive and the inside of the building was double-lined and plastered to prevent anyone breaking in.

The receptionist smiled up at them. Disconcertingly, one of her false eyelashes had slipped up her eyelid. It made her look as if she was rotting.

Leonard took the woman's name and home address, asked her how long she had worked here. Three years, said Wendy. Leonard asked if they had a nightwatchman. They did. Wendy gave her his details too. It was irrelevant because the fault in the post office alarm system had been discovered on the morning of the robbery, but they knew Morrow would ask them anyway.

Wendy buzzed through to Russell for them.

A lock buzzed loudly on a far door and a tall man, denim-shirted, beige-trousered, came out to meet them.

'Russell Crossan,' he said, his hand out. 'This has never happened before. It's really worrying.'

Routher reassured him. 'It's just routine, Mr Crossan, we're exploring a number of avenues.'

But it wasn't routine and they all knew it.

'Can you take us into the back office?'

'Of course!' said Russell.

Taking ostentatious care, he covered the key pad with his body and typed in a security number, making the door fall open, telling them that he, personally, changed this number every week, he was the lead engineer and a partner in the firm and he chose the number. Then he blushed, appreciating that he was narrowing the frame to include no one but himself.

He led them through to a low-ceilinged open plan office. At the far end a glass wall looked into a brightly lit storage area. The two other engineers who worked for him were out on calls, their seats empty but their desks stacked with tidy piles of manuals and newspapers.

'You have a lot of cameras outside,' said Leonard.

'And inside,' Russell insisted. 'I mean, it's our office but we use it to showcase security equipment.'

He pointed to cameras in two corners of the small room and a red blink came from the smoke alarm in the ceiling. 'Back up,' he said.

It didn't seem to have occurred to Crossan that they might suspect him of telling the robber about the alarm. Leonard thought that was a good sign.

He offered them tea but they said no and sat with him to fill out the interview form, getting his contact details, his recollection of the day, notes of any speculations he might have about the incident. He didn't have any worth noting. Russell wasn't an imaginative man.

Routher asked him to talk them through the procedure when he got a call.

Russell warmed to the task: well, the call came direct from the manufacturing firm. Then they sent the details in an encrypted email. Routher asked why the details and job order were given separately? Because phone calls could be intercepted, explained Crossan, and email bugs always left a trace. They could triangulate any leaks, but there weren't any in this case. Was the post office address in the email? Russell said absolutely not: they never told him the address in advance, just the approximate journey time, fifteen or fifty minutes, just like that. Then he, or whoever was doing the job, whoever had a specialism in that sort of system, waited in the office for the part to arrive. The manufacturer ordered the taxi for them.

'So you never know where you're going?'

Russell said no, the manufacturer didn't tell them. This part was being flown in from down south. A taxi would come from the airport, pick them up and take them.

Leonard listened, letting Routher ask the questions, nodding when he looked at her, nodding when Crossan looked at her, nodding, nodding and nodding.

Russell Crossan smiled at her and Leonard suddenly thought she might throw up again. She shifted softly in her chair and nodded.

'Mr Crossan,' she was surprised at the calmness of her voice, 'could you give us a list of other companies you've performed this duty for?'

'Certainly,' said Crossan. 'Absolutely, good idea, so you can ask them about us? Absolutely.'

'May I use your toilet?'

Crossan took her back out to reception and showed her through a door to a very cold bathroom.

She thanked him, locked the door and slumped against the wall. She stayed there for a long time.

Russell Crossan gave them a huge amount of paperwork: printed lists of clients, references for the company's work, for Russell's previous employers, his own personal credit check – he was applying for a mortgage and had looked it up anyway – maybe they would like it? They left with a folder full of paper, DVD footage of the inside and outside of the office, front and back for the entire week before.

Russell stood by the door to the warehouse, anxiously waving them off.

Leonard pulled out, leaving it to Routher to wave back.

'What do you think?' asked Routher as they turned onto the main road.

'Dunno, what do you think?'

'Keen to help.'

'Yeah.'

'We should find out if the taxi driver had been given the address.'

'Could it be such a specific part,' wondered Routher, 'that he could work the address out? That post office had that problem before.'

It was a good point, a smart point, they both knew it.

'Worth checking out, I suppose?' said Routher, sounding as if he was fishing for a compliment.

'Yeah.'

'You still feeling ill?'

'Very.'

'Maybe you should call in sick.'

'Yeah, I think I'll have to.' She glanced up and found Routher smiling again, the way he had smiled on the way there. She realised that he wasn't grinning because he had one over on her. He was smiling because he was a decent man and he liked working with her. All that other crap was her own.

9

Morrow looked down the street at an unremarkable row of domestic tenements. It was the last Victorian man standing in a bleak industrial area by the river. It looked innocent, the red sandstone was stained deep burgundy by the incessant rain, but the uniformity of the net curtains hinted at the institutional nature of the building. That and the prison-level security on the entrance; a white metal cage with a lock the size of a paperback and a steel door behind it.

Morrow would have sent someone else but she was checking out a hunch from the old Anita Costello case. She couldn't send anyone else because she wouldn't know what she wanted to ask Anita's daughter until she got there. These calls were what propelled most officers to seek promotion, she thought, not ambition, not the need to serve on a higher level or a burning desire to piss about with politics, but the craven need to avoid calls like this: face to face with the lost.

This homeless unit was not for families down on their luck or single men and women seeking work. It took wet cases, drunks and drug users, masters of chaos, people with open sores and transmittable diseases, those struggling with unsympathetic mental illness. A lot of the residents were recently released prisoners with nowhere else to go. A good proportion of them would have been left to die under bridges in a more brutal time. The city had opened the unit in this cash-and-carry wilderness because there were no residents to object and nothing for them to steal.

Harris had called ahead and someone was watching. The cage over the door buzzed as they approached. They stepped inside and had to shut the cage behind them before they could open the front door.

A man was waiting for them inside. His skin was grey but his ginger stubble was as fresh as monsoon grass. 'Keith Beckman.' He held out his hand, chin jutting aggressively.

Keith looked each of them in the eye as he squeezed their hands, yanking them down hard as though they were having a secret arm wrestle. He smirked at the end, as if he had won.

Morrow looked around. The hallway was an old close, cold and grey as a prison. A noticeboard was nailed to a wall next to a museum-piece vandal-proof telephone with phone books resting on a shelf below.

Keith took a breath to speak, when a door opened two feet from them. An old man's face appeared, cheeks slash-scarred and his nose flattened. He jumped when he saw the three of them standing there, and slammed the door shut.

Licking his lips unkindly, Keith looked to them for a reaction.

Morrow touched her face. 'Duelling scars?'

Beckman snickered at that, puffing the sour smell of cigarette smoke at her. 'Good one.' He looked back at the door and laughed unpleasantly again. 'Good. Come in here.'

He showed them into a communal space that smelled of strong urine and weak disinfectant. Armchairs were arranged around a boxy television pinned to the wall and in a mesh cage. Resting on the arm of a chair, the filthy remote was held together with a gaffer-tape girdle, the sheen of black worn clean in the middle of the buttons.

'You know she's had a head injury?' said Keith.

'I didn't know that,' said Morrow.

'Yeah, car mowed her down.' He shrugged. 'She fell asleep walking across a dual carriageway.' He smirked at that and Morrow thought that she would give up her pension to get away from people like Keith. His bitterness had a sadistic tang to it.

'Well,' she said, 'that's very sleepy.'

'She used to "get sleepy" a lot.'

'Not any more?'

'Hard to tell with some of them. Just moved in, we'll see. I'll get her.' He left.

Alone in the room, Morrow and Harris looked at the arm-chairs. They were purple plastic, waterproof presumably, with a design of triangles and squares that looked like an abstract representation of vomit. Harris shook his head and stayed on his feet.

'No,' she said, 'me neither.'

By the window a flimsy table had three wooden chairs set around it and they sat there, Harris pulling the third chair out for their interviewee before taking his own.

Keith's voice echoed down the corridor outside, 'Yes!'

A woman muttered something in reply.

'Get in!' shouted Keith. Harris and Morrow shook their heads at each other: Keith shouldn't be working here, he was badly burnt out.

The door banged open and Keith hustled a woman in.

If Morrow hadn't read the case files she would have thought Francesca Costello was thirty-something. The seventeen-year-old was missing four of her front teeth and her top lip collapsed over the gap. She was fat, had cut her own black hair very badly, brown flaky something was dried on one side of it. She was dressed in a faded pink velour tracksuit, the top zipped up and her fists meeting each other in the pockets.

Morrow could read Francesca's sorry history: she was hiding her hands because they were heroin-puffed, keeping them fisted in her pockets in case of an attack. Francesca got fat, left her teeth out and made herself unattractive, because to be attractive was to be prey.

Alex Morrow did not want to know these things. She didn't want this in her head when she went home to her boys, didn't want Francesca on her mind on Christmas Day. She didn't want to look at her presents on her knee and wonder where Francesca was or how she was feeling or if she was safe. Her discomfort made her angry with the ugly woman, disgusted with her, as angry as Keith, and she recognised it as a shared primordial need to blame the luckless for their fate.

'Francesca?' she asked.

'Cry me "Frankie".' The girl couldn't raise her eyes to Morrow's. She remained standing.

'Frankie, I'm DS Alex Morrow.' Morrow held her hand out. Frankie looked at the hand and puffed a laugh, her top lip ballooning out, but Morrow kept her hand out, giving it a little rehearsal shake as if to show Frankie what to expect.

Keeping her eyes on the fingers, Frankie pulled one hand out from the haven of her pocket and took hold of Morrow's fingertips, giving them a coy little tweak. The skin on Frankie's hands felt spongy, bags of pooled blood because the valves in her veins were ruined. Morrow invited her to take the chair and sat down herself while Frankie sized up the situation and decided whether to join them or not.

'Sit!' barked Keith.

Francesca shuffled awkwardly into the space between the chair and the table and sat down, hands tucked away, and back bent so she was facing the table top.

Sensing their disapproval of his method, Keith explained, 'A lot of our residents are suspicious if you're nice to them. Best just be straightforward.'

'Aye,' said Harris, and Morrow sensed he was finding Keith heavy going too. 'Can we just talk to Frankie alone now?'

Keith swithered. 'Well . . .' He looked at Morrow, thought about it. 'OK.' He stepped towards the door and turned back. 'I'll be just out here.'

'Thanks, Keith,' said Morrow, enjoying the defiant gleam in Francesca's eye.

Keith shut the door behind him and Francesca raised her

head. She looked at Morrow, not as if she was a person, but as an object, eyeing her hair and her clean pressed coat, her handbag containing keys to a house, chewing gum, tissues for in case.

'Frankie,' said Morrow, 'I wanted to ask about your mum.'

'Huh.' Her eyes fell back to the table.

'Would that be all right with you?'

She shrugged long and hard, looked up to the dark television and muttered, 'Nob'dy cares who done that anyway.' The void of front teeth muffled her voice.

'It was more about the robbery beforehand.'

Frankie looked straight at her then, wary. 'How?'

'When was that? Just three years ago?'

Frankie looked back at the TV, a conversational habit, Morrow thought, from always being in rooms where a TV blared in the corner. 'Is it?'

It seemed like it had been a long three years.

'I wanted to ask about the guy who robbed your mum. You were there that night, weren't you?'

Slowly, Frankie brought her puffy hands out of her tracksuit pockets, put one fist on top of the other, and rested her chin on the fleshy tower. 'Georgie Mac.'

'Is that his name?'

'Aye, Georgie Mac robbed us.'

'What's Mac short for?'

'Dunno.'

'At the time, your mum said she didn't know who it was. Was that true?'

'Aye, she never knew. He telt us after she died.'

'Why didn't she know? Was he a stranger?'

'He'd a mask.'

'What kind of mask?'

Frankie moved a hand over her face. 'Grey. A hole . . .' she said, her finger tracing part of an oval on her face. Her eyes were animated and bright as she remembered and Morrow could see then that she wasn't brain damaged. She wondered what it was about Keith that made Frankie pretend she was.

'Why did he tell you it was him?'

She rolled a shoulder. 'Just telt us.'

'Was he sorry?'

Frankie looked confused. 'Fur wha'?'

'Robbing you.'

'Never robbed me, robbed my mum.'

'He took her money, didn't he? We always assumed she'd been killed because she couldn't pay her debts, so he was kind of responsible. Am I wrong?'

Frankie looked vague. She must have thought about it, must have railed against him in some way. 'My pal from St Helen's knowed him . . .' She tailed off. St Helen's was a secure unit for kids who were in danger or beyond parental control. Most of St Helen's alumni graduated seamlessly to prison.

'He just telt us.' She scratched her head hard.

'Were you in care before your mum was robbed?'

She tutted indignantly. 'Nut. Good mum, my mum.'

'But you were after?'

'After she died, aye.'

'You didn't have any family you could go to?'

Frankie grinned, giving them the full benefit of her gums. They looked raw, as if she'd lost her teeth recently. 'Granny. Couldn't keep us in the hoose.'

'What's your pal from St Helen's called?'

'Sheila.'

'Sheila what?'

'Dunno.'

She knew, Morrow could tell, but she'd never tell them. They could find out if they needed to anyway.

'Where did you meet this Georgie Mac?'

'Party.'

'Whereabouts?'

102

'Dunno.'

They looked at each other and Frankie excused herself, 'Ye cannae do him, anyway, eh? Over now.'

'Was it a lot of money?'

'Cou'le o' hundred.' Frankie smirked. 'Aye. Never needed the money neither, he says.'

'Why did he do it then?'

Frankie smiled up to the ceiling. 'Dunno.'

'You're smiling, Frankie, why do you think he did it?'

'Jus' having a laugh, I suppose,' she said flatly.

Outside, on the wet pavement, Morrow and Harris walked down to the car in silence. It was ridiculous, Morrow knew, to worry about carrying the sorrow of Francesca home on her cuffs, but she did.

'Does that bother you, ever?' said Morrow quietly.

Harris sighed, squinting up at the stream of cars two blocks away, queuing for the motorway. 'Sometimes. There'd be a lot more like her if we didn't do this.'

She was irritated by the pat, party line answer. 'But why us?'

Harris heard her this time and stopped walking, looked at her. 'If we don't do it the Keiths will,' he said.

They walked on. Harris drew a breath to speak but Morrow interrupted him. 'Check for "George Mac" or "Georgie Mac" in connection with robbery or guns. And anyone called Sheila resident in St Helen's over the past three years.'

'I've heard the name "Georgie Mac" somewhere, in connection with something. Can't remember . . .'

'Yeah?'

He shook his head at the ground. 'Something about Gourock.'

'Rings a bell. Didn't Pavel say something about an Ayr accent?'

'Aye.'

She stopped at the door of the car. 'You can drop me in the town. I'm meeting my brother.'

He reeled, surprised that she had said it to him. 'Danny McGrath?'

'Yeah. Today just keeps getting better and better.'

10

Kenneth Gallagher and Annie drove to his parents' house in a dazzled silence. It seemed as if every small conurbation of shops they passed on the way to Jordanhill had a poster outside carrying the headline 'CLASS TRAITOR'– GALLANT GALLAGHER FIGHTS BACK.

Neither of them could quite believe how public everything was this morning, how a deeply private argument seemed to have ruptured out of their family kitchen into the public domain.

Kenny slowed down as he drew into his parents' street. He didn't want to be here but Annie had insisted that they speak to Malcolm before scheduling the press conference. She was calling Kenny's bluff, banking on abrasive Malcolm making him drop the law suit if he was lying and saving them all from ruin.

Kenny could see that his recklessness scared her, this clever, beautiful woman, but not suing would mean admitting he'd fucked Jill Bowman in a stationery cupboard at his constituency office, in a B&B in Inverness, that she'd sucked him off in a car outside the party conference. Annie would leave him and McFall would fuck her. Gallagher's life's work, the glory, the sacrifices, the love of the people . . . it would all be lost. Malcolm would be proved right: he'd end up teaching. He had to sue.

Looking up, he saw his mother framed in the window of the front room, arms crossed below her breasts, watchful, waiting. Her eyes followed the car as it pulled slowly up the street. A shadow moved behind her, drawing her away from the glass: Malcolm, his stepfather, pulling her into orbit.

Kenneth's parents' house was slightly better than the

neighbours' on most counts: bigger garden, corner plot, larger windows, two-car garage. They could have afforded a much larger house, up in Lenzie, nearer Malcolm's golf club, but they wanted to stay where they were, though they didn't like the neighbours or the neighbourhood.

Kenny drove around the corner to the back and the dank, sunless alley behind the garage. They passed the back gates and saw Malcolm and Moira watching for them from the conservatory.

The garage door was open and Kenny parked his Honda next to Malcolm's Jag, turned off the engine, looked out into the lane he had skulked in as a boy, smoked in, gone and come from school, from uni, from marches. He came back here from the Battle of Bath Street, with fresh stitches on his swollen cheek, not knowing about the press photo, or what he had just become. Everyone called him Kenneth then. It was the press who dubbed him 'Kenny'. Even now, he could tell where people knew him from by how they addressed him. Annie called him 'Kenny'. Everyone in the Labour Party called him 'Kenny'. It sounded boyish to him now. He was getting too old for it.

In the dark of the garage, Annie turned in the passenger seat and looked at him. Kenny couldn't look back. He got out, walked through the open side door and waved to his mother at the window. Moira raised her hand in reply, fey, dropping it to her side, keeping her eyes on them as if she was unsure whether they would come in.

Annie overtook him. Kenny trailed after her across the lawn and the gravelled side path, across to the conservatory door. He walked heavy-limbed, falling behind, dreading a discussion of his sexual behaviour with his mother.

Moira stood guard by the door, opening it before Annie reached the step, wanting to get them in before the neighbours saw them. 'Whatever is it?'

'Go inside and we'll talk about it there.' Annie slipped past her. When they stood next to each other he noticed how slim his wife was, how sleek her dark hair, the blue-black gleam of her bob as it sliced across her slim neck. And his mother, broad, square, stumpy-necked and ashamed of it, the Hermès neckerchief disguise serving only to draw the eye to the offending area. Her immoveable hair was styled solid blond.

Moira looked past Annie. 'Kenny. How are you, darling?'

She held his chin and kissed his cheek softly, hand lingering there as if he was a sweetheart in a film about the war.

'What's happened now?' Malcolm had stayed in the conservatory but came now into the kitchen. He was tall but not as tall as he acted: he stooped as if no room was tall enough for his incredible stature, hands behind his back as if he had been in the army, which he hadn't. His cardigan was buttoned and flattened, his shirt open at the neck revealing the root of his sagging wattle and a string of grey chest hair. He would have done the top button up if Annie hadn't come.

Kenny walked through the warm conservatory into the seating area of the kitchen, dropping his eyes as he passed the wall of framed photos of himself. They were from newspapers and magazines, sometimes Moira wrote in and asked for proper stills, sometimes she cut them out of the mag. Kenny and Tony, Kenny and Gordon, Kenny and Ed. Gallant Gallagher wins! Kenny and Annie Gallagher Show Us Their New Home. Kenny Gallagher enchanting an audience in suits. Kenny Gallagher with Nelson Mandela. That was a print. They gave you that when you met Nelson, his photographer gave you that. There were no photos of Annie or the kids on the walls. One picture of his half-brother, James, the photo the papers used when he was run over and killed. The biggest picture was facing the door, the Battle of Bath Street front page in a modest clip frame. The newspaper was yellowing and Moira had cropped the bottom of the page with scalloped scissors and then folded it over to make it tidy. It always bothered him that she left it like that.

They all slid onto the twin benches flanking the breakfast table:

first Kenny and then Annie, first Malcolm and then Moira. The table was too low for Kenny's legs, always made him feel trapped. It had been built for himself and James and Moira when the boys were little. It wasn't a fit for men.

'So . . .' Malcolm was yet to make eye contact. Hands clasped together, he leaned into the middle of the table, taking up all the space and forced himself to smile: '*What is going on?*'

Annie stood back up and, in a moment of effortless elegance, twisted her torso, looked down her right arm and her coat slid from her shoulders into her waiting hands and the old dynamics were back: Malcolm hating her and loving her, Moira hurt because she knew he'd had affairs with girls like that, common girls like that. She was already on the edge of tears, ready for another slight from her jailer. And Annie, proud, knowing the shadow she cast, powerful.

'Malcolm,' she said softly as she sat back down, 'I don't know if you've heard but Kenny's in the papers again—'

'I am well aware,' said Malcolm.

Annie stalled but continued. 'They're saying he's had an affair with a party worker called Jill Bowman—'

'I do know about that.' Malcolm looked at Kenny, scowl on his lips, a smile in his eyes. 'McFall made the allegations. I should have let him join, shouldn't I?'

Malcolm had blocked McFall's membership of the Kintail Golf Club three times, despite his being proposed and seconded by different veteran members each time. It was personal. McFall would have said something to Malcolm, something Malcolm could not forgive, so it could actually have been anything. He might have parked a newer car next to Malcolm's. He might have flirted with a waitress Malcolm was after. Malcolm said it was because McFall couldn't play golf. So now Kenny's entire career was hanging in the balance, all because Buchan had stumbled on a rival of Malcolm's, all because of bad feeling about a golf club membership.

'Kenny wants to sue the newspaper for defamation,' Annie ploughed on. 'He's scheduling a press conference today.'

Malcolm kept his eyes on his stepson. 'Is that wise?' He dropped his voice, as if they were keeping it from Annie. 'Are you proposing to sue?'

Kenny watched his wife drop her coat over her knees, smooth the silky lining as she crossed her fine legs.

'I am,' he told Annie. 'I'm suing because it's not true.'

Malcolm huffed, as if he was laughing. 'How are you proposing to pay for that? Legal aid?'

'No,' said Annie. 'We won't get legal aid.'

Proud, Moira's eyes widened at her son. 'Because you're earning too much?'

'No,' said Annie, 'there is no legal aid for defamation.'

'I hope you don't think we're going to support you,' said Malcolm loudly. 'Legal action is very expensive.'

Annie caught Kenny's eye and smiled briefly. It was word-for-word what Malcolm said when they told her Annie was pregnant. Wanting to linger in that warm memory, Kenny repeated what he'd said back then: 'We'll find the money somehow.'

'As long as that somehow doesn't include me or your mother.'

Moira said, 'Well, I'll get the tea.'

She went to the counter and reboiled the kettle, poured the water into the waiting pot on a tray and brought it back to the table with four mugs and a plate of caramel Rocky biscuits arranged in a fan. She always served them when Annie was there, not the usual Marks and Spencer's Extremely Chocolatey Rounds. On better days Annie and Kenny laughed about it.

She had picked the mugs instead of teacups, mugs that looked a little like teacups, with pink flowers and stumpy stems. She stood by the cramped table and put the tray down, held the plate of biscuits out to Annie. Annie took one, feigning delight.

Moira watched, monitoring Annie until she opened the biscuit wrapper and took a small bite. Then Moira gave a triumphant little nod, reminding them all that she'd once caught Annie slipping a biscuit in her pocket, when she was dieting.

She offered the plate to Kenny and he took one, glancing up to catch the glint of joy that he always saw on his mother's face whenever he ate anything. Malcolm took two. 'I like these,' he said.

This annoyed Moira. 'You could just have one ...' she said and stopped, looked down.

Malcolm had hit her only once or twice, early in the marriage. 'Different in those days,' Malcolm would say when the subject of domestic violence came up now. Moira, pregnant with James, cowering in the kitchen, a black eye swelling slowly over the course of an evening in front of the telly. She never again asked Malcolm why he was at work all the time or spent his weekends at a golf club she wasn't allowed into.

Keeping her eyes down, Moira slipped quietly into her place.

Malcolm had to eat both biscuits now, because Moira had suggested he have one. His mouth was full but they sat in silence as he opened his second biscuit and crammed it in, jawing his way through it, joyless, glaring at his wife.

Kenny usually enjoyed enmity between his parents, especially when Annie was there. She didn't put up with that sort of crap from him. Their relationship was quite different, but today he saw that it was not helping his cause. Annie was thinking about leaving him and she might be glad never to sit at this table again, watching Malcolm chip away at Moira.

'So,' said Moira, giving the sort of martyred smile that would make anyone want to give up smiling altogether, 'why did you come if you don't want money? What can we do for you?'

Kenny looked at Annie expectantly.

'It was my idea to come. I want Kenny to talk to you about it before he decides for sure. I think he could do with your input, Malcolm.'

'My input?' He looked flattered.

'Because you're an outside eye.'

It sounded hollow. She might as well have said it was because Malcolm was a philanderer and knew what a man like that could get away with. Kenny smiled twitchily at his mother, trying to pretend he didn't know what she meant either.

Annie stood up. 'I'll nip to the loo.'

Moira stood up quickly, blocking Annie's exit. 'I could come with you.'

But Annie didn't want her to. 'I can go to the toilet myself, Moira. You should stay . . .' she said, trying to step past her.

'No, I'll come . . .'

'I'm going to the *lavatory*, Moira.' It sounded aggressive the way she said it, without moderating her accent, giving them her flat Castlemilk vowels.

Moira sat back down, watching Annie's knees as she moved past her. Kenny watched them and knew that Moira was furious at Annie for refusing to protect her from this, for bringing him here, like a cat bringing in a dead bird.

Annie walked out of the kitchen to the hall. They all listened for the toilet door clicking shut.

'She's going to leave you,' said Moira.

The Rocky turned to gravel in Kenny's mouth.

Malcolm twitched a smile. 'What'll happen to the children?'

'We're not splitting up.'

'Why did she bring you here then?' He suppressed a triumphant smile. 'What do I know about it?'

'She respects your opinion . . .'

'No, she doesn't,' Malcolm huffed and looked out to the hall. Then he looked back at Kenny. 'You know why she brought you here.'

'Oh, why would that be, Malcolm?' He heard himself sounding like a teenager.

'She wants to humiliate you.'

'She's furious,' added Moira.

'Yes, she's furious.'

Kenny struggled to chew the biscuit. The chocolate felt as thick as feathers on his tongue.

They all sat for a moment, at the table, as the wall clock ticked softly.

Malcolm broke the deadlock: 'Who is Jill Bowman?' He raised an eyebrow.

'I barely met her.' But he couldn't look at his stepdad.

Malcolm smirked. 'You know: McFall will fight dirty but he's not a liar.'

Kenny took another bite of his biscuit. Malcolm was thinking that Kenny was him, he always did that, but Kenny wasn't him. He was a better man by far and it sickened him to be thought of that way.

'Where's she from, the Bowman girl?'

'Knightswood, I think,' said Kenny and then remembered he probably wouldn't know that, if he barely met her. He was sure he was blushing.

'Still, nicer than Castlemilk, I suppose . . .'

'Oh, for God's sake.'

Malcolm dropped his voice. 'I've been treating these people for forty years, Kenneth, I know these areas.'

These people. Another dead argument, another unsayable.

'Anyway,' said Kenny, blithely, 'never mind me. How are you?' He looked hard at his stepdad. He was retired and so obnoxious and bullying that even his old practice didn't want to use him as a locum. No one wanted him to work for free on any of the committees or historical societies, even the Kintail Golf Club had passed a motion for him to be removed from the board.

'Did you have that girl? Are you suing them on the basis of a lie?'

'No.'

Malcolm narrowed his eyes thoughtfully. 'You'd better have

thought this through, Kenneth, as a *potential future leader* of the Labour Party.'

It was an odd thing to say; Malcolm never gave him credit.

'I have thought it through . . .' said Kenny tentatively.

'*You cannot win*. It's too expensive and you'd have to take a year out of work to bring it. Losing is inevitable.'

'I'm just—'

Malcolm dropped his voice again. 'That is your line. The election's coming up. They've come after you because you are a future star. You never could win against them. *That's* what you tell them before, during and after you lose.' He glanced at the toilet door in the hall. 'And transfer the house into her name, if you haven't already.'

A losing speech. A great losing speech. Malcolm smiled at his stepson and Kenny smiled back as the toilet flushed.

'Transfer it?'

Malcolm stood up, stepped across the room. 'They can't take it when you lose.'

The toilet door opened but Annie paused in the hall, listening. She switched the light off, came back in and sat down at the table without speaking. Pointedly, she lifted the nibbled chocolate biscuit, pulled the wrapper flat over it and put it back on the plate.

Moira looked at her inquiringly.

'I never liked to say so before,' Annie said primly, 'but I don't really like Rockys, Moira.'

Moira looked at the half-eaten biscuit. 'Oh?'

Annie smiled at her. 'I really prefer Markies' Extremely Chocolatey Rounds – have you ever had them?'

Moira shook her head vaguely, as if she had never heard of Marks and Spencer, or chocolate, or things being round before.

Annie blinked slowly. 'They're very nice.'

Moira nodded. 'They sound nice.'

Annie was smiling now and looked at Kenny. 'So, did you talk about the legal action?'

'Yes.'

'What's the conclusion?'

'Going ahead with it.'

She looked at Malcolm. Malcolm nodded at her, a small curt nod. The tension went out of Annie then; she looked at her husband and smiled, her eyebrows twitching an apology. Kenny finished his biscuit and smiled back.

'You two must have been under an awful lot of pressure,' said Malcolm, nodding at Moira. 'How about we pay for a nanny and let you two go away for the weekend together? Where would you go?'

Annie and Kenny smiled at each other. They couldn't do it, Andy had asthma, but it was a nice idea.

'Port Patrick,' he said. 'That seafood restaurant.'

Annie added, 'And that wee hotel on the cliff?'

'With the trouser press?' They laughed at that. The heating was broken when they stayed there and they kept the trouser press on all night to keep them warm. They bought Christmas tree decorations from a shop on the quay, gorgeous glass balls with little ships in them, only three of them, one for each of the kids as it turned out, because they were very expensive. They told the kids about the trip every year when they put them on the tree, pretended they knew there would be three of them. It was the first joint purchase they ever made.

Suddenly doubtful, Annie broke off eye contact. 'Seriously, are you doing this?'

'Yes,' he said.

Annie asked Malcolm, 'Can we win?'

Malcolm shrugged. 'I don't know. But I suggest that you separate for a while, Kenneth can move in here, into his old room and you should transfer the house into your name. That way, if you lose, you'll have a better chance of keeping it. But if you *win*,' he smiled warmly, 'you'll be facing a large award, I suspect.'

Annie liked that, both the relief of a pretend separation and the possibility of a big cash payout. Possibly the separation more than the money.

Kenny's mobile rang out in his pocket, and he straightened his leg and felt for it, mumbling an apology because he always did when his phone rang. He slid along the bench and got up, walked over to a corner of the kitchen, knowing they would listen anyway.

It was Peter, his press secretary. He didn't waste time with greetings and his voice was muffled. 'Meehan from the *News* phoned here for a reaction. Now the constituency party have called a closed emergency meeting. They're all leaving their work *now*. Kenny, what the fuck did you say to Meehan?'

'I'm suing them.'

'You're *what*?'

Gallagher resisted a cringe. 'I'll get there in an hour.'

And he hung up.

'They'll dig up anything they can,' Malcolm was saying to Annie. 'Are you ready for that?'

An emergency meeting. Through infighting and schism the constituency activists had dwindled to retired trade unionists, lesbians and lovelorn middle-aged women.

'*Kenneth!* Are you ready?'

'Yes!' He was startled to attention.

'If you've had at any of those girlies,' Malcolm's eyes were bright, 'some drunken tittie fun at a Christmas party . . .' Moira gasped and looked away. 'Well, don't listen if it bothers you, Moira, for heaven's sake. What I'm saying is that you'd better be ready, Kenneth.'

'I am ready, Malcolm.'

Annie crossed her legs. 'Moira, we're going to hear worse.'

Moira looked at Annie, gave a terse smile.

Annie said, 'Everyone knows what a lady you are, Moira. Just keep your head up.'

Moira liked that. She smiled, glanced at Annie's ample chest and smiled wider.

Annie let the slight go. 'This could work out well, Kenny. Really well.'

Everyone was smiling. Everyone was happy. Annie would get away from him. Malcolm would come to the court, play the angry father of a great man, and get his picture in the papers.

Kenny Gallagher, Gallant Gallagher, the Greatest Living Scot in two polls running, smiled back.

II

Morrow watched her brother walk into the café like a mayoral candidate, waving to other customers, clamping the proprietor's hand in a two-handed shake, nodding to Morrow as he swapped pleasantries with the man's wife.

Danny suggested meeting here because this was how he wanted her to see him: popular, belonging, accepted. The café owner looked up to him smiling, slightly awe-struck. Morrow knew then that Danny owned part of this business or had lent the man money. The man didn't like him, he owed him. Maybe Danny didn't register the difference.

It was positive, in a way, that he wanted her to see him as a good guy, instead of in a big car or with totems of his wealth around him, and it was probably a big deal that he came alone, or almost alone. She could see a man sitting in the driver's seat in the big car across the road, but Danny had left him out there.

Still, the café business was a cash business, perfect for cleaning up the vast sums of money Danny and his associates were generating every day. The drugs trade was worth more than a billion pounds a year in Scotland. Some estimates said four billion but the source of that number was looking for more funding so she wasn't sure about that. Whatever the absolute number, it was telling that cash businesses were being taken over. Hairdressers, sunbed shops, nail bars, cafés, pubs were being either taken over or opened up to give a credible source for the tidal wave of dirty notes. Some high streets had row upon row of tanning salons right next to each other to account for various people's income.

Even nurseries, Morrow had heard, even there the gangs were using businesses and claiming for fifty ghost children attending, all doing 8–6 every day, all paid for in cash.

Still having his hand pumped by the café owner's, Danny smiled over at her, and Alex smiled back. Despite everything, Danny and Alex had always liked each other.

They looked alike, both tall, same blond hair, same deep dimples. They even mirrored one another's laconic temperament. But Danny's mother drank to Olympic standard and took up with whichever nasty man she woke up next to. He had told her that when he was sent to Polmont Young Offenders' Institution it felt like Disneyland because they had hot food three times a day. He even liked it when they locked the door at night because no one could get in to hit him. He was seventeen, already a celebrity thug and had a three-year-old son, JJ.

Morrow and Danny stayed away from each other until JJ was sent to prison for a brutal rape. When Morrow was called upon to give evidence about the boy's background, she saw that they were part of each other, deeply. She became a police officer because Danny was a thug; she married Brian because he was dark and quiet and gentle. Her life was always a mirror to Danny's. Her mother's anger had coloured her whole life and Morrow wanted more for her boys. She didn't want their lives to be shot through with rancour the way hers had.

She stood to meet Danny coming across the messy little café towards her. He looked her in the eye and touched her upper arm, an infinitely tender gesture from him.

'Let me get you a coffee,' he said and turned back to the café owner who was watching expectantly, chin pointing at them, lips parted in readiness.

'A latte for me, Malik, and,' he turned to Morrow, 'latte?'

'Aye.' She smiled as he looked back at the man and told him to make that two. Lattes used to be called milky coffee, but again here was Danny, showing her he knew about lattes, that he had a sheen of sophistication, that he was no longer filth. She thought it was positive that he was keen to impress her.

He turned back and sat down next to her on the low faux-leather settee, leaving a respectful space between them.

'How are ye?'

'Good, Dan, how's you?'

'No bad, keeping busy. How's the boys?'

'Both great, Brian's well.'

'You looked fucked.'

'I'm getting about five hours a night.'

'That's a good sign, then, eh?'

'Aye.' She smiled. 'Good sign. How's Crystyl?'

'Oh.' His face clouded. 'She's not a happy woman. Wants more money, always wants more money.'

He had finished with his long-term partner and she was squeezing him for a pay-off. Morrow supposed that there must have been an implied threat that she would take him to court: Danny couldn't afford to have his income drawn attention to. But they would settle it: Crystyl might imply a threat but Danny was a threat.

'She'll be fine.' He shook his head as if he didn't believe it.

'JJ?'

'Causing trouble, mostly for himself. Won't talk to me. He's changed his surname from McGrath.'

'To what?'

'His mother's name.' He looked at Morrow and they both smiled at the table as the coffee machine shrieked into the milk. JJ's mother was a nutcase. It was probably fitting.

'Aye,' he said when it quietened. 'She never had a chance, that lassie.'

It was a nice thing to say about someone who was never very nice to him. Morrow changed the subject: 'Can you make the boys' christening, then?'

He grinned wide. 'Bought a kilt and everything.'

'Oh.' She frowned. 'Aren't kilts for weddings?'

'Ye can wear them for christenings.' His voice lowered to a defensive growl.

'No,' she reached towards him, 'don't – it's fine. What tartan did you go for?'

'Black leather,' he said, nodding.

Morrow nodded along with him, making a mental note to warn Brian so that he didn't say the wrong thing.

Malik arrived with the coffees on a tray, and a plate piled high with biscuits. They were courtesy biscuits, wrapped individually in slippery cellophane; there were too many on the plate and they spilled all over the table as he set them down next to the coffee cup. 'There ye are, Danny, because I know ye like them.'

'Thanks, Malik, man,' said Danny. 'I do like them.'

He looked at the plate and at Morrow, offering the offering. His expectation of deference made her think of Rita Lyons, the mannered acceptance, as if it was routine for people to anticipate their needs.

Morrow didn't want to see that in him. They drank their coffee and ate the biscuits, rolling through the christening arrangements; it was a few weeks away, after Christmas, but they'd all need to be there for one thirty.

Then Danny talked about people they knew when they were young, the people they had in common from school, Lan and Brody, who'd had kids recently, who was ill, but these were not the people they had in common. There was a whole pool of commonalities they couldn't touch on: officers who had arrested Danny, friends of his that she had investigated, mutual acquaintances who had been murdered or who had OD'd. They skirted carefully around the pot holes.

With the shadow of Francesca over her mood, Morrow began to feel that she was trying to keep her feet dry on a marsh. She saw that her being here was unsustainable, a fiction. Danny was selfish, predatory and vindictive and it was wrong to be here with him, in this café where he was laundering the fivers and tenners paid by the poorest of people, notes snatched from the mouths of their children and the meter.

And the poor, obsequious café owner still watching them, looking for a need to anticipate. The man was a bankrupt, but not yet, homeless, possibly, but not yet, given a stay of execution by the beneficence of Daniel McGrath. He watched them with a half-ready smile, happy that he'd spotted a penny under the tongue of a lion.

But Alex wasn't here for herself, she was here for her boys. After the christening, she thought, she could leave longer and longer between the meetings, let Danny slide away. What she wanted was for her boys to know who they came from, for Danny to be an interesting ancestor, for the shame to stop with her. She was here to ask him to be godfather. It was meant as a hollow compliment but still it stuck in her throat.

She was astonished at the courage the second chance at motherhood gave her. Not wanting the twins to grow up ashamed as she had, she called her union rep and her bosses together for a formal meeting a month before the twins were due. She met them and admitted that Danny was her half-brother.

Danny McGrath was serious enough to prompt an investigation into her entire career. They had to ensure that her failure to disclose the connection was sincere on her application: they hadn't been in touch then – he was in prison – she thought he'd disappeared in Spain. They needed to know that their relationship had never affected her professional decisions.

Three months later they'd found nothing. The depth of the inquiry had left her the most trusted, vetted DS in Glasgow and put the shame of her past behind her.

She could admit to him. They named the youngest twin after him. It seemed to have affected Danny. He was moving into legitimate businesses now, owned a block of student flats and a string of pubs. Morrow felt sure, like everyone else, that the pub business was a cash conduit to clean ill-gotten money. No one like Danny could own a cash business without incurring suspicion but he had been investigated and it looked clean.

Danny was telling her about a crossed-eyed boy from their class who'd become a grandparent a week ago.

'A boy,' said Danny.

'What age is she, the daughter? Fifteen?'

'Thirteen.'

'My God, is she keeping it?'

Danny huffed indignantly, 'Aye, for as long as they'll let her . . .'

They looked away from each other, one on each side of the 'they' divide. He started telling her about a foster mother who'd hit the children in her care.

It was a stupid, badly drawn lie: bad premise, one-dimensional characters. It was the sort of story bad parents told each other to justify attacking the social work when they came to take the children away for their own protection. What the story really told a cop ear was that Danny was likely to have children taken from him and he didn't trust the authorities. Morrow watched him tell it, saw him realise how he sounded to her and slow the telling. A spark of shame flared in his eye, then anger at her for calling him on it.

'I can't get a taxi licence,' he said, out of nowhere.

''Cause of your previous?'

'Aye.'

He didn't seem to expect her to fix that, he said it as if it was just an observation. Danny was not used to talking to people who didn't want anything from him. He didn't talk to equals very often and it was hard for him, she could see that. She wondered why he was here. He might want it known that his sister was a cop, but she wasn't the sort of cop people suspected of moral grey areas. Her bosses knew that. Danny's people knew that. This was hard for him and now that they had the occasional talk beyond

'Dad's dead' or 'My son needs a witness' she could see he often found himself out of his depth and uncomfortable.

'Danny, I want my boys to know where I come from,' she said, straight. 'But why did you meet me?'

Danny glanced at the café owner, who smiled and raised his hand like a kid waving to his mum from a ride.

'I'm getting older,' he said simply. 'Need to learn how to talk to people.' He looked at the café owner who was gesturing – did they want more coffee from the machine, no problem, he'd get it, he'd like to get it. Danny ignored him and looked back at her. 'I don't want this to be my life.'

She knew what he meant. Maybe he spent time with Francescas every day. Maybe Danny deserved more.

'So you're practising on me?'

He grinned. 'Wee bit.'

'I can see it isn't easy for you.'

They both flinched from that. Too close, too intimate, too much pressure behind the dam.

Danny hesitated and then looked at her, a sad smile twitching at his mouth. 'Was this easier before?' he murmured.

She couldn't remember. 'A bit. Was it?'

'This.' He flicked a finger between them. 'Because of this . . .' He blinked and looked away. 'I'm getting out of it all.'

Alex watched him blink heavily though his eyes were dry, rubbing his hands together in a mimic of regret.

'You being friendly to me, owning up to me; you've made me feel different about everything, Alex, you really have.'

She watched him and wondered how he'd been so successful, when he was so poor at lying. He looked back at her to see if it had taken. Alex blinked back.

By the time she opened her eyes again Danny was looking at the door where his driver was standing. A tall, scrawny, shaven-headed thug, mean faced. His eyes were opened too wide as he scanned the dark interior for his boss. He spotted Danny, met his eye and raised his eyebrows, nodding when he saw he'd been acknowledged, backing out to the street and turning back to the Audi A3. All the gangsters had the same cars because someone in the finance department was fluffing the proceeds-of-crime checks. She half thought about teasing Danny about it but stopped herself.

'I need to go,' said Danny standing up, oblivious that something had shifted in her. 'I'm buying Crystyl a flat and I need to see the surveyor.'

That was a lie too. Morrow knew that Crystyl was living in a flat that Danny owned under a company name. She'd moved all her things in a week and half ago, had placed an advert for hair extensions to the address and wasn't moving anytime soon. He caught her unaware when he said, 'You on that post office thing?'

He was nodding up the road to the area of the robbery. It wasn't that sinister, everyone knew about that. It was all over the papers. Without waiting for an answer he said, 'He was into stuff, Brendan Lyons.'

'Did you meet him?'

She hadn't meant it that way but he heard it as an accusation. He stood up and nodded an end to the conversation. 'See ye, then.'

As he walked out he batted a wave to the owner, brushing off his good regard.

Morrow waited until his car was out of sight before she left, realising when her feet hit the street that she hadn't asked him to stand godfather. She was glad.

12

The call came through as Morrow and Harris were driving to
Pavel's in the genteel heart of Kelvinside: Georgie Mac was a
known alias of a George MacLish from Greenock. It sounded
promising: he had a long rap sheet, mainly for violence, fitted the
height and build description of the post office robber. He was
due to sign in with his parole officer this afternoon. Two cops
from a neighbouring division were on their way to bring him in
from Greenock for questioning.

Greenock, near Ayr. Ayr-ish accent, Pavel had said. The
accent wasn't that specific, not to her ear, but it might be to an
outsider. It made her suspicious that Pavel knew that, psycho-
pathically disengaged, as if he was watching them in a petri
dish.

She hung up. 'We might get home for tea this evening. Might
even get Christmas Day off.'

Harris tutted, greedy for overtime. He had four kids. He
smacked his tongue against the roof of his mouth. 'I can still
smell those armchairs from that place. It's like the smell got in
my mouth and it's stuck there.'

'Stays with you, doesn't it?' Morrow looked out of the window
at the nice houses.

'The smell?'

'The everything.'

He let it go for a minute. 'That's shit about her mum being a
good mum, you know. All that would probably have happened
anyway.'

Morrow's voice was muffled by the rain pattering on the

windscreen. 'Don't want to be near that any more. Don't want my kids near that.'

'Well,' he sighed, 'you could get a desk job, a transfer to training or something. Regular hours, anyway.'

'Yeah.' She had always thought of those jobs as bullshit jobs and she knew he did too. They were admin roles, not real policing and there seemed to be more and more of them. Real police, like them, felt they carried those other roles.

'It's legitimate,' he said. 'You know, with the kids.'

'Yeah,' she muttered at the window, 'legitimate.' She thought back to Danny. He said Brendan Lyons was involved. She only half believed him but she wondered, just for a moment, whether Danny was someone she could trust one day.

They were on the grand residential end of the West End, passing restrained neoclassical terraces and stand-alone bombastic mansions, all gorgeous, all sandstone and all together.

But these weren't houses any more. Converted into flats, the gorgeous ballrooms were now the hard-to-heat living rooms of galley-kitchened apartments. Libraries and music rooms served as living quarters, low-ceilinged servants' quarters were bijou flats. All the social gradations and flow of authority through the mansions had been chopped up, like the end of a tragedy welded onto the start of a joke.

Harris took a right at a slow set of lights, pulled the car up a steep hill, and took a left into Martin Pavel's street.

Here the mansions seemed intact. Grand front doors had single doorbells and long-established hydrangea bushes in their driveways.

Morrow was surprised. Pavel had a shaved head and a lot of tattoos, he looked like a low-level foreign hood. Since they found out that he wasn't registered at the university she had assumed the slippery accent and hints about the US were grandiose bullshit, that the accent was the result of a chaotic family life, stepfathers and foster placements and midnight flits.

'Rehab,' said Harris, looking up at the houses and thinking the same. 'Bet he's in a rehab.'

Morrow pondered. 'D'you think?'

'Yeah, early release or something.'

'*Here* though?'

He scanned the big houses. 'Private rehab?'

'They're expensive, though, aren't they?'

'Don't they all take charity cases, even if they're quite exclusive?'

'Hm.' She couldn't imagine the neighbours tolerating that. 'What about the ULF? If they're an anti-abortion campaign from America, they can be quite rich, can't they? Sponsor him to come over here, get a movement going, maybe.'

'Like, part of a church or something?'

She shrugged. It didn't sound that plausible. 'Maybe it is rehab . . .' She stepped out into the street, waiting until Harris was out and had shut his door. 'Anyway, rehab for what?'

'Not drugs.'

Harris was right: Pavel was muscled and healthy-looking. 'Gambling?' suggested Morrow, and looked at Harris innocently. He avoided her eye: there were rumours that Harris like a wager.

'Maybe it's sex or something?' he said quickly.

They both winced, thinking about the same offender. A young man, good-looking, middle class, everything going for him. He had been caught fucking a dog behind a bus shelter by an off-duty police officer. It should have been funny but it wasn't. He was mute with shame when they booked him in but, left alone in the cells, he howled like a soul in torment.

She shrugged the memory off. 'What number did Pavel give?'

Harris checked his notebook. 'Thirty-six.'

They looked for house numbers. The odd numbers were on the higher side of the road, separated from the evens by a small rock garden.

'Should be up there.' Harris frowned up to the crescent. 'Do we need to speak to him that much?'

'I'm just wondering something.' She'd been rolling it around her mind all day: if Brendan Lyons, the gunman and Pavel were involved in a strange insurance scam Pavel would be the one to talk. He wasn't dead or guilty of murder. All he had done was a mild assist.

There was nothing functional or institutional about number thirty-six. They took a small set of steps through the rockery and crossed the road. Thirty-six had a single brass bell, well-kept windows and a small front garden with two feet of trimmed box hedging separating it from the street.

A large bay window was on one side of the door, and on the other a flat window of equally grand dimensions. The curtains were open in both.

They knocked on the door, a glass panel etched with a Grecian urn, and waited for a moment before stepping over to look in the bay window.

It was a very big room, furnished with a prim spindly legged settee in striped yellow silk and two matching armchairs designed for perching not slouching. No TV, no Xbox or PlayStation. No cups left on the white coffee table. No personal effects of any kind.

They sidled to look in the other window. A dining set with elaborately carved chair backs on a giant gaudy red and blue rug. Day chairs with wooden backs sat at the corners of the room, watching the empty table.

'This isn't his house,' said Harris.

Morrow knew what he meant. Even if Pavel was living here, the house belonged to someone else.

Harris pointed at a large antique doll in a pink dress propped in one of the chairs, her stiff little hands sitting on the armrests. 'Christ, maybe he's a serial killer.'

Morrow stepped back to the door and rang the bell this time. A sonorous toll echoed around the hallway.

They waited, staring at the door expectantly. Nothing. No

shuffling noises inside the door, no movement behind the frosted glass.

Morrow looked across the road at a villa with a huge Victorian conservatory on the side. The windows were strung with net curtains, blocking the view from the road. It didn't look very nice. She felt quite smug about her little house, an honest thirties semi, built for purpose.

Harris raised his eyebrows in a question and Morrow nodded him up the road. 'Neighbours.'

One door up had a videophone. This house looked warmer, less strained: cushions were arranged along a window seat under the bay window. A book had been left open on a table inside and the dark wooden panelling on the walls compensated for the huge dimensions of the room.

A wavering voice answered through the speaker, 'Who is calling?'

'Strathclyde Police.'

The clumsy crash of a hurried hang-up was followed by footsteps in the hall. The door was opened by a slim, elderly man in a flowery tabard, worn over a shirt and tie. He looked angry. 'What is it?'

They introduced themselves, showed him their warrant cards as he held onto the door and peered out at them. 'Has there been a break-in?' He was very well spoken.

'No, we're looking for your neighbour. He lives at number thirty-six, next door.'

'I don't know them.'

'Could you tell us who lives there?'

'I don't know them.' He was getting agitated, was obviously in the middle of doing something and keen to get back to it. Morrow slowed her speech down to calm him.

'I see. I'm sorry to bother you, but we need to know: is there someone living there?'

He opened the door a little, looked down the street to number thirty-six. 'Yes. There is.'

'Could you describe them to me, sir? Sorry to be a bother.'

He liked her calling him 'sir' and apologising, and he softened a little. 'James Cardigan and his wife. She has cancer. They've gone to Houston for treatment. He's tall—'

'So they're not here at the moment?'

'No. They've rented it out. To a man who is covered in tattoos. I thought he was a sailor but he isn't. He's very strange.'

Harris asked, 'Why did you think he was a sailor?'

'Because he's covered in tattoos,' he said, as if the answer was obvious.

'And in what way is he strange?'

'Well, he's covered in tattoos, but he's not a sailor.'

'I see. Is he tall?'

'Six foot?' He was treating it like a test now, reading her face, to see how he was doing.

'What age is he? I'm just asking because I want to be sure we have the right address.'

'Early twenties? He runs a lot. Goes jogging.'

'And he lives alone there, does he?'

'Not alone exactly. I've seen five people, older, all American, coming and going. No tattoos, though.'

'They live there?'

'Visiting, I'd say. All dressed the same.'

'What do you mean?'

'You know, American. Informal. Slacks.'

'Five of them?'

'Two men, two women, all about the same age. And another man. Wears a blazer.'

She caught Harris's eye, both of them thinking of a church committee. 'Two couples and another man, then?'

'No. More like a set of four and their boss. The four all dress the same sort of way: slacks, shirts, all the same sorts of colours. Pastels. They bring a lot of luggage each time as well. A lot of luggage.'

'So they're coming from quite far away, you think?'

'No, more luggage than that. As if they're moving things. They have steamer trunks with them, one each.'

'Steamer . . . ?'

'Trunks, big boxes, leather corners.' He wrinkled his nose. 'New ones, not proper.'

Morrow couldn't be entirely sure he was talking about the trunks instead of the people.

13

Tamsin Leonard knocked on the door and stepped back to look up. She had imagined a slightly angry, messy house but it looked well tended: the windows were clean, the curtains tidy. Wilder's name was on the door so it was definitely the family home. She felt a little more respect for him, seeing the little puff of bushes around the edge of the garden, the weeded space between the pavement slabs.

She knocked again and saw a bedroom curtain upstairs shimmy like a signal to a lover. She took out her mobile and called him: if they asked she'd say she asked him if he'd been sick again.

From inside the house she heard the thumping run of someone bolting down the stairs. She heard him through the door and the phone at the same time: '*Hello?*'

'Wilder, can you open the door, please?'

He hung up, hesitated, and opened the door.

He had changed back into a beige T-shirt and beige jeans. His hair was a dull yellow brown, his face the same sort of creamy colour. It wasn't a good look.

'Hello,' he said formally, keeping her at the door.

'You give my number to someone?'

'No.'

'Were you texted this morning?'

'When I was at my locker . . .'

'That why you left?'

'Aye.' He slumped against the wall. 'I couldn't face . . .' His voice trailed off. He blinked hard at the floor.

'Who sent it to you?'

He shook his head. 'Unknown number. It was Boyle.'

Tamsin leaned in. 'Where did he get my number? I only got a new number three weeks ago and I can count on the fingers of one hand the people who have this one.'

'Well, I've got it.'

'I know.' She tried not to sound aggressive but he heard the undertone.

'I didn't give it to him. Is it on your personnel file?'

'Work don't have this number. They've got my house number.'

Wilder hadn't considered that. He opened the door. 'Come in.'

Leonard stepped into the house, found it as bland as his clothes: magnolia paint, small table in the hall with a little vase and a fake flower in it. Pictures of paintings on the wall. He led her through to a small square kitchen and then stood there with her. She felt he was unused to having visitors. In the sink sat a dirty mug, 'World's Best Dad'.

Wilder followed her gaze to it. 'Sorry for the mess.'

She looked to see if he was being sarcastic. He wasn't. 'Was it a deliberate set-up?'

He looked at her, wild-eyed. 'Boyle? He did it to get the photo?'

'What if we're not the only ones? What if they're targeting officers from our division?' she whispered.

'Why would you think that?'

'Barrowfield. They must have got my number from your mobile: someone at work has been through your phone.'

He considered it. The Barrowfield investigation was uncovering a whole drug distribution network, taking them far enough up the food chain to include Benny Mullen, a man wanted by Interpol as well as the Dutch and French police. At first they were all surprised that the case hadn't been taken over by another glory-grabbing agency but less so four long months into it: no one would testify against Mullen. At worst the labour intensive investigation was an irritation to him. He kept having to change phones.

133

'Didn't it seem too easy?' she said. 'Stopping him, pulling him over, getting the phone off him and the number?'

Wilder nodded. 'Bait.'

'Yeah, bait. He was sent to get us. And why us? Who are we? Nothing special. DCs, I mean, who else have they got to? Think about it. If they're targeting the squad, that's the smart thing to do – get a little something on everyone and call in favours. One person loses a file, one person turns a camera off for ten minutes, one person forgets to give a warning. Who had access to your phone this morning?'

'No one. Wait, no! Boyle!' he said. 'Boyle! Did you leave your phone in the car with him?'

'No.' She'd wondered about that on the way over. 'Phone was in my pocket the whole time.'

'Well, what about the phone company?'

'They could get it from there but they'd need to know my name to check it there, wouldn't they? Someone at work would need to tell them who was on our shift and in our car for them to have my name. Be easier for someone to check your phone this morning. Did you leave your phone at the locker?'

'Just for a second, to go to the toilet. The room was empty, there was no one but McCarthy there and then I came back and got the text. I mean it wouldn't even be long enough for him to get the phone, note the number ...'

He shook his head at the carpet. Next door, through the wall, a baby began to cry.

'Wilder, we need to go and tell the boss.'

Wilder's panicked eyes skitted around the floor. 'She'll think we're only confessing because we got caught.'

'We are.'

They both knew the procedure: they'd be suspended. They'd be made to stay home until a disciplinary committee was called. Then they'd be keel-hauled, pictured in the papers, shamed. Criminal action would be threatened but not brought because they'd handed themselves in. They'd lose their jobs, be unemploy-able and broke.

'I can't lose this house,' whispered Wilder. 'It's all I've given them. I'm not . . .' He covered his eyes with a hand. 'She ran off with her best friend's man. Everyone around here knows about her.' He sobbed, spittle spluttering onto his chin.

Leonard heard what Wilder was saying: we are already ashamed. We cannot survive this.

She wanted to reciprocate the intimacy, tell him something shameful about herself, but she wasn't ashamed of anything, not really. Not of Camilla or the fertility treatment, not of her youth-ful political activism or the failure of her first company. By the time she had run through her few reservations about herself the moment had passed. Wilder had stopped crying and dropped his hand.

'We can't go to her,' he said.

She leaned against the countertop, looked around the floor. 'Why did they send us that picture? Think about it: what's the next move? They'll ask us to do something.'

'Like what?'

'What do you think? Nothing good. And if we refuse, what then?'

'But even if they send the boss the picture, we can explain it. It just shows us looking in a boot . . . ?' He looked hopeful, as if he'd been comforting himself with the thought all morning.

'Then they'll investigate all our purchases. Ingoings and out-goings. We can't spend that money. We can't touch it. We've got nothing. It might as well be tissues. We've got nothing.'

His eyebrows rose sadly as it dawned on him that she was right. But he didn't want to hear it. He picked up the dirty mug and ran the hot water, squeezed half an inch of washing up liquid into it and rubbed it around the inside of the mug. Unsatisfied he used a scourer pad on it, working his elbow back and forth.

'There has to be something else we can do. There has to be. I can't lose the house . . .'

He was going to cry again. Leonard reached into the sink and took the mug off him, putting it on the draining board to dry.

'Wilder,' she said firmly, 'if we don't do something now losing your house will be the least of your problems. Get your coat.'

'No—'

'You can't hide here for ever, cleaning the same cup.'

He blinked hard at the floor.

'We made a stupid mistake,' she said. 'If we do nothing it'll turn into a catastrophe.'

Still he didn't move.

'Wilder,' she said it firmly. 'Get the money and get your coat.'

Leonard didn't want to get out of the car. Everything about the Milton made her uneasy.

The low scheme cowered under a threatening sky. The houses were old and worn, thrown up in the fifties and showing their age. A nearby block of flats had verandas stacked with bikes or bags of rubbish. At the very heart of the housing scheme was a large stretch of bare grass, pockmarked with the scars of small bonfires.

Wilder had been crying on the way up but he had stopped when they passed the cut-off for their station. Then he slowly dried his face, never asking where they were going. He just sat with his mouth hanging open, exhausted.

She looked out of the window at Abernathy Street. 'He was right, wasn't he? "Not nice."'

'Who?' sniffed Wilder.

'Boyle. He said "Abernathy Street: not nice."'

Wilder looked sadly out of the window. 'Did he?'

His self-pity was exhausting. Tamsin sighed, trying to stop it being audible. 'OK, let's find this little shit. Where's his house?'

136

'Round the corner,' said Wilder, gesturing to a bend in the road.

Tamsin pulled the car out into the street, passing a primary school behind a chicken-wire fence with coils of barbed wire on the roof. 'Glad I didn't go to that primary school.'

'They bring it on themselves,' said Wilder absently.

Leonard glanced at Wilder, head resting on the window, miserable. When she was ten years old a group of bigger boys took to shouting 'fucking dyke' at her as she hurried home from school, so her mum bought her a personal CD player. Then the boys started chucking stones at her and her mum had to drive to the school every day to collect her. One day, safe in the car with her mum, she saw them and gasped. Her mother heard her, stopped, got out of the car and walked over to the scary boys, grabbed the biggest one by the ear and sort of swung him around. Her mother, a lifelong member of the WI, who once embroidered vestments for the Bishop of Birmingham, never told her what was said. She never mentioned it again. Leonard didn't see the boys again. What she did remember was her mother's face as she turned on an upward swing towards the car. Her mother was very angry and she was smiling. And Leonard felt now that she could hurt Wilder and stay smiling. She felt that very much indeed.

As Abernathy Street turned away from the primary school its character changed utterly. The road narrowed and the short run of houses were hung with fairy lights draped over Christmas trees, around windows, coiled around fences. In one garden a nativity scene of pious figurines gathered around a brightly lit stable. Low metal fencing separated the gardens from each other but three consecutive houses had matching benches under their front window. This part of Abernathy Street was a community.

An old man stood in his front garden, hands resting lightly on a spade handle, talking to a woman and a small child over the fence. The woman and child were dressed in matching blue anoraks, their hoods up against the threat of rain.

The man's eyes followed their car, spotting Leonard in the driving seat, reading her. It was a police reflex to a direct challenge: Leonard stopped the car and held his eye as she got out.

'Hello,' she said, approaching him.

His spade was far too big for the tiny garden. Tamsin wondered if he could have stolen it from his work.

'I own a building firm,' he said, answering her enquiring look. She realised then that he'd clocked her for a cop.

The woman had turned to watch Tamsin approach, her face eclipsed by the unwieldy hood.

'See ye later, anyway,' she said to the man, gently slapping the back of the wee boy's head as a prompt.

'Cheerio,' piped the boy. His mother took his hand and they ambled away.

The gardener waited until they were out of earshot. 'I suppose you're here about him?' He nodded across the road to the only grim house on the street, number nine, Hugh Boyle's house. The fence had been removed and the garden levelled as a parking space, the concrete slabs tipped up and down at the edges.

'Hugh Boyle?' asked Leonard.

'Aye.'

'Yeah, I am actually. Is he around?'

'Well, the boy doesn't walk anywhere. If that bus he drives around in isn't parked there, then he's out.'

'Do you know when he'll be back?' She looked over at the empty driveway, uncertain of the tone to take with the man.

'You the polis?' The man watched the hooded woman and her matching son move away.

'Yes.'

'Hugh Boyle's a drug dealer, ye know.'

'Right?'

He slid his eyes to her. 'Did you not know that?'

'Uh, can't really say.'

'Hmm.' He looked guiltily at her. 'Well, he is. I'm saying to him: what would your mother think of ye?' He nodded over the road. 'That's her house. Dead at fifty-three. A really lovely woman. Doted on him.'

Leonard thought back to Boyle at the boot, pleading to be allowed home to care for his mother.

'Did she die recently?'

'Three years? Two and a bit ago.'

'I see.'

'Devoted to him. That was the cause of the trouble. The shit that wee fucker put her through, you wouldn't believe it.'

'Has he been in trouble?'

'Nothing official, that I know of.' The old man frowned. 'Speaking frankly, the boy thinks he's due a mansion for breathing.'

Leonard looked across at the rundown house. The PVC front door was scuffed and dented near the bottom where someone had kicked it, the glass grey with dirt. A corner was missing from a pane on the second storey window.

Leonard tipped her head. 'Who's he working with?'

'I've no idea. They're not coming to the house, whoever they are. But he's nothing and then, one day, he's driving around in that car.'

'Where did he get it from, do you know?'

The old man followed her eye and looked at the house again. 'I thought he was just driving someone, but it seems to be his.' He stared intently at the ground and lifted his spade, bringing the edge down on the concrete with a loud clang that echoed off the neighbouring houses. He'd cut a slug in half, its opaque orange insides spilling out over the translucent green of its skin. He looked up, pleased with himself. 'I think he's bought it on credit and it'll get took away.'

She didn't know what to say to that. 'Are you slug hunting out here?'

'No,' he smiled up at her, 'I'm on guard.' He pointed at the Christmas decorations in the street. 'The audacity of hope.'

Leonard really liked him. 'Well, thanks for your help anyway. Have a nice Christmas.'

'I'm Patrick Gilchrist.' He winked at her kindly. 'And anything I can do, you know. You can come to this door *anytime*, day or night, and ask anything.'

He wasn't offering Tamsin support, he was offering it to the police.

Freshly shamed, she crossed over the road, catching sight of Wilder's panicky stare in the front seat of the car. Every minute that passed made her situation worse. If it wasn't for him she would have already gone to the boss and she knew that.

She stood on the uneven paving stones and looked up. Hugh Boyle's house was elevated over the road, five steep concrete steps up to the front door and a white plastic council handrail along the side for a disabled person to haul themselves up. The council weren't exactly responsive in providing equipment like that: his mother must have been ill for a long time.

The narrow house had one window on the ground floor and a smaller one above. Boyle wasn't looking after it: Tamsin could see ceilings tattooed with grey.

Reluctantly, she went back to the car and Wilder was on her right away. 'What? What did he say?'

She didn't trust herself to answer Wilder in a moderate voice. She held the steering wheel tight and looked out at the street.

'You seem very tense. I don't know what you're going to do,' he whimpered.

'I'm thinking.'

She turned the key and started the engine, gently let the handbrake off and pulled out.

'Where are we going?'

Tamsin took a left and followed a long, empty road past a block of high flats. She had done this, she put her hand in there and took the money. It was not Wilder's fault; it was her fault.

Theirs was the only car on the road. Even at the bottom of the high flats there were no parked cars, just the burnt-out skeleton of a van.

Leonard wrestled with her temper as she drove, looking all around, going through the physical motions of policing. A man on a bicycle rode away from them up a side street, hands warming in his pockets. The road they were on swerved and then swept uphill for half a straight mile, suddenly bordered on one side by waste ground.

She looked up and saw Hugh Boyle's giant beige Audi turn towards them at the crest of the hill.

Wilder shouted, 'Look!' and lurched forward in his seat so that his face would be visible through the windscreen.

'Sit back,' said Leonard.

'It's him!'

'SIT BACK OR I WILL SIT YOU BACK.'

An awful hush fell in the car. She hadn't actually known that her voice went that loud.

She let Hugh Boyle drive past her, not even looking to see his face, and then swung the car in a perfect curve, following behind him, gradually drawing near as they came to the kink in the road. Hugh's eyes flicked at the rear-view mirror, registering the car but not realising that they were police officers. She flicked the siren on for a single wail and he dipped his head down and pulled carefully into the side. The brake lights came on. He stopped. Then, after a moment, the hazards. She knew then that he had no idea who was in the car behind.

'What are you going to do?'

She stepped out, walking up the body of the car, keeping to his blind spot. She took a chance that it wasn't locked and yanked the door open in a swift move.

There sat Hugh, hands passively resting on the big leather steering wheel, shoulders down, face turned to her with a little smile on his face. Owl eyes, and even now he made her want to laugh. He looked vulnerable, with his squint, and now he wasn't wearing a hat she could see that he was balding in a haphazard manner. He saw it was her – 'Oh! Ha! Hiya!' – and that she was furious. 'Oh. I'm in trouble. Right.'

He widened his eyes, looked sorry. '*You* took it, though.' He looked to see where her hands were, looking for a gun or a night-stick. 'I just showed you the money and walked away. It was you that took it.'

'That doesn't mean you can threaten me.'

'You know, you taking that money means anything can happen. It wasn't me that threatened ye.' He seemed to mean it and sat straight in the seat again. 'I didn't. I just took your picture.'

'Why did you send it?'

'I didn't.'

'How did you get my mobile number?'

He looked out of the windscreen. 'OK, look, I don't have your number. I just took the picture.' He turned to her and smiled. 'See, what you have to appreciate, is that business is business. These things have a market value, I mean it was too good to just pass up, eh? No harm, eh?'

She saw, then, the spark in him, saw his eyes scan the modest street, slinking from window to window, looking to see who was watching him. If it meant turning a profit, Hugh Boyle would have sold them all for parts.

'I was sent that photo this morning.'

'Not by me.'

'Who sent it then?'

'Auch.' He half yawned and raised his arms in a faux-casual stretch. 'It was just an auction in the end. I don't know who got it.'

'What do you mean by "an auction"?'

'On the internet. It was an auction.'

'How would . . .' She didn't even really know what to ask about it.

'Chat rooms,' explained Hugh, rubbing the tip of his nose. 'No one's using their real name. You just let it be known you've got something. You know . . .' He gestured to her. 'And then you, sort of, go off and do a deal. If there's a few folk interested it becomes an auction.' He shrugged. 'I didn't mean to upset ye or anything, it's just business.'

'Where did you get the boot full of money from?'

He widened his eyes, amused that she would ask him that out-right. 'I'm not stupid.'

'Hugh, you gave us your home address.'

'Yeah, OK,' he frowned at the steering wheel. 'I am quite stupid.'

He wouldn't do that the next time. He was learning. Leonard thought for a moment. 'Give me your car keys.' Hugh did. And she stepped back. 'I'm driving. Move over.'

14

Martin had run for a full hour and a half. He had run through the burn in his legs; he had run past the rain and through the cold into a warm and safe rhythm. Rosie had been a really genuine connection, a genuine human connection, and the smell of her cigarette smoke lingered in his nose for the longest time, fading into memory as the wind and rain washed it from his skin. He felt refreshed, replenished, human.

He didn't take the time for a cool-down walk, afraid his calves would seize up, but felt another burst of energy as he approached the incline towards his front door and went with it, enjoying it, conscious of his lack of self-care but not frightened by it.

It was in the midst of this conflict that he saw his mom standing in the window of the house, smiling hopefully, smoothing her hair as if he was her date and she had been there, waiting for him to come and approve of her.

Martin stalled at the sight, his throat tightening with dread.

The front door was opened by Philippe, a man who embodied the dignity they themselves should have had, as if he was trying to lead by example. Philippe stood waiting, keeping his eyes down but a smile twitching on his cheeks.

'Philippe,' said Martin, a sudden greasy sweat engulfing his body.

'Mr Martin.'

Martin stepped over the threshold and his mother ran out into the hall.

'Oh, honey.' She was drawling slightly, not Xanax, something else. 'Honey, honey.' She hurried up to him, cupped his face in both her hands. 'You look terrible. What happened to you?'

Martin wrestled himself away from her and saw his dads standing in the kitchen.

'Marty.' Stepdad was drinking again. He wasn't drunk now but he had that bitter air about him, the sort that preceded a vicious fight.

'Son.' His dad kind of smiled, secretly pleased to see him, but hiding it because he ought to look solemn.

They always travelled with a million suitcases but they weren't in the hall. They must have put them in bedrooms already. They weren't supposed to have a key to this house.

'Where's the luggage?' said Martin, drying his face with the hem of his T-shirt.

It was too much for her, his mom began to cry. 'We know, honey, you don't want us turning up all the time, so we booked into a hotel.'

'Really?'

'Hon, really. You see? We're trying to do it your way.'

Hooking arms with him she pulled him along towards the kitchen. 'Let's have a little breakfast together.'

They walked down the hall, past the breakfast room, down through the second dining room to the back kitchen. It looked out on a small courtyard and the servants' quarters at the back: a mews cottage with small windows. It was not a nice view, not the Pacific or the Rockies.

His stepmom was sitting at the table. Even in the draining blue light of a Scottish winter she looked beautiful. She was the youngest of them, barely eight years older than Martin, Greek-Australian. Martin tried never to be alone in a room with her. Sensing his discomfort, she mistook it for dislike and avoided his company. She was not pleased to have been brought here. 'Hello, Martin, how are you?'

'Hi.' He looked away, flustered, and went to the cupboard

for a glass. 'I asked you not to come back. How come you're all here?'

'We heard what happened yesterday.' She said it before she remembered she shouldn't know, that it told Martin they were having him watched.

Stepdad snapped at her, 'Just shut up.'

She muttered a 'sorry'.

Slowly, Martin took a glass from the cupboard and put it on the side. They were watching him, waiting for him to say it.

'You have someone following me?'

His dad coughed. No one would look at him but his mom. 'This city is not a safe place, honey.'

Martin took the carton of orange juice out of the refrigerator and poured it. He shut the carton and put it back in the door. He shut the refrigerator and looked into his glass. 'It's as safe as anywhere.'

His mom exclaimed: 'You were in a shoot-out! Is that safe?'

'Yesterday was not about me. Anyway it wasn't a shoot-out. It was a robbery.'

'Marty,' she said, 'you could have been killed. Suppose people find out who you are? That front door isn't even alarmed.'

'The front door *is* alarmed.'

His dad chipped in, 'The windows aren't.'

Martin picked up his glass and drank, needing to breathe in but still drinking. Swamped. He thought of Rosie Lyons and rain dropping from a grey sky and sausage rolls and Lallans Road.

'I mean,' his mom gestured to the window, 'just look at that yard. There's a wall all around it, no alarm on the window, if one of them scaled that fence and got over—'

Martin slammed the glass down on the counter and turned to face them, holding on to the worktop behind him. 'I'm staying.'

His stepdad leered at him. 'We know you're not at college, Marty.'

Martin was embarrassed at being caught out. 'I'm attending lectures.'

His dad: 'You're not working towards a degree though, are you?'

His stepdad: 'You're wasting your time.'

His mom: 'It's a hobby, Marty. It's not *purposeful.*'

Martin muttered at the floor, 'There's no point in my getting a degree.'

'Marty!' said his mom.

'What are you saying?' asked his dad.

'Well, what's the point?' Martin was uncomfortable. 'I'm never going to have a job. I want to learn, is all.'

'What do you want to learn?' Everything his stepdad said sounded reproachful.

But Martin would never work, he could never have a job and long for promotion, meet colleagues as equals, strive. That's what he had been robbed of, the capacity for longing, the capacity to strive. And now they resented him for it. He turned and shouted at them, '*What am I supposed to do?*'

His words filled the room. A mistake, showing that level of emotion. He would seem unbalanced. He felt as if his dad was making notes of his mental state, scouting the rest of them for witnesses.

'Honey,' said his mom, 'would it kill you to get a degree?'

It was important that he answer calmly now, rationally: 'So what? So you can tell people I'm not a bum?'

'Marty!' wailed his mom.

Their behaviour seemed nuts actually: he had a case for saying they were crazy too: 'Why are you having me followed?'

'Why are you lying to us?' she said. 'All we want is to be part of your life.'

They had had this discussion a hundred times. 'I need you to go.'

'That fat girl, the smoker, are you dating her?' His stepmom said, smirking at him. She had been shown the file, a photo of Rosie emailed to them before Martin even got to his front door.

She added, 'Is she the girlfriend you're spending Christmas with?'

Martin wanted the chaos here right now, with the gun, he wanted the weight of the gun on his hip bone and the trigger kissing his finger and to spray them with bullets, spray them and watch the mist of their blood settle all over the bland white kitchen. He understood then that this was what he saw in the chaos, a way out of this trap with them, this swamping story.

He said it quietly: 'If you all go away right now and leave me until after the holidays I'll transfer a million US into your account.'

'We don't want that money,' said his mom uncertainly.

Martin looked at her. She resembled him, she had been a pretty woman once. She was ossified now, as if she had glimpsed Sodom and was turning to stone terribly, terribly slowly; only her eyes remained expressive and they were in torment. He was her only child and they had been close at one time.

'Is that a million each or . . . ?' Everyone turned to look at his stepdad and he smiled, bitterly, pretending he had been joking. 'What? It's a joke.'

Everyone looked away.

'It's a joke,' he said quietly.

Martin knew his stepdad in this mood. He'd be shouting in a minute, infuriated. 'So, where you guys planning to spend the holidays?'

'Here.' His mom's blank face begged him.

Martin said flatly, 'I don't want you to.'

Then he didn't add to it or threaten them, but when he looked around at them he knew they'd be gone by this evening. They'd dress it up for each other, say they respected his privacy or he was a grown-up now. Then his stepdad would say something crass, tell the truth, say he wanted the money or something, and they'd put it down to his drinking.

'I'm going to take a shower.'

He passed Philippe in the hall and muttered to him, 'How's your nephew, Philippe?'

'Much better, thank you. I sent your lawyer his medical results from the last series of tests.'

'I got that, thank you. And a lovely letter from your sister.'

For just a moment Philippe held his eye, humbled, diminished by gratitude.

Martin blurted, 'It's, like, *nothing*, Philippe,' trying to redress the loss to him.

'No, Mr Martin,' said Philippe. 'It's everything.'

The power of life and death. The responsibility horrified him afresh. 'No, but to me, it's nothing. Really.'

Philippe stood aside to let Martin pass. As if following an order, he climbed the stairs to his room, glancing back to see Philippe still with head bowed, like the grandfather the day before.

He hurried up the last twenty steps and shut the bedroom door gently behind him. He pulled a chair over behind it. He stood back and looked at it. Four of them and Philippe. He moved the chair away and pushed a small dresser over instead, jamming it under the handle, so it couldn't be turned.

Watching the door, he backed away to the bathroom, entered, shut the door and locked that too.

Martin sat on the toilet floor. Cold from the marble tiles seeped into his buttocks, into his thighs, his legs began to throb as the muscles cooled down and he tried to concentrate on that. He stayed there, mapping his pains, until he heard the front door slam shut downstairs and the cars pull away.

15

The Lyons lived in a small house in a small street, with the bright glow of Christmas lights at the window.

Harris parked across the road from the house and they looked over, noting the black scorch stain on the side of the postbox and the glassy texture to the tarmac next to it. A car had been burnt out here, a while ago by the looks of the postbox: the blistered red paint had been scraped off and repainted in patches of grey primer.

They got out of the car and Morrow looked back up the road. She couldn't see any CCTV cameras and it made sense: stolen cars were usually burnt out in places the thief was familiar with, knew were safe but had no investment in.

'I want the incident details.' She pointed at the scorched tarmac.

Harris scribbled it in his notebook.

'Get someone to ask the neighbours as well.'

'I'll get McCarthy on it.'

The front garden of the Lyons' house was behind a shoulder-high hedge which had been burned in the fire. The blackened hedge had been trimmed back hard, baring the branches. It was recovering: little yellow winter bud-leaves struggling to clothe the plant. Through the sparse foliage they could see a concrete square, a tricycle tucked behind a flat green plastic turtle sandpit.

The large window was framed with red and white blinking fairy lights. Inside, a fibre-optic Christmas tree shifted colour softly in the dark, blue to green, green to orange.

Morrow looked at it. 'They all live here?'

Harris nodded. 'Mother, daughter and grandson all lived here with Brendan.'

Morrow followed him to the gate, the three steps across the garden to the front step, and Harris rang the bell.

The door was opened immediately by a very small, very old woman in a long nightdress. Her vertebrae seemed to be fused and she had to bend back at the waist to look up at them. 'Hello?'

Rita Lyons' daughter appeared further down the hall.

'Hello, Rosie, is your mum in?' asked Harris.

Smiling amiably, the old lady looked from one to the other.

Rosie looked at them both and paled. 'I saw you two at the hospital when I picked up Joseph.'

'That's right.' Morrow flashed her warrant card. 'Is your mum in?'

'Aye.' She stood behind the old lady, still smiling. 'This is my granny.'

'I see – do you all live here?' she asked the grandmother, because it seemed as if she was ignoring her.

'Well, I'm wearing a nightie,' she said, her voice a shrill trill, 'try and guess.'

Rosie smiled at that, watching her gran turn and trundle back down the hall to the kitchen.

'Is that your dad's mum?'

'Mum's.' She invited them in with a hand to the mat.

Morrow and Harris brushed their feet and stepped into the house. It was her parents' house, their style. The hall was salmon pink with a big brass-framed mirror and table. The kitchen door was ajar and they could see brown units against turquoise walls. The smell of warm sugar wafted through to the hall.

'I met that guy,' said Rosie. 'The one who was with Joe at the hospital. I met him this morning.'

'Martin Pavel? The tattoo-guy?'

'Yeah. I bumped into him outside the newsagents up there.' Her head bobbed up the street. 'He was waiting . . .'

'Waiting for you?' asked Morrow, trying to sound nonchalant.

Rosie looked confused. 'I don't know. No, I don't think so.' She seemed quite sure. 'Not me . . .'

'What did he say?'

'Well, I sort of suggested we sit and have a cigarette and a chat.'

'Right?' Morrow tried a neutral prompt. 'What was he saying?'

'How social obligations are determined by stories.' She looked a little confused. 'Narrative . . . Stuff . . .'

'Did he mention anything about yesterday?'

'No.' She looked troubled and shook off the thought, cleared her throat and shouted to her mother, 'Mum? Some, um, people are here to see you.'

Rita came out of the kitchen, hands held high like a surgeon, her fingers powdered with flour. She looked exhausted, as if she had been baking all night since they saw her. Her eyes were red and sunken, hair tousled and brittle from the dye.

'Yes, hello,' she said heavily, resigned to speaking to them but not eager. 'If you don't mind, go in the front room and I'll be with you in a minute.'

'Of course.'

A small boy's voice called from the kitchen, 'Done it!'

Rita turned to the kitchen door, rolled her shoulders to correct her posture and lifted her voice half an octave, 'Good boy, now the next one.' And she went back in.

Rosie held the living room door open for them. 'Tea? Coffee?'

Harris did the rebuff and they walked into a front room that was dated but comfortable: an overstuffed beige leather sofa unit hugged the corner. A hexagonal coffee table with shiny black glass, reflecting the ever-changing colours of the fibre-optic Christmas tree.

'What was Martin Pavel waiting for?'

'Auch, he was out running,' said Rosie, her cheek softened blue, green and yellow from the tree. 'He's got an injury, shouldn't be running. It's weird, actually, because he lives quite far away but he happened to run down here. He was asking about Joe.'

Morrow watched Rosie's face and saw it dawn on her that his interest could be sinister.

'Did he ask to see Joe again?'

'No.'

'Did he ask how he was?'

'Yeah.'

'Well, sometimes,' said Morrow, 'when people go through something as traumatic as that, they feel bonded.' The 'Beast' tattoo on Pavel's neck came to her mind and she saw her reflection in the window, saw her eyes widen. 'Did Joe ask about Martin Pavel?'

'No. I didn't say I'd met him but Joe's making biscuits in there and he wants to give some to "that man from yesterday".' She nodded tearfully through the wall to the kitchen. 'Hope you don't mind my not saying "police". We're trying to keep as much as possible from him. I don't know if we're doing the right thing.'

'That's probably the right thing to do,' said Harris.

She looked back at the door. 'It's hard to know what's right. He seems more tired than teary. Just wants to know where his papa's gone now he's dead. I can't very well tell him he's in heaven – my dad was a lifelong communist.'

Harris nodded. 'Do you tell him there's a Santa?'

'Aye.'

'Well, you're not worried that he'll believe in that when he grows up, are you? Why not tell him there's a heaven? If it's a comfort. Help him process it.'

She thought about it, nodded and seemed comforted by that. 'Just hope my dad won't haunt me. Anyway,' she held her hand out to the settee, 'sit down, sit down.'

Morrow and Harris took a seat next to each other and Rosie pulled over a footstool to sit on.

Harris leaned towards her. 'You always stayed here? With your mum and dad and gran?'

'Aye, I never got around to moving out. I was young when I got pregnant with Joe. It's worked out well. It's great to have help with the wee man and Mum and Dad needed help with Gran. She's not that nimble, never goes out and can't really be left alone. And now,' she nodded sadly, 'well, I'm glad I'm with Mum.'

'Joe's dad's not about?'

'No.' She dropped her eyes. 'No, he's not about.'

'Does he have contact?'

She could see Rosie remember that they were police officers, that they weren't here for a chat. 'His name's Lawrence, he's from Lyon. I met him on holiday and we lost touch.' She opened her hand towards them. 'Not my choice.' She hadn't wanted to talk about that and squinted uncomfortably at them. 'Aren't you here to ask about my dad?'

She looked to Morrow, as if she was counting on her to be cold and distant.

'Yes,' said Morrow, obligingly chilly. 'We've been wondering about your dad, if he recognised the gunman and if so where from.'

Rosie thought about it and looked at the Christmas tree. 'He doesn't know bad people, gangsters . . .' She rubbed her eyes. 'I mean, I don't know where he could know him from.' She caught sight of herself in the window, gave herself a warning. 'I just don't know.'

'What about locally? Was he a man for the pub?'

'No. My folks don't go out much.' She couldn't look at either of them.

'Why?' asked Morrow.

'Auch, they're always saving up to go back to Mallorca.' She smirked and dropped her voice to a whisper, 'They rent the same house there all the time. It's like a caravan. It's bloody horrible.'

'So, he's not about the local area so much?'

'Well, he could have met him at the nursery gates. He walks Joseph up in the mornings.'

'The nursery?'

She frowned at that. 'It's a council nursery, a lot of kids get sent there by their social workers when they're months old. It means they're definitely getting fed and they're not in front of the telly twenty-four seven.'

'You don't think he'd know him from somewhere he worked?'

'I'd say the nursery gates is most likely.' She looked up, seeing if the misdirection had taken, and then repented: 'But they're probably not capable. Mostly junkie nuts.'

'What's "junkie nuts"?'

'Auch, you know: laughing loud one day, weeping the next, hoods up, eyes down. Sad really. Sad for the kids. Wee bits of things in dirty jerseys and shoes that don't fit. One boy up there, four years old and every second word is the 'c' word. Effing c. His mother laughs about it, she thinks it's funny. Kids coming in with bruises and no lunch, you know?'

Harris seemed to have taken his parental-advice win to heart. 'Would it be too expensive to move Joe to another nursery?'

Rosie looked at him with her mother's regal bearing. 'You can't just pull out and leave those kids to their fate, can you? Not responsible. You have to participate in your community.'

Morrow thought of the boys. 'Most people's principles change when they have kids, though. Who wouldn't compromise themselves for the good of their kids?'

Rosie smiled, wistful, as if it was a discussion she'd had many times. 'But you could use that to justify anything, couldn't you? Say murder – that robber from yesterday might be taking the money home to this kids. Doesn't excuse his behaviour.'

'No—'

'Nor should it,' continued Rosie. 'Children need an ethically healthy environment as much as a physically healthy one.'

Morrow read her face. It had the beatific gleam of the truly religious. She looked at her and tried to think like her: Rosie might approve of her father defrauding an insurance company, but not having himself murdered. That would be 'unhealthy', probably.

The door opened and Rita Lyons paused before she came into the room.

'The biscuits're in the oven,' she said solemnly. 'Just give them ten minutes.'

'Sure.' Rosie got up. 'If I think of anything else I'll let you know.' She nodded at Harris, sensing perhaps that he felt scolded. 'That's lovely advice about Santa. Thanks.'

Harris pressed his lips together modestly as she left. She shut the door firmly behind her.

Rita was a lot less warm than her daughter. She stood, hands clasped in front and looked down at Harris.

'What advice was that?'

Harris looked back at her. 'We were talking about how to explain death to a child. I've got four myself.'

'I see.' Rita sat down on Rosie's footstool, crossing her legs away from them. 'And so, is this interview a continuation of yesterday?'

Morrow sat forward. 'I suppose it is.'

'OK.' She folded her arms defensively but said, 'Ask me anything.'

Morrow looked her in the eye and Rita blinked. A telltale tic. Rita was hiding something. 'Well, as I said last night, we think that Brendan and the gunman recognised each other. We're trying to think of places he might have met someone like that.'

'The nursery?' Rita was adamant. 'Did Rosie suggest that?'

'She did.' Morrow nodded.

'Because we talked about it this morning and we both thought maybe there. You should go up there.'

'We'll look into that. Can you think of anywhere else?'

'Like where?'

'Brendan's retired?'

'From being a driver. Special buses for day centres and schools, you could check that out.'

So, not there either then, thought Morrow.

'But, you know,' said Rita, 'we spend a lot of time in Mallorca, he hasn't worked more than an odd shift for a year or so. I mean, it really could have been anywhere at all.'

'Maybe you met him in Mallorca?'

'Was he Spanish?'

'Are there Spanish people left in Mallorca?'

Rita didn't find that funny. 'He doesn't sound like a Mallorca man. If anything he sounds like a Costa Del person.'

Morrow and Harris were both aware of the irony of a Communist Party widow parading her snobbery.

'Anyway, it won't be there.'

'You seem very sure. It's a shame, we were both hoping for a wee trip out.'

Harris grinned at her and Rita conceded a small smile, as if she was the Queen of there,. 'Yes, it is very nice. Even at this time of year the climate is lovely.'

'So,' Morrow carried on, 'maybe they knew each other from a while ago? When Brendan was involved in politics?'

'Well, true, Bren used to be very active with youth groups but honestly, that's a long time ago – those guys'll be in their thirties and most of them were sharp as tacks. They're not hooligans, those guys.'

'Was Brendan ever in Greenock?'

Rita blinked. 'No.'

'Are you sure?'

'Yes.' Another blink. 'Why?'

'No reason.'

Harris's phone rang and he took it out, looked at the screen and raised his eyebrows at Morrow before excusing himself to Rita. He stood up and answered it, shuffling off to the corner of the room by the window, muttering single word replies.

Morrow saw Rita Lyons' eyes slide to the side, listening, so she asked her: 'Was Brendan worried about anything?'

'Like what?'

'Debts?'

'No. Brendan always paid his debts.'

'Renting a house in Mallorca must be expensive.'

'Not really. EasyJet there, book in advance. We know the family who own the house we rent. Get it for fifty pounds a week. It's cheaper than living here, actually. We used to dream about buying that house. Irony is we could afford it now, with his life policy.'

'He had a policy?'

'Yes.' Rita wasn't aware of saying anything significant. 'Sixty, seventy thousand or so, I think. Don't really want to buy a place there now, not without Bren. Won't come through for months anyway.'

Rita glanced at the ceiling and her face contorted with grief suddenly. She fought it and won a couple of times, only to lose control again. She covered her face and waved a hand, telling Morrow to come on. 'Ask,' she muttered, "mon, *ask*.'

'Um, that taxi driver who picked you up last night was from Abbi Cabs? He seemed to know you well.'

'Donald?' Rita sniffed and pulled herself upright. 'Yes.'

'He seemed very impressed with you and Brendan.'

'He's nice. Fan of Bren's.'

'A fan?'

'Brendan was famous. Gave a famous speech at the TUC.'

'The Trades Union Congress?'

'Mm.' Rita took out a cotton hankie and dabbed her eyes. 'It was on the news.'

'What did he say?'

'About demarcation in the steel industry. "Though diverse in our method, we converge in our aim" – that was his phrase. Brought them to their feet.' She ran the handkerchief under her eye. 'That's a defunct skill now, I suppose, oratory. Engaging a room full of people isn't that useful now, like a lot of things. Still, I hope people remember, hope a lot of people'll come to the funeral. He'd like that . . . He liked a party, even kids' parties.' She looked suddenly exhausted and Morrow saw her chance to do a bit of housekeeping.

'You've been told it'll take a while for the body to be released?'

'Yes, the man last night told me.'

'I'm sorry about that but it gives us our best chance to find the man responsible.'

'How long?'

Harris hung up, swung to look at her and Morrow could tell from the wideness of his eyes and the tightness of his mouth that he needed to talk to her right now.

'It's hard to say, Rita.' Morrow stood up. 'I'm afraid we need to go, but we'll be back and I'll be keeping in touch.'

Rita stood up and flattened the thighs of her trousers. 'I'll see you out.'

She followed Morrow to the hall and opened the front door for them, leaning on the door frame, ready for a lingering good-bye but Harris was down the path and had the gate open.

'Thanks, Rita.' Morrow held her hand out for a formal fare-well, and Rita put her hand out, palm downwards again, again as if she expected her to kiss it.

Morrow pressed her fingers. 'Goodbye.'

Rita nodded. If Brendan Lyons was involved in an insurance conspiracy, Rita knew nothing about it.

Morrow caught up with Harris at the car door. 'Gobby's called in. They were sitting surveillance in Barrowfield and a twelve-year-old kid chapped the van door. When they opened it he chucked in a Morrison's bag full of twenties and legged it.'

'Where are they now?'

'Sitting sweating in the van with about two hundred grand in readies.'

16

Annie Gallagher pulled on the handbrake and looked over at a mean-windowed bunker of a building. The Hillhead constituency office was now in a long-defunct pub. During the property boom they kept having to move to cheaper spaces and they were on the very edge of the ward now, by the north shore of the River Clyde, in an area that had once been home to grain stores and warehouses. The area was up and coming, a new transport museum had been built by a world famous architect and roads had been moved to accommodate it. They'd have to move from here too, soon.

'There *they* are,' said Annie, watching the corner.

Kenny saw them, two middle-aged women, footfalls perfectly synchronised, a matching pinch to their mouths. He was sure they were behind this, them and the Emoticon, that they had called this meeting. He understood, really. Marion, the older one, would be heartbroken. If Marion died unexpectedly and the police went to her house, if they found out that she had a mannequin dressed as Kenny Gallagher in her living room, that she dressed it every morning and bathed it at night, Kenneth wouldn't have lost a breath. She caressed cups that he used. He had seen her do it. And here she was with her apostle, member of the party since she was thirteen, a devotion born of the need to have somewhere to go. She took no positions herself but would kill in support of other people's.

The pair of them hurried down the road, on their way to save the day and ruin his. Their fat blond friend must already be in there. He was all over the place, emotional, painfully sincere. Pete called him the Emoticon because his fat face was always busy expressing something, but Kenny said that was unkind. He knew what Pete meant though. The Emoticon had a crush on Kenny too. In the early days he'd given an interview to Radio Scotland and said that he could literally feel it when Kenny was anywhere in the building, because Kenny was so charismatic. Kenny pretended he hadn't heard it.

Of the twenty or so members of the union who followed Gallagher to the Hillhead Labour Party constituency, only the female union members remained. It had been agreed before they joined: they would work as a group, sway the party to the left, represent the working man with Gallant Gallagher as their public face. Now those women were trying to get rid of him, but he knew it wasn't about Jill Bowman. They wanted to hijack the constituency to meet their own interests.

He watched Marion and the Apostle take the front door.

'You hate them, don't you?' said Annie quietly.

'Because of how they treat you,' he spat. 'I mean, feminism – fine – but treat other women with a bit of respect. You've been an active member of the party for just as long as them. The way they just dismissed you out of hand.'

'Yeah, but you know maybe they were right, though, maybe it wasn't the right move—'

'No, they rejected you out of hand because you're my wife. And in front of the constituency.'

'They had a point. It does look unprofessional. I shouldn't get the chair just because I'm your wife. Especially after Malcolm headed that fund-raising committee. It looks like nepotism.'

'You were right for it. They just dismissed you unanimously on the first vote.'

She took his hand in hers and squeezed it. 'Don't get angry before you go in.'

She was right. Kenny wanted to stay here, under her forgiving eye. He couldn't. This was the second meeting they'd called to discuss this McFall controversy. He had made an excuse not to attend the first one but he'd heard the rumours from Pete, from Mikey, from Hank: they were furious, they were going to try and deselect him. This was for his political life.

'See you soon.' He tried to smile for her but his face was too tense and his expression soured into a leer.

Annie smiled for him. 'Good luck.'

He got out, waiting on the pavement as she drove away, waving when she reached the end of the street and took the turn. Annie disappeared around the corner.

Kenny stood, watched the empty corner. Annie knew. She had to know, but she would forgive him, to save face and for a pay-off. He was disappointed in her, again.

He crossed the street, head down, stormed the doors. Ignoring the smattering of people hanging about in reception, he battered through the door to his office like a man coming up for air.

Inside, a jumble of files and stacks of papers everywhere. Normally he savoured the business of it, but today it looked unprepared and amateur. He often thought democracy could easily fall apart if the electorate discovered how ramshackle and petty the whole thing was.

In the middle of the messy office sat his secretary, Peter. He was a big man who dressed like a country singer in a denim shirt and jeans, his sumptuous head of grey and blond hair swept down his neck, and incongruous gold half-moon glasses hung on a Rasta-coloured cord around his neck.

'Pete.' Kenny swung his bag to the floor and stepped over to his desk. 'What's going on?'

Pete glanced behind him to check that the door was shut. 'The motion is to deselect you on the basis that you had an affair with Jill Bowman. If you play it wrong they might expel you for bringing the party into disrepute.'

'OK.'

'The fuck are you doing making off-the-cuff statements to journalists like Meehan?'

Kenny tutted. 'An affair? For God's sake it's not the first time they've said that about me, is it?'

'You sell yourself as a family man, Kenny, this is the price if you have an affair.'

'I didn't have *an affair.*'

'Kenny, three members of the exec saw you take her to your room at a B&B in Inverness.'

He was outraged. '*That is a lie.*'

'They said they saw you.'

'Who?'

'The names I have so far are Marion and the Apostle. The Assassin is a given. Possibly the Emoticon, but he was pissed and his nephew was in hospital so he's not sure.'

'They're *lying.*' He thought back. Jill had left the bar at the same time as him and they walked across the road to the B&B, but Hank was with them and Hank saw them go to separate bedrooms.

'Since when did we all pry into private matters like that? We've never done that. Who decided that change?'

'Kenny—'

'When was that voted on? This is personal, they're trying to *destroy* my family and using McFall, for Christ's sake—'

'Kenny—'

'They're insulting my *wife*, my *children*—'

'No. *You* insulted your wife.'

Kenny and Pete looked at each other. Kenny suddenly understood that Pete must fancy Annie. He felt surprised that he hadn't realised before. They would have known each other before Kenny met her.

'Anyway, who's leaking this stuff? I'll tell you, Pete, it's the radical feminists who are leaking this stuff, they've put McFall up to it.'

'No, they haven't.' Pete was looking over his glasses like the college lecturer he once was. There was a lack of warmth in that look. Pete was loyal, always, but he was a career man now. They both started with the Battle of Bath Street but they weren't boys any more.

'We need to keep our eyes on the prize,' continued Kenny. 'We need a united—'

'Kenny.' Pete took his glasses off, shut his eyes tight and pinched the bridge of his nose. 'You fucked Jill Bowman.'

Kenny swallowed. 'OK, but not in Inverness. They're lying. Hank was in Inverness, he knows nothing happened there. He'll go witness.'

'But you fucked her and she's seventeen.'

'It's legal.'

'It is legal,' Pete conceded, 'that's true.'

'It was all consenting, Pete. I always asked before and after: "are you sure?" Always, whatever was going on. And never when she'd been drinking: I'm not a rapist.'

'No one's saying you are a rapist. No one's even brought that up. It's not about consent.'

''Cause she's nearly eighteen . . .'

'Look, let's not lose sight of the big picture: you fucked Jill Bowman. She's little more than a child and you're a married man who trades on his image as a family man. Now you've told a national newspaper that you're suing them because you *didn't* fuck her.'

'I didn't tell the *Globe* I was suing them. I told the *News* I was suing the *Globe*.'

Pete put his glasses back on and straightened the papers in front of him. 'Keep quibbling about details they'll flatten you on the major facts.'

It was good advice. Kenny calmed himself, good advice. Pete always gave it straight. Good political advice.

Pete looked at his watch. 'It's time,' he said sadly and stood up.

'Pete.'

Pete couldn't look at him.

'Pete, tell me what to do here.'

Pete's shoulders dropped. A door slammed out in the corridor. Pete looked at him. Pete never lied.

'Take the deselection.'

'No.'

'Take it, Kenny, and don't sue.'

'No!' Kenny was on his feet, he was hot and angry and Pete was making the end of his career a possibility by saying that. This seat was his life's work; he hadn't skimped his responsibilities, or made friends with businesses with an eye on afterwards. He had no other skills, no other way of making a living. He had no other way of being Kenny Gallagher.

'Kenny, man, if you start a war with the papers they'll find the other women.' The skin under Pete's eyes darkened. 'You know there's photos. I've seen them.'

They both froze at the thought. All those bits of women: in cars and hotels, with friends, at clubs, in toilets. Some of them he knew, some were pals, but some he didn't know at all. He couldn't even go back and speak to them.

A naked woman, a thin woman, not young, maybe in her forties, rolling away from a man on a tousled bed, her tit sliding across her body as she rolled, seeing Kenny lying there, ready for her, and the recognition flaring on her face. She kept looking back at him as he fucked her. But it was all consenting, it was all grown up. They couldn't accuse him of doing anything except what everyone else wanted to do. He wasn't ashamed and he wasn't a predator. He had always lived with integrity.

Pete lifted his jacket from the back of the chair, ending the discussion. 'Take the deselection. We'll talk about the press conference after.'

He opened the door and held it for Kenny to follow him. Kenny did.

166

Through reception, empty now, through double glass doors into the main saloon bar.

Chairs were ordered around the walls and they were all in there, waiting, clutching mugs of tea. The room was dim.

Standing at the door, Kenny looked around for the clipboard: Hank was chairing, thank God.

Marion in front, next to the Apostle. The Emoticon almost weeping already, sitting next to them, his hands clasped between his knees. A smattering of irrelevant people, retirees, members they had roped in to coming this afternoon so that there would be a quorum, and the Five Lesbians. A fist. Sitting together, calm. Of course they were here: they were all lecturers or self-employed, three of them artists. And their nominee for his seat: Alison Collins, the Assassin. She was sitting on the window ledge, framed and backlit. She wanted his job. Even through the gloom he saw her staring straight at him, breasts straining at a flimsy shirt. At first he thought she might be up for it. He'd said something to her at a party once but she'd stared him down. The straining bra was not a come-on but a cold technique, to distract the eye while she stabbed you in the belly.

The Emoticon stood up from his chair to greet him, starting to smile through force of habit, but caught himself. He pulled a chair out into the centre of the room.

'Kenny,' he said, standing behind it, kneading the backrest with unquiet fingers.

'How's your mother, Garry?'

He beamed. 'Better, Kenny, thanks for asking. They took the tube out.'

'That's great.'

Kenny took the chair, turning it to face Hank who held his clipboard tight. Pete stayed by the door, on his feet.

Sitting in the centre of the circle, Kenny felt like a mouse at a parliament of owls.

'Kenny,' said Hank, a 'sorry' hanging around his eyes. 'Thanks for coming.'

'Of course.' Kenny moved to cross his arms but thought it might look defensive. He dropped his hands to his lap, kept both feet flat on the floor.

'This is item two,' Hank told the room. 'Should have been item one but . . .' he glanced at Kenny who had been late, 'circumstances dictated a change in the agenda.' Hank looked at his clipboard for courage. 'Kenny . . .' He hesitated.

'Yes?' Kenny allowed himself a mildly sarcastic tone.

'Um . . .' Hank took a deep breath.

'Just read it out, Hank,' the Assassin called over. She was hugging one knee, pressing one ample tit on either side of her raised leg as she stared Kenny out. She knew, she fucking knew what it did to him.

Hank read from his clipboard, 'The meeting has been called to discuss the newspaper coverage of you and Tam McFall's dispute regarding the expenses for Jill Bowman's—'

'That's not the issue.' It was the Assassin again.

'But I'm reading it out,' whined Hank.

'Just to be clear: who's chairing this?' said Kenny.

The Assassin piped up, 'Hank is. I missed the vote for the chair because I was dropping the kids at nursery.'

Kenny tried not to roll his eyes: she was always using her childcare issues to demand special treatment.

'What Hank means,' she said, 'is that your sexual behaviour is endangering this party's election campaign in the Hillhead—'

'Hold on,' said Hank. 'Hold on. I'm chairing this. Let the man speak.' Mumbled concurrences rolled around the room. 'Kenny, what have you got to say about this?'

Kenny looked at his knees. Don't get stuck in details.

'OK,' he said, chewing his cheek. 'OK. This is hard to talk about with you, because it's private. And even a politician has his, or *her*,' he nodded respectfully at the women, 'private life. Thomas McFall is a long-time rival of my stepfather's—'

The Assassin couldn't stop herself. 'You fucked Jill Bowman.'

'SHUT UP, ALISON.' A sympathetic heckler, a woman. The Assassin was starting to lose the room. The Lesbian Gestapo turned to face down the heckler.

Kenny continued, 'This movement has been my whole life. We have given hope to the hopeless—'

'Don't give us your election speech.' The Assassin again.

Kenny turned to her, moving only his head so it looked awkward and difficult. She didn't flinch.

'A lot of people in this room,' he kept looking at her, speaking slowly so that she would hear the undertone, 'have had sexual contact with other comrades. There's no law against that.'

Shocked, the Assassin looked away. Kenny remembered the time. It was eight years ago and they were all fresh to party politics, couldn't believe how easy it had been to take over a constituency, and expected it to be the same with the national party. They were wrong. They'd done nothing but drift since then. But back then they were euphoric at finding one another, half in love with the collective. Alison had fucked Hank just once, but Hank confided in Kenny immediately afterwards. She didn't know he'd told Kenny, and she was flustered.

Blow dealt, Kenny turned back to Hank: 'I'd like to ask when our private lives became the concern of the party. If that's the case we're going to need full disclosure from everyone about their histories, not just me.'

The room fell quiet as each looked to his conscience.

The Assassin spoke more quietly this time, 'You're being slippery.'

'Alison,' he said and tried to sound warm, 'it's the press. They're trying to cause division and disarray in this party through lies. We're letting them set the agenda here. Since when did we trust them?'

'Kenny, man' – a kind voice from the back – 'there's a Twitter storm about it already.'

Pete managed Kenny's Twitter accounts. Kenny didn't really understand Twitter.

He moved on to something he did know about: 'And this meeting, a meeting about a member's private life, should never have been called. The press can't prove a single allegation, not one. I wasn't even in Inverness that day. I was at a meeting for supported housing with thirty other people. Jill Bowman is a legitimate representative of the youth committee, she had every right to have her expenses paid for her. How can we ask young people to fully participate in the process if they have to pay their own way? The press are trying to disenfranchise working people through process.' He raised his voice for the climax, raised his hand in a fist, tempering the aggressiveness of the stance by pointing his thumbnail at Hank. 'We must resist that!'

One clap. Marion, who had forgotten that she didn't love him any more. The Apostle then clapped once because Marion had clapped. It sounded like a slow clap, worse than nothing, then complete silence. Kenny was shocked. It had been a good speech and he'd expected at least a cheer, a low 'yes!'

'So,' he added uncertainly, 'we can't take this sitting down—'

'*Lying down*,' the Assassin sneered quietly, 'the phrase is "take this *lying down*".'

'Is anyone concerned,' an old man standing tall at the back of the room, pointed around at them with a rolled-up newspaper, 'about us attempting to rein in the power of a dying medium when working men and women are again being made to foot the bill for the mistakes of the wealthy?' But no one was listening because he was old, though everyone made a show of listening because he was old.

Kenny was trembling with emotion as he continued, 'I *am* going to sue—'

'No!' It was the Emoticon. He stood up, stood in front of

Alison the Assassin and waved his arms around. 'You can't sue them! Kenny! Kenny? They'll rip you apart!'

'I have the right, the basic human right to stand up for myself. I have the right to defend my family, since I'm being questioned here. My wife and children—'

'Oh, God,' the Assassin drawled, 'he's off.'

Kenny was on his feet, three steps past the Emoticon and the Assassin unfurled her long legs slowly and slipped off the window ledge, meeting him tits first.

'You,' he said loudly, 'are staging a putsch to make this party a platform for your own agenda.' The irony wasn't lost on him: it was what they had done together in the first place.

'We need a new candidate,' she said. 'We need someone who is hungry for change. Who understands people's troubles and can challenge. Who doesn't just float about being charming.'

'This is about your own agenda, Alison.'

'Which is what?' She kept her voice flat and emotionless. 'What's my fantasy agenda, Kenny?'

Cunt. He took a deep breath. 'This movement, this party, is not going to be hijacked and undermined by Trotskyite infiltrators obsessed with gender and sexual orientation—'

'Sexual orientation?' She waved a hand around the room. 'Who's gay here?'

The Lesbians all smirked. He couldn't point them out. Unless they stood up and claimed it themselves, he couldn't say anything without looking as if he was picking on them.

A sudden sharp sob, stifled: the Emoticon covered his mouth with his hand and began to weep. Until then Kenny had never known whether the Emoticon actually knew he was gay, he was never with anyone. His sexuality was forever shrouded in misery.

The Assassin continued, 'We don't speak for the people, we don't speak for women or gays. We speak for wee guys who like footba' and beer and shagging birds.'

'Manners, Alison,' heckled someone.

She ignored them. 'And that's not a quest for social justice. That's self-interest masquerading as something noble. Your sexual behaviour *matters*. If ye remember Lenin said there can be no mass movement without the women and your behaviour is excluding and objectivising and predatory.'

Kenny threw his hands up. 'Well, if Alison's not happy let's all give up and go home.'

'Where are the women? Who made the tea today?' she said.

Even Hank groaned. 'No, not the fucking tea question again.'

'Who made the tea?'

'I've brought a can of juice,' shouted a joker at the back.

'We do all the graft and you take all the glory.'

Pete stepped forward, though he had no right to speak. Everyone looked at him. 'This is a pivotal campaign moment,' he said, loud, staccato, as he always did when he needed to be heard. 'We cannot lose this election over petty, feminist point-scoring.'

At that the room erupted in shouts and roars, old resentments dressed up as doctrinal points were shouted from dark corners, defended in bawls, the calmers-down shouting, adding to the furore.

Kenny sat back down in the centre of the circle and waited. In among the tumult someone threw a mug at a wall. It was chaos. There was no chairman, no discipline, no direction. They were getting a taste of how it would be without him and Kenny saw that it would get worse: Alison would take over for a while but no one liked her, so she'd lose the next vote. Then a puppet leader, Marion maybe, or a compromise candidate, Hank maybe, but they'd lose too eventually. The confusion would be tiring. They'd lose heart, they'd come to miss him.

If he let it happen and then came back, his position would be strengthened, but it would have to be at the right time. Just after the second candidate. The important thing was not to get expelled from the party. He tried not to smile.

Sensing that the fight had began to run out of steam, Kenny

stood and held up a hand. The fight slowed and stopped. Everyone was listening and he spoke softly.

'I'm suing them for defamation.' Before they had time to draw breath he added, '*I'm going to lose*. And I'll make a speech, explaining the injustice of the defamation action, how ordinary people—'

'Kenny, it's a Twitter storm, it's all over the internet . . .' interrupted someone but was shushed down.

Kenny ploughed on. 'How ordinary people have no defence against the monsters of the press. But I'll keep my profile, and my reputation. And in pursuit of that,' he looked at Pete, 'I'll take the deselection and step aside.'

17

Morrow was undoing her seat belt as Harris pulled into the London Road car park. He stepped on the brake suddenly, flinging her forward, banging her shoulder off the dashboard.

'Bloody hell,' he said.

Facing them, right in the centre of the brick-walled police station car park, was a solid car: the tyres were big, it stood four foot eight from the ground. The Audi Q7, a cop in-joke, and it was sitting right in the middle of their compound.

Tamsin Leonard and George Wilder were standing in the rain next to it, and they'd been watching for her. Leonard held Morrow's eye and made her way over, an entreaty on her face. Wilder followed behind, chin down, shoulders hunched. It wasn't good.

They waited by Morrow's car door, hands behind their backs as if they were on parade, the rain running silver off Leonard's black waterproof jacket.

Morrow opened the door, stepping out into the hard rain.

'Ma'am,' said Leonard formally, rain dripping off her prominent nose, 'we need to—'

'What is *that* doing here?' Morrow jabbed a finger at the Trojan car.

Leonard blurted it. 'That's the Audi we stopped last night on the motorway.'

'Why's it *here*?'

'Ma'am, last night, the boot was full of money. We took it.'

'You *took* it?'

'We took it. The driver of the car is in the cells for you to question. His name's Hugh Boyle.'

'You brought him in?'

'We did, ma'am. And the car.'

Morrow whispered, 'You've spoken to him since it happened?'

Tamsin saw then that it was a mistake and was flustered: 'Just to bring him in.'

Morrow looked at the car while she considered the possibility that Leonard had primed the witness. She'd spoken to him, possibly to make him lie and say this was the first time she'd taken money when it wasn't, to say that she took X amount when she took XX. Morrow didn't want to believe it of Leonard but the woman had taken twelve hours to report an attempted bribe. The drab rain turned to manic racing pearls on the bonnet.

Morrow could hardly look at them. 'Where is the money now?'

'We production-bagged it and it's in my car boot over there,' whispered Leonard.

'Give me the keys.'

Leonard reached into her pocket and handed over cop-car keys.

Morrow pointed at the beige giant. 'And for that car.'

Leonard reached into the other pocket and handed them over.

Morrow checked her watch; it was two thirty in the afternoon. She forced herself to look at Leonard and then at Wilder cowering behind her. She had never liked him. 'Get in, dry off and get upstairs.'

The interview rooms were upstairs, she was going to interview them like criminals, on tape, under caution. Wilder looked at her and his mouth flapped a silent objection.

'Don't you dare,' she growled.

Leonard turned and walked away, head bent so low the rain was bouncing off the back of her neck, and Wilder followed her.

They were in the office, leaving Leonard and Wilder to sweat upstairs, leaving Hugh Boyle sitting pert and happy in a back cell. They'd watched him on the desk sergeant's monitor on the way through the back bar and found a balding, would-be-G scratching his balls, unaware that he was being filmed. They ate their lunchtime sandwiches and tried to foresee all the angles.

'That can't be his car.'

'Claims it is. He's been driving around in daylight with it, parking it outside his house. It's not reported stolen.'

'That doesn't mean much. Benny Mullen didn't lend it to him?'

'Quite indignant about that suggestion, apparently. He's not attached to anyone. Name comes up all over.'

'Freelance delivery boy?'

'Looks that way.'

'Must be lucrative. Nice paintwork.'

'I thought that.' She smiled a little. 'That paint looks new but the reg is a year old.'

Harris smiled back. 'Should we give it a wee scratch and see what's underneath?'

'Good, yeah.'

They looked at each other and the smiled faded from both their faces. Morrow said what they both knew: 'We've got to call them. Tell them what's happened. They'll have to come in.' She was talking about the Professional Standards Unit. They were high-handed, accusing and loathed by everyone.

'They won't send Bannerman, will they?' Harris looked genuine.

'Here? Don't be daft.' She gave him a reproachful glance. 'They won't want all that to come out on appeal.'

But Harris wasn't embarrassed and he didn't look away. Harris wasn't sorry for what he had done to Bannerman, though it was wrong and mean. He had orchestrated a campaign of anonymous claims of bullying against him by various members of the team and Bannerman was whipped out and moved to the Professional Standards Unit. And now PSU would have to come here. Since the phone call at Rosie and Rita Lyons' house they had both known Morrow would have to get them in: any big attempted bribe necessitated a proper investigation.

176

Harris looked at her. 'D'you think Wilder and Leonard confessed because they heard about Gobby?'

Morrow had been wondering about that too. If they had heard a bag of money had been shoved in the van with Gobby then they'd know PSU were about to be called in, that they would get caught. It was strange that Harris said it aloud though. He wasn't just stating the obvious, it was more than that. Letting him play it out, she hummed and took another bite of sandwich, watching him out of the corner of her eye. He lifted a KitKat out of his pocket, sliced a fingernail down the centre and snapped it in half. 'Might explain why they came forward.'

He looked at her as he pulled the wrapper off one side, crumpled it into a tight little ball and bit his biscuit. As his teeth sank into the chocolate his eyes narrowed. 'We should ask who knew,' he said. 'Who was told? Could it have leaked? Hard to keep a thing like that quiet.'

Morrow hummed non-committally again, wondering if he was just trying to change the subject from Bannerman or if he hated Tamsin Leonard, or Wilder. She'd never noticed him taking against them especially. He'd often said Leonard was an exceptional officer.

'They did look panicky,' he added. 'Didn't they? At the car, when they met us, they looked scared.'

Now he was trying to make her think about Leonard and Wilder, taking her back to the emotional state in the car park; he was creating a distraction.

She ate quietly. It felt strange to have that double perspective in this room, in her warm, dimly lit office, to have to calculate the gulf between what was said and what was meant.

Harris went for it again: '*I* thought they seemed panicky, anyway.'

They did seem panicked. Obviously they seemed panicked. They'd done a terrible thing. Even if they both walked from a charge the stain of what they had done would follow them for ever. They'd be stupid not to panic. But Harris was looking hard at her, trying to force her to agree.

'You're right,' she said. 'They did seem panicky.'

Harris ate the rest of his KitKat. He was being a bit harsh. Most cops with his length of service could at least empathise with their situation. It was hard, a week before payday, to see work-shy shits with big motors and suitcases full of cash. It felt unjust and Morrow knew that the shadow of redundancies was corroding the solid sense of cop-identity that many of them had. No one knew where the scalpel was going in and they were all imagining other futures for themselves now, identities beyond being cops.

She looked at Harris, scowling at the floor, thinking about Bannerman. Even when he was whispering in the canteen, listening to complaints and telling them that Bannerman's behaviour constituted bullying, goading them to call the hotline, he must have known that no one stayed gone. Strathclyde was a small force. The venom against Leonard and Wilder was a misdirect: a wife hit because a boss was cheeky, a small man punched over a slight by a giant.

She finished her sandwich and brushed her hands clean as she stood up. 'Better get on.'

He stood up to meet her, his face intense, as if he was already in the middle of a fight.

'You phone PSU and tell them what's happened,' she said, 'and get someone to check the Vehicle Identification Number on the Audi's engine, see if it really is his.'

Harris's cheek twitched. He was standing too close to her, hadn't moved away when she stepped out of the chair and he was blocking her passage to the door. He didn't want to do the things she ordered, he wanted to come up to the interviews with her.

She leaned into him, spoke with great force and formality. 'DC Harris?'

Corrected, he stepped back. Morrow waited until he followed

her out to the corridor and shut the door behind them. 'After you report to PSU, get Routher and bring him upstairs to the viewing room.'

'Will I ask around about Gobby and the van? Who would have heard and when?'

She almost laughed but his expression told her he wasn't going to let it go. 'If you like. Get the VIN into the computer first. And scratch the paintwork, see if there's another paint job underneath.'

She walked upstairs, glad to get away from him. Christmas time was heavy for lots of people: too much family, getting into debt, nasty cases. Even a simple domestic murder, with the boon of a quick and easy clean-up, could take on a sinister pall at Christmas. But he'd been trying to distract her from talking about Bannerman and it made her wonder if he knew something about Grant Bannerman that she didn't.

Upstairs in the viewing room she watched Wilder on the TV monitor. He was weeping softly in interview room two, glancing up at the camera every so often, wondering who was watching. Leonard, in room three, sat in her chair, staring unfocused at the table top, shoulders slumped, looking exhausted. She had less to lose, she had been in the service for a fraction of the time Wilder had. Morrow decided to interview Leonard first.

Routher came in with Harris at his back.

'Harris: PSU?'

'I called. They're coming tomorrow morning at ten a.m.'

He nodded her away from Routher, wanting to speak confidentially. He needn't have bothered: Routher was mesmerised by the show on the monitors, his mouth hung open with dismay.

Harris whispered, 'It was Erskine who called us at the Lyons'. He was in the van with Gobby and called us direct. Said he didn't tell Leonard and Wilder or anyone else, but you know what he's like.'

'Leaky?'

Harris whispered reluctantly, '*Excitable.*'

She had never seen Erskine being especially excitable, except when looking at car magazines and even then he was more happy than excitable. She liked the guy: he was a good worker.

'D'you get the VIN order in?'

'I'll do it now.'

'OK.' It was a twenty minute job and he'd spend the rest of the time asking about Wilder and Leonard. 'And I want the report on the burnt-out car outside the Lyons'.'

She turned back to Routher who looked back at her, sadly. She jabbed an angry finger at him. 'Get that look off your face right now.'

Harris was walking away but she called him back. 'Also, Harris, get McCarthy to follow up on the ULF lead, find out who rents the house in Cleveden Road. Don't like Pavel going up to the Lyons.'

He nodded sharply and walked away. She waited until he was gone before she told Routher to turn the monitors off. She needed to tape the interviews but, out of decency, she didn't want anyone remote-viewing two cops being questioned as if they were the opposition.

As Routher unplugged the monitors: 'Did you background check the airport taxi driver who got the call for the alarm? Any previous?'

'Mother of two, works days only, clean as a whistle.'

'How are you working that out?'

'Well,' he looked vague, 'she's just a working mum . . .'

He was sucking up to her. Morrow tutted. 'Check her out properly, for God's sake. Look for previous, dodgy boyfriends, dad, neighbours, that sort of thing.'

'Sorry—'

'Get on it right after this. She's the only person who had the address, Routher – come on, that's shabby.' She was being aggressive, expressing the annoyance she felt at Harris, another misdirect.

Morrow led the way out to the corridor. As they passed the open door to the interview room Wilder was sitting in, she leaned in the door. 'Stay there,' she said firmly, 'someone'll be with you shortly.'

It was a pro forma, something they said to suspects all the time. It meant nothing more than don't kill yourself, don't smash the place up, because we might walk in on you. Wilder must have said it himself a hundred times but now he nodded obsequiously and sat up tall at the table.

In the next room, where Leonard was sitting, Morrow skirted past her chair, leaving Routher to shut the door carefully. In silence, Morrow sat down and arranged her papers carefully in front of her. Tamsin sat still, staring at the table top, not even watching her. Morrow started the tape machine and read the laminated rights sheet out slowly. She put it down and looked up at Leonard who met her eye.

This was why she liked Tamsin Leonard: almost uniquely among the officers in the division Leonard never asked Morrow to engage with her emotionally. She did not want to be friends. She did not curry favour. She didn't even seek eye contact more than would be usual in the course of police business. Aware of these prejudices, Morrow steeled herself.

'You're entitled to a lawyer present,' she said flatly. 'Want one?'

'No, ma'am.'

'Sure?'

'Yes. Is this being filmed?' Tamsin glanced anxiously up at the camera.

'It is. You won't be remote-viewed by anyone in the station, though the tapes may be used later. We're calling in PSU.' Leonard nodded. 'I need to know what to tell them about last night. I want the facts, just the bare bones.'

'OK.'

They looked at each other.

'Now?'

'Now,' said Morrow.

So Leonard told her that they stopped the car, about the slip road and Hugh Boyle and how he prompted them to look in the boot, though he seemed unlikely to be behind the plan. And she told Morrow about the bag of money and how they divvied it up in a street nearby without counting it, half each. And she told her about the incriminating photograph being texted first to Wilder, then to her. She had a new mobile, new number, not known to many people, not registered at the station yet. She didn't know how they got it.

'"They"?'

Boyle said he had auctioned the picture on a website. He sold it to the highest bidder. He didn't know who had it. Wilder got the text this a.m. before roll call—

'That's why he left?'

'Yeah.'

'Where did he go?'

'Home, I think. That's where I found him.'

'What time did you get the text?'

'Ten something.' She reached into her pocket and took out her phone, slid it across the table. 'It's in there. I was with Routher.'

She nodded at Routher, sitting next to Morrow with his mouth hanging open.

'You were sick,' he said.

'Yeah.' She looked ashamed about that, more so than taking the money.

'She got a text on her personal mobile,' Routher explained, 'in the car, before we went into TSF Electricals and then she was sick.'

Morrow looked at Tamsin's phone for a moment. She wasn't sure if she should touch it. 'Show us the picture.'

Leonard swung it around to face her, pressed a few buttons and opened the picture. She picked up the handset to turn it to landscape and gave it to Morrow.

It wasn't incriminating. Morrow could see that the bag had something in it, but she couldn't have guessed it was money if she hadn't been told.

'What made you come in and admit it?'

'That.' Leonard nodded at the phone.

'Because you'd been caught?'

'We weren't caught, we were threatened,' she said softly.

'They threatened you as well?'

Leonard tapped her fingernail on the face of the phone. 'That's the threat. They were going to ask us to do something.'

'*Did* they ask you to do something?'

'No. They were letting us know that they would, in the future.'

Morrow nodded. 'What time did you leave Routher?'

Tamsin nodded at Routher. 'He dropped me here at eleven thirty-five. I drove to Wilder's house. Ten minutes there. Went to the Milton. Spoke to a neighbour. Got Boyle and came back here.'

'What time was that?'

Leonard shrugged and looked at the ceiling. 'Not sure. We went straight to the booking bar with Boyle. Sergeant said you were on your way back and we went back out to the car park to wait for you.'

It would all be on the booking bar CCTV.

'Anyone tell you about Gobby?'

Her forehead lowered. 'Gobby?'

'Gobby.'

'Is he OK?'

Morrow wrote a note to get the CCTV and ask the desk sergeant who they'd spoken to. When she looked up Tamsin was looking hard at Routher, trying to work out what had happened to Gobby. Routher wouldn't look back.

'That photo: they give you any idea what they wanted you to do?'

'No, ma'am.'

'What do you think?'

Leonard held her breath and flushed. 'Evidence spoil?'

'Why are you blushing?'

'I'm embarrassed.'

Morrow liked her for saying that. The fear of getting caught was a base motive. Next to that, the fear of being corrupted seemed quite noble.

'How much did you get?'

'A hundred and sixty-three thousand each.'

Morrow made a big play of writing it down. 'Tell me again?'

'One hundred and sixty-three thousand each.'

'And that was half of the whole stash?'

'Pretty much. They were all twenties. We didn't count it, we just split it by volume.'

'Out of you and Wilder, whose idea was it to take it?'

Leonard shrugged sadly and thought about it. 'We took it,' she said finally. 'We did it.'

Wilder was crying, swatting thin tears from his cheeks. 'Leonard said "Let's take it." I knew it was a mistake—'

Morrow didn't look at him. 'Word for word what did she say?'

'She said "Let's take it." We were looking at the money in the boot and I said "That's a lot of money" and she said "Let's take it."'

Morrow stared hard at Wilder. His face quivered a long and boring story about how sorry he was for himself, how terrible it was that he was in this situation, how he would tear everyone around him if it meant he didn't have to take responsibility for what he had done. She felt he'd deny having a nose if it saved his pension.

'Got your mobile on you?'

He took it out, trying to catch her eye as he handed it over. Morrow took a production bag out of her pocket and nudged it inside with a pencil.

'What did you do with the money?'

'I took some, she took some, we just shoved it into bags, we were in a hurry. We didn't count it.'

'How much did you get?'

'I handed it all in.'

She sat back and looked at him. 'That's not what I asked: how much did you get?'

'Eighty thousand pounds.'

She picked up her pen. 'Say it again.'

'Eighty thousand pounds.' Morrow wrote it down. As she did Wilder said, 'We've worked together a long time, haven't we, ma'am?'

'Have you been offered money before?'

'No.' That much was true, she could see a marked contrast between the story about Leonard forcing him to take it and the open faced 'no'.

She stood up to leave.

'Haven't you got more questions?'

'What do you think about Gobby?'

His eyes skittered around the desktop. 'He's a . . . good guy?' He looked up to see if he'd got the answer right. 'Is he getting promoted?'

'Stay here,' she said to Wilder, nodding at Routher to follow her.

Routher shut the door behind them. Looking back she checked they were out of hearing. 'Get the booking bar CCTV for this morning. The bit with them and Boyle in it. And get me a warrant for Wilder's house.'

She didn't like Wilder. She never had.

*

185

Alex Morrow sat in front of Hugh Boyle, trying to gather herself. When Harris told her who the VIN traced Boyle's Audi back to, it told a story that made them both laugh out loud with surprise. Usually, when she interviewed a suspect, she wanted to know whether they would tell the truth or lie. This time, whatever Boyle had to say, she just couldn't wait to hear it.

Hugh Boyle was a familiar type with a twist: a strip of piss wearing what little money he had, showing off his Adidas this and Ted Baker that because he came from nothing. She'd seen a hundred of them, but Boyle had charm: the slight squint and big glasses gave him a boyish air and he had a readiness to laugh at himself that was unusual. His strawberry blond hair was receding, showing off a large, square, babyish forehead.

'Mr Boyle, you've got a lot of previous for theft,' she said looking over the forms.

'I'm just trying to turn a crust,' he said and his face broke into an uneven, guilty grin as he said to Routher, 'Youth unemployment being what it is . . .'

She flicked through her papers. 'Cars, provi cheques, moved a bit of cannabis, you're always on the edge of things.'

'I'm not a joiner.' He smiled. 'Although, ironically, I am a joiner.'

Morrow tried not to smile back. He'd never done substantial time and it was to his credit: he must have been smart, she thought. Hugh Boyle was still smiling at her. 'I'm no one serious. I'm just a freelancer.'

'You're someone now, Hugh.'

'Am I?' he seemed flattered.

'New act came in last year: bribery gets you ten years.'

Boyle's face fell. Morrow addressed her notes. 'Maybe that's why they called in a freelancer. They wouldn't want to do that to one of their own.' It was her turn to shoot him an unreciprocated grin. 'How did you get the officer's mobile numbers?'

'Ah, but see, I never sent the texts.'

'Who did?'

'Ah, well, see . . .' Before he even began the story she knew he was lying. Hugh could sense it wasn't working but he ploughed on nonetheless: he cringed and said that he took that photo of them, right? Yeah? [lopsided grin]. And then he went on an internet chat room, yeah? [Smirk] and what you can do is [anxious giggle] that you offer the photos up for sale, yeah and if they like it, these anonymous criminals, they have an auction.

Morrow didn't bother listening to the rest. It was rubbish. He said he was paid in Tesco's vouchers and the nice thing about Tesco's, yeah, is you can get anything, clothes, electrical goods, fags or food, anything.

'That's a very complicated story.'

Hugh hesitated and then his face broke into an honest grin. 'Too much, was it?'

'You don't seem worried about losing the money. That tells me it's not yours.'

Big grin. 'You're smart. Can see why you got promoted.'

'Whose cash is it?'

'Ah, see,' Hugh was regretful, 'I can't tell you that.'

'Really?'

'I'll get in awful trouble.'

'Go on. You can tell me.' It was Benny Mullen. They both knew it was.

Hugh lifted his hands helplessly. 'They'll fucking kill me.'

'That would be very sad . . .'

Hugh grinned and reached across to her. 'Come on. You know they will.'

Morrow sat back and looked at him. 'OK, let me guess how it works: someone calls you to come over, they fill your car boot with cash. They know we're watching. They call you from a certain number, knowing that will alert us. You drive off. We send a car after you.'

Hugh's eyes widened, telling her she was right. But he'd never say it was the Barrowfield mob. They couldn't get anyone to stand

187

witness against them because Benny Mullen was a nutcase. He got rid of people the way other people dropped sweetie wrappers. Bodies never even turned up. A previous investigation suspected they were carting corpses off in the same containers they used to ship loads in. That's why Mullen was still out there. No one lived to tell.

Hugh sat up and licked his lips. 'Look, I'm a small player here,' he said as quickly as he could. 'I've not met . . . anyone important.' He grinned awkwardly. 'Ten years is a long time but I'd be lucky to live ten weeks if I said a word out of line.'

Morrow grinned at him. She liked this bit: 'I've checked the VIN on your motor.'

'Vim?'

'Vehicle Identification Number. Stamped into the chassis. On the metal. Every car has a unique one. Can't file it off.'

The colour drained from Hugh Boyle's face so fast she thought he might faint, found herself leaning forward, ready to catch him.

Hugh opened his mouth. Hugh shut his mouth. She could hear his tongue rasp as it moved. It sounded very dry. She hoped the camera was picking up the details of Hugh being turned inside out because she knew she'd want to watch it back.

'You want a drink of water?'

Boyle nodded. She nodded Routher to the paper cups and he poured the dying man a drink. Boyle's hand shook as he raised it to his lips. He drank it in one and asked for more. They gave it to him.

'So,' said Morrow, 'what possessed you to nick Benny Mullen's car?'

Hugh slumped over the table. 'I never knew it was his car!' he whispered. 'Never knew until I was away with it. I got it repainted straight away. I even nicked three other Audis that same night to cover myself—'

'He'll kill you, Hugh.'

'I know. I know he will!'

'Still, there's always the hope that he doesn't find out.'

Hugh looked through her. Small beads of sweat began to form on his large forehead.

'I need a witness and we can protect you.'

'No, ye can't, not from him. No one can protect you from him. He's everywhere.'

Morrow looked at him. It was blind panic. They would protect him. If he complied with their orders they could keep him safe, move him out of the city. Up high would love them for this. Up high might well overlook Tamsin and Wilder's twelve hour hiatus because they had delivered Benny Mullen to them.

Boyle looked back at her tearfully. 'Cow.'

'Now, now,' she said, trying not to grin or cheer. 'This situation is of your own making, Hugh. You know it is.'

He did know. He gave a small nod. He glared at her, saw she was his only hope of living past January.

'I'll give you what you want,' he said quietly and added in a whisper, 'Can I keep the car?'

Conscious that the cameras were running Morrow didn't tell him to fuck off. She said a quiet, 'No' and shut her folder.

18

Kenny Gallagher walked from the brittle squall of a winter afternoon into the soft and warm cocktail hour. On a raised dais in
the bar a young man played lobby jazz on the piano, languidly
reaching for the end of the keyboard, too young to understand
the timeless comfort he was affording his audience of middle-
aged, afternoon drinkers. A group of office workers in Christmas
hats and tinsel scarves were gathered by the bar and spotted
Kenny coming in. Too drunk and jolly to remember his disgrace
they started to chant 'There's only one Kenny Gallagher' at him
as he passed to the lifts.

Kenny smiled, waved, said 'Merry Christmas' and pressed the
button.

The chant grew louder as he waited, nodding an acknow-
ledgement, smiling at the steel doors, enjoying the comradeship
unique to a drunken afternoon, until the doors opened on an
empty lift and he got in.

The doors closed on the choir, which was sliding from the
football chant to 'Oh, Little Town of Bethlehem', just as rowdy,
just as joyous. Kenny pressed the button for floor seven.

The lift was old-fashioned. It gave a little dip down before it
took off upwards. Kenny felt as if he shed something in that dip,
anxieties for the future and the past. Annie and Moira, McFall
and Bath Street, the Assassin and Pete were all left in that dip.
The lift ascended and so did he, lighter and lighter, becoming
present, real, honest. He needed this.

The disembodied voice announced 'floor seven'. The doors
opened to the hourless gloom of a hotel corridor. Kenny stepped

out onto the hush of the thick blue carpet, fingertips trailing the walls of padded blue hessian. He passed doors to other worlds, other lives, other possibilities. He stepped around a tray left outside a room, a linen napkin draped over the plate, a bottle of ketchup, egg yoke dried and cracked on a fork and a milk-dirty glass. He passed a newspaper welcome mat. He walked to the end and turned the corner.

The lights were even dimmer here, or at least he felt they were dimmer. It was quiet, only the squealing crunch of carpet fibres beneath his step. His mouth was wet, his breath shortening, heart rate rising slowly.

Room 723. He knocked twice, stopping himself from a third, slightly frantic knock, dropped his hand. And he stood there and waited, listening to his own shallow breathing. A whistle in through his nose, past the hairs, the mild constriction of nasal passages swollen from the air conditioning, and then a puff out through his open mouth, a small puff, as if his chest walls were collapsing. A small puff, whistle and puff.

The door was opened by a paranoid stranger, a trickle of white powder under his nostril. His eyes were flicking about all over the corridor and he held his body back from the door, only his neck and mad face visible. Derek stepped into view, naked but for socks, his erection bold and honest. He looked out at Kenny and held his hands up, helpless, and they laughed as Kenny slipped into the room and shut the door behind him.

The paranoid man behind the door was wearing boxers and looked from Kenny to Derek, head juddering around the room for an explanation.

'Less sniff,' advised Derek kindly. 'Take a whisky or something.'

The man went over to the impromptu bar set up on the coffee table, a bottle of cheap malt, one of vodka and a carton of orange juice with the corner ripped and hanging off. The chairs and dirty glasses were arranged around the television. They'd been watching a film and Kenny wished he'd been here for that.

191

'Man.' Derek hadn't moved, stood unashamed where he was, as naked as he was.

Behind him a wall of tinted glass overlooked the city, turned the foul afternoon into a glittering midnight. They were high over the river, facing an unfamiliar view. They could have been in any city, at any hour, anywhere in the world.

'Drink?'

'Got stuff to do, after,' Kenny said, regretting the intrusion of that other world into this.

Derek dipped his head towards the bedroom door. 'Come and see what we've got.'

Kenny dropped his jacket to the floor and pulled off his belt as they walked to the bedroom. Whatever was in there he was going to fuck it. He was going to fuck it in places it didn't get fucked and he was going to fuck it more than twice, three times, four times, fuck right through it, lose himself in the skin of it, lick it and fuck it.

Derek whispering over his shoulder, 'Get stuck in, man.'

Sometimes, like right now in the dark of a taxi on a low-sky afternoon, Kenny saw Annie's face in Andy. It was his expression more than the shape of his facial features. Sad and angry at the same time. The boy was faking a stomach bug and sobbing to get home. A nine-year-old boy shouldn't cry that much; he was drawing attention to himself, making himself a target for bullies. And it was just Andy's dumb luck that the nurse was in that day for something about lice, took his temperature, pressed his belly and said that she honestly didn't think there was anything wrong with him.

Andy continued to lie and hold his stomach and cry as they walked out of the school but dropped the act the second they got in the cab.

'Let's get your seat belt on.' Kenny reached across Andy to the belt above the window and the smell of his afternoon lifted up and hit his nose: perfume, cig smoke, a woman's sweat, ethanol high notes from other people's vodka. 'Heeeere we go.'

As he pulled the belt down and clipped it around Andy, he saw his youngest son look down to watch, his chin disappearing into his neck in a roll of fat. His top lip was chapped, red and dry, his eyelashes clumped from crying. Kenny found it hard to get on with Andy because the child was quite unprepossessing and he'd always been a popular child himself. Young Kenneth was a bit more his type. He'd have been friends with him at school. Marie, in the middle, was very close to her mother.

'Are you feeling better, sweetheart?'

Andy nodded, sniffed, and leaned his head on the window.

'Well, let's get you home.' He leaned forward to the driver's hatch and gave him the address.

The taxi rumbled to life and the driver took off. Gallagher was glad it was an old cab, loud and rattly. He didn't much want to talk to Andy. He was afraid that Andy would ask about the papers. The taxi driver had the radio on to a phone-in show about headaches, otherwise Kenny would have made conversation with him.

'My tummy's not really sore,' Andy whispered.

'Oh,' said Kenny, 'that's good. Wait till we get home and we'll have some ice cream, watch some cartoons. Think that'll cheer you up?'

Andy gave a weak smile and a nod. 'Dad?'

And Kenny thought *Oh Christ, here it comes.* 'Yes, sweetheart?'

'Boys at school are saying you've got a girlfriend.'

'That's rubbish.'

Andy sneaked a look at him, his mother's look, not believing him but wanting him to go on. 'Listen, Andy.' He took his son's hand in his and felt how pudgy and unformed it still was. 'Mum asked me to come and get you so I could talk to you about this—'

'Mum's at the gym.'

'No, I know, I said Mum's probably at the gym and that's why she wasn't answering her phone when you called her. What I mean is she asked me to talk to you about this. About the stuff in the papers. That's what this is about, isn't it?'

Andy nodded.

'What the papers are saying about me?'

He looked, waiting for another nod but Andy just licked his chapped lip. 'Well, Andy, did you know your daddy is famous?'

Andy carried on licking his lip as he thought about it. He looked sad and then he seemed to give up on the conversation, and just turned back to the window.

'When you're famous the papers think they can say anything they like about you. They make stuff up. Andy?' Andy was watching the parked cars as they passed the window, his head flicking a short 'no' every ten feet. 'Andy, listen to me. Listen to me, Andy.'

The boy turned to him, his whole body facing Kenny, but he wouldn't look at his father.

'They think they can say anything, but it isn't true. I'm going to take them to court and I'm going to make them admit it. I'm going to make them admit that they lied. What do you think about that? Me and Mummy are going to make them admit it in front of everyone and then the boys in your class will know that what they said wasn't true. How do you think they'll feel then?'

The taxi took a sharp turn into their street, tilting hard on the turn, forcing Andy forwards so that he craned into Kenny. Their faces were inches apart but he kept his eyes down. The taxi drove a hundred yards down the street and stopped, flicked the meter off and the driver looked back at them expectantly.

Kenny was relieved to see Annie's car in the driveway. He needed to get back to the office but he'd get brownie points for picking Andy up from school.

'We'll make them admit it's a lie in front of everyone, OK?'

Andy sniffed and nodded and licked his dry lips. 'It's a lie,' he echoed.

'That's right, sweetheart, it's a lie.'

Kenny paid the cab, told him to keep the change and asked for a receipt as Andy undid his seat belt. He got out of the cab and turned back, holding out his hand for his son.

Andy took his father's hand, looking down at the ground from the jump door. The boy stepped out, suddenly leaning his entire body weight on Kenny's hand so that Kenny's elbow buckled. They collapsed towards each other and as they fell Andy caught his father's eye and Kenny saw in it a shocking flash of anger, saw Andy blaming him for his weight, his fall, every mistake he would ever make.

The boy's foot hit the ground and when he looked up again his face was a child's but Gallagher felt he had witnessed the birth of something terrible, a shadow that would hang over them for the rest of their lives.

They walked up to the door, both acting as if nothing had passed between them. Kenny felt for his door keys.

'Dad?'

'What, sweetheart?' The keys were stuck. His trouser pocket lining had folded over as he sat in the cab and a small key was jammed in there.

'You had a girlfriend before, didn't you?'

'No!' Kenny laughed as if it was ridiculous, his fucking keys jammed in his pocket. 'No, not at all, what on earth makes you say that?'

'Mummy said.'

'Mummy was angry but then she realised that it wasn't true.' He couldn't get the keys out, he tugged and tugged at them until he was sure he was ripping the lining. When he finally managed to free them he'd scratched a welt in his thigh. 'You talk to Mummy about it, sweetheart, she'll tell you.'

Annie must have seen them drawing up, or finally got all the messages on her phone, because she threw the front door open. 'Oh, Andy, are you ill?'

195

Andy stood absolutely still. Annie hadn't been to the gym. Her hair was dry. She bent down and held Andy's cheek. 'Are you ill? Nurse said you've got a sore tummy. Have you?'

'Yes,' said Andy quietly, 'I've got a sore tummy.'

19

Martin Pavel felt strangely elated as he turned into Lallans Road. He kept to the wrong side of the street, aware of the bright pools cast by the street lights, dodging them in case he was spotted in a stray glance out of a window by Rosie, or worse, Joseph.

He stopped for a minute in the darkest portion of the street, gathering himself, and walked over to the Lyons' house. He opened the gate and approached the front door, keeping his eyes down, not wanting to meet anyone's eye through the window.

It was a modest house but by no means poor. The front yard was tidy and cared for and he could feel the heat coming off the glass. On the ground, by the side of the concrete front step, was a small ashtray, four half-smoked cigarettes laid out in a neat row, filters by filters, the burnt tips concertinaed. They made him think of diagrams of slave ships.

He pressed the bell and waited, nervous as a suitor.

'What are you doing here?' Rosie had opened the door in a swift motion.

'I, um, just came to visit you.'

Impassively, she looked past him, up the road to the shop. 'Were you passing?'

'No. I, um, just came up to see you. To see if you were all right.'

She looked at him, reading his face, and asked again, 'What are you doing here?'

He stalled. 'I came to see if I could help?'

'Help who?'

He wasn't sure. The hall behind her was cluttered. The radio in the kitchen was tuned to Radio 3, a channel he loved himself. 'I'm not sure.'

She slumped on her hip and tipped her head at him, her hand on the door relaxing a little but she sounded exasperated. 'What if we don't need help? Are you wanting me to help you?'

'No.'

'You know,' she looked past him and the rims of her eyes flushed pink, 'I've got an awful lot on my plate at the moment.'

He said, 'I'm trying to help you.'

She looked at him, almost pitying. 'Why are you doing that?'

'I'm trying to add to the sum of . . .' Martin's mind blanked. He looked behind her. He really hadn't had much sleep. 'I don't know. I just want to help.'

She huffed air slowly out through her lips, as if he had asked her to lift something terribly heavy, and opened the door. 'I'm not letting you in. Let me get my coat on so I can have a smoke.'

She left the door open and went into the kitchen, re-appeared drying her now wet hands on a kitchen towel. She looked troubled.

'I know it must seem kind of creepy, me coming here,' Martin called to her. 'I'm not a stalker or a creep or anything.'

She picked up her cigarettes and lighter from the worktop and walked towards him. 'I'm saying this to get it out of the way: you're not my type.'

'I'm not here for that.' He didn't elaborate because he couldn't think of anything to say that wasn't hurtful and alienating: you're fat, I hate your hair.

They looked at each other and she laughed, covering her mouth at how awkward it was, and Martin smiled back. It was good to have it out of the way, off the table. It could be awkward when it wasn't.

She took her red coat down from a hook and smiled at him. 'I think we handled that quite well.'

Martin smiled. She was honest. 'We did,' he said, waiting for her to ask again what the hell he wanted if it wasn't that. Rosie didn't. She slipped her coat on, the same red calf-length Puffa he had seen her in at the hospital, and came out to stand next to him on the step.

She shut the door behind him and brought out her cigarettes, holding them open to him. 'Do you smoke?'

'No, thanks.'

'Thank God for that.' She took one out, put it in her mouth and held it with her lips, pinching them tight, making her look old. 'It's so expensive in this country, you're always dreading people taking one.' She struck a match and held it to her cigarette.

When the flare died and she dropped it into the ashtray, they stood in the dark, looking out like sentries. Rosie exhaled a stream of frosty smoke.

Lallans Road was steep. Uphill to the right were the bright street lights and the headlights of cars and buses passed on the busy road. To the left, three more houses down, the short street dropped into a dark netherworld beyond the canal, a long stretch of industrial waste ground. The land had not been shaped by wind and rain but thoughtlessness and industry: it was unofficial landfill, white goods and rubble covered over with soil. Grass grew in defiant clumps, scraggy trees, winter-bald, struggled hard there. The discarded shells of cars pitted the heath.

'They get deer over there, you know.' She smiled.

'For real?'

'Yeah, there's a corridor of empty ground between here and the Trossachs. Gangs of deer get all the way down here and just run around. There's not much there for them. They usually fuck off after a while.'

'It's not called "a gang".'

She didn't like that and took an irritated draw on her cigarette. 'Is that what you came here to help me with? My collective nouns?'

He always found this bit hard. 'OK, so I don't want anything from you. I want to help you.'

She looked at him, suspicious. 'With what?'

'I dunno, I thought maybe a job.'

She smiled at that.

'Maybe I could set you up in business or something.'

She smiled, said nothing, and looked at him.

'You don't want a job?'

'I've got a job. I'm a nurse.'

'Oh.' He'd assumed, because she was a single mom. 'Oh, I didn't . . .'

She turned to look at him. 'What job do you do, Martin?'

He shrugged awkwardly and looked away.

'D'ye have a job?'

He shouldn't have assumed that, it was patronising.

'You don't talk about yourself much, do you?'

He didn't know what to say. He could feel himself blushing and knew she would see it too.

'Are you just out of prison?'

He snorted with surprise.

'It's OK if you are,' she said softly. 'Except if it's anything to do with kids—'

'It's not.'

'We all have our troubles but I'm Joseph's mum, you know.'

'It's nothing to do with kids, I'm not just out of prison. I've never been to prison. I told you before, I'm not a criminal.'

'Well, Martin, you're something. Are you hiding from someone?'

Martin slumped against the cold outside wall. He'd got that so wrong.

'When I turned twenty-one' – his voice had dropped, he noticed, lips tightened – 'our lawyer called me into his office. I'd inherited, um, well, *a lot*. I, kind of, ran.'

He couldn't look at Rosie. He had witnessed the change in so

200

many people when they found out who he was, he didn't think he could watch it again. Her hand rose to her face and her cigarette flared orange. She exhaled towards the waste ground.

'Why did you run?'

'Kind of freaked. My grandpa, he skipped my parents and gave it to me. It was . . .' he shook his head, '*big* . . . They were expecting it, had organised their lives around getting it. They were in terrible debt. No way of making money . . . He took great pleasure in calling them and telling them what he had done.'

'That's a bit shit.'

'Yeah, he's . . .' Martin broke off. He didn't know what to say about that, how spiteful his grandpa was, how much he hated his feckless son and all the vacuous things he had made. But he understood it. His grandpa was self-made. He'd tried to save his son from every hardship he himself had suffered, and made a man he had nothing in common with. At least Martin's parents left him alone, until Grandpa told them where the money was going.

'There.' Rosie pointed the orange tip of her cigarette at the dark lumpy meadow. 'Some deer were there last summer and a wee ned went down with a crossbow and he was trying to shoot them, just to kill them. And all the worthless, scrawny drunks who gather down there in the summer, all the wine-drinking jakies, they got his crossbow off him and threw bits of it all over the place.' She looked at him, kindly. 'Protecting the deer.' She turned back to the dark. 'He came back with his dog. Set his dog on them, the wee bugger. They weren't sorry though.'

'Did the dog bite them?'

'Oh aye. Those bloody dogs can kill you. Their jaws lock.' She sighed heavily. 'So you were saying you ran?'

'Yeah. My parents . . . They weren't much interested in me before but then they wouldn't leave me alone. It was like a zombie movie. They made me go everywhere with them, got me a psychiatrist. I was in Boston, at some charity dinner and my table were debating where we were all going to winter, where all the Fiscals were going—'

'Fiscals?'

'Fiscal nomads. Don't have residency anywhere. No tax liability. I just' – he held his hands up, trying to articulate the sudden, completeness of his epiphany – 'I, kind of, sobered up and thought *I've got to get out*, that's what I kept thinking, *I've got to get out of this story*. And I ran.'

'Here?'

'No, I've been all over . . .'

They stood in silence until she added, 'In other stories.'

He was glad she wasn't looking at him because he felt so raw. 'My parents appeared at my house when I went home this morning. They're watching me.'

'That's not nice.' She was looking at him. 'Can't you just give it all away?'

'They'll have me hospitalised. I've been depressed before.'

'No wonder.' She looked at him. 'Different over there, isn't it, adolescent psychiatry? It's a business.'

'Yeah, the tattoos don't help, I suppose.'

'Yeah, you do look a bit nuts. Do you know what that means?' She was flicking a finger at her neck but looking at his.

Martin touched his neck. '"Gods and Beasts". It's from Aristotle: "Those who live outside the city walls, and are self-sufficient, are either Gods or Beasts".'

She was grinning. 'But, pet, you can only see "Beast". A beast is a paedophile here, you know.'

Shocked, Martin covered it with his hand. Rosie smoked and laughed. 'Backfire.'

'I didn't know that,' he said quietly.

'Yeah,' she snorted, 'I guessed that.'

'Fuck. That's terrible.'

'Yeah.' Rosie smiled. 'I'm treating a fat guy for recurrent gonorrhoea and he's got "Living the Dream" tattooed on his forearm.

Kills me every time.' She finished her cigarette, leaned down and stubbed it out, laying it next to the others. 'Martin, I'm wondering now if you're a fantasist and this is a load of shite you've made up.'

He smiled at that. 'Yeah, maybe.'

'What do most people do, that have money?'

'Hand it over to a trust fund and go off to live somewhere. Keep enough by to piss their lives away.'

'Most people's dream, isn't it? Not to worry.'

'If it doesn't worry you it's because you don't know what happens to it. See here?' He showed her the third dot on his wrist. 'She was in rehab, a girl I was at college with and she needed rehab. I paid. She met a guy in there, a rich guy. They fell in love and cut out, started using again. They both died. This . . .' a black dot near his elbow, 'Haiti: two hundred interim shelters to replace tents. They were building the water pipes when cholera hit the camp.'

She softened and looked at his arm again. 'Some of them must have gone right.'

'Oh, yeah.' He pointed to a dot on his wrist. 'Look.'

She smiled and pretended to read it. 'Brilliant. Well done, her.'

'Well, them, really.'

'Aye,' grinned Rosie, 'well done them.'

'And him?' He pointed halfway up his arm.

'That was great!'

'Brave guy.'

'He was brave, wasn't he?'

'See, if you hand it over to a fund you learn nothing. You become my grandfather. He doesn't understand why no one cares about him. He's lonely. Alone. Detached. It's the practice, the effort that teaches you courage and honesty and humility, all those virtues.'

She looked askance. 'You sound a bit religious.'

He held up his hands. 'I'm *so* not. I'm referring to virtue in the Aristotelian sense.'

Rosie laughed and made him say 'Aristotelian sense' again. She said she was going to drop it into conversation whenever she could. Then she looked at him and, apropos of nothing, said, 'I love that they did that, took his crossbow.' She smiled to herself. 'OK, Mr Moneybags, you up for a bit of local colour?'

Martin shrugged. 'Sure. Where are we going?'

'Get the wee man from nursery.' She dropped heavily off the step and walked over to the gate, holding it open for him.

Martin followed her out, glancing back at the dark waste ground, imagining herds of glowing neon deer galloping down from the hills.

They walked up to the main road, following the pavement around and along, passing the shop and the municipal playground on the other side of the road.

Cars roared past them, headlights blinding in the dark, buses rumbled by, windows steamed with breath and the cold felt good on his face and hands. Every few steps the smell of her, of Rosie, a mixture of lemony perfume and soft smoke, would catch his nose. He wanted her for a sister. A bossy sister. And he realised then that he trusted her. *Of course,* sausage rolls.

Rosie seemed to shrink as they turned down a side street. She kept her head down as she stopped at a row of railings where other parents had gathered in twos and threes, all eyes trained on the low brick building beyond the locked gates. A woman on the other side of the gates saw them and smiled, her eyes lingering on Rosie's face, trying to say hello, but Rosie kept her face down.

Martin felt he should say something that wasn't about him. 'Today felt months long, don't you think?'

Rosie nodded. 'Yeah,' she muttered, 'long.'

'Think you'll sleep tonight?'

'Dunno. I brought him in late,' she nodded at the nursery

windows, brimming with cotton-wool snow and snowflake cut-outs, 'just to wear him out, so he'd get tired and sleep at a normal time.'

Martin looked back and saw a small man on the other side of the street. The man had hunched shoulders, his hands in his pockets, and he was staring at them. Thinking for a moment that he might be the PI his parents had set on him, Martin turned to face him full on but the man didn't flinch. He wasn't interested in Martin. He was staring at Rosie.

'There's a man staring at you over there.'

Rosie leaned her head against the railing. 'Leave it, Martin.'

'Is he an ex or something?'

'Just turn away. Please.'

Martin turned away. 'Is he trying to frighten you?'

At that moment the doors to the nursery opened and Joseph and the other children filtered out into the playground behind a purposeful nursery teacher who took the chain off the gates and checked each parent as they came in to collect them. Rosie tucked herself into the scrum at the gate and picked Joseph up, carrying him off down the road without a word.

Martin followed her as she hurried along, catching up at the gate to her house. 'Rosie?'

She looked back as if she had forgotten he was there.

'Can I help you?'

She was panting from the effort of carrying Joe. 'No.' But as she reached into her pocket for the keys the child slid from her hip, his leg dangling, his arms pulling her over by the neck. Martin reached over and took him easily and Joe looked up.

When he saw it was Martin he gave a little 'You!'

'Hi, bud,' said Martin. He didn't like the company of children. He felt they could see right through him.

'I'm not a bud.' Joe frowned. He pushed himself down and stood near his mother as she opened the door. 'My grandpa died and you're here now. You got blood all on me.'

Reflexively, Rosie's hand came out and tapped him on the back of the head. 'Manners. It wasn't him that did that.'

Martin didn't know many kids, he couldn't hear the adult voice siphoned through him. He found Joe a little charmless and odd.

An older, more glamorous, version of Rose was waiting in the hall. 'Hello, pal.' Joe ran to her, nuzzling her groin like a dog. Then he dropped his coat in the hall and ran into the kitchen. The woman looked up. 'Who are you?'

'Mum, this is Martin, the guy who looked after Joe at the post office. There was a guy glowering at me outside the nursery.'

Frightened, the woman looked out to the street and whispered, 'Did he follow you?'

Rosie was red, on the brink of tears and shaking her head. 'Didn't need to.'

'Go have a smoke outside, pet. I'll see to the wee man.'

They sat this time, on the step, and Rosie smoked with her coat pulled tight and her knees by her chin.

'Who was that?'

She didn't want to tell him, or she didn't want to say it out loud, he couldn't tell which.

'You know, I can easily pay for him to go to a private school. The Academy's just down there ...'

She left a pause and said thoughtlessly, 'My dad hated that fucking school.' She sat up. 'Used to spit on the gates. Embarrassing.'

He didn't know whether she meant that she hated it too. 'Want to have a look at it?'

Rosie smoked and left another long pause. Then she started to cry, or at least he thought she was crying until she looked up and he saw that she was laughing. 'We could. We could have a look at it.'

'Sure,' he said, a little confused. 'We can have a look.'

She laughed again but then she took a draw on her cigarette and her mood shifted violently. She started to cry, exhaling at hills, watching the wind swaying the grass silver then black. When she spoke her voice sounded different, low, coming from her gut. 'They don't know what's happening in this city. How deep it runs.'

'Who?'

'Police.'

'How deep what runs?'

'The corruption. How deep it runs. That guy yesterday. He's just the tip. The city's polluted with it. That guy at the nursery? Letting me know it'll be Joseph next if we do anything.'

Martin suddenly had the feeling of being completely out of his depth. It was a feeling he'd had many times before and he knew what to do. He stood up, brushing his backside. 'OK, so I'm going now.'

Rosie looked up at him. 'Could we look at the school tomorrow?'

Martin shrugged, zipped up his top, pulled his hood up. This was going to be one of those ones that felt bad all the way through. A thankless intervention with no pay-off for either of them, nothing at the end but her resentment and his guilt.

'Sure,' he said. 'I'll call 'em.'

20

Tamsin Leonard was shamefaced as she stopped Morrow in the corridor: 'George MacLish is upstairs, ma'am. Room three.'

'OK.' Morrow knew Leonard would have been hiding out in the station and she could tell from her manner that she hadn't heard about the Benny Mullen collar.

'Also,' Leonard dropped her head forward, 'Gobby got a photo texted to him.'

Morrow stopped: 'What's it a picture of?'

Leonard shook her head. 'His phone's kind of old, we can't get the photo open.'

'I'm amazed he has a phone.' Gobby rarely, if ever, spoke.

Leonard smirked miserably. 'He says his wife gave him it so she can call and ask what he wants for tea. He's got three numbers in it.'

Morrow stepped past her to McKechnie's door. 'Stay available, Leonard.'

'Yes, ma'am.'

She knocked briskly.

'Come!'

Morrow opened the door on to a chummy scene: two very senior officers sitting with McKechnie – his boss and his boss's boss, all on first-name, golf-course terms, all delighted to see her.

She shut the door and let a wide smile break over her face. McKechnie stood up to meet her. She could tell he wanted to hug her. 'Alex,' he said, hands open to her, head listing with awe. 'My gosh. Benny Mullen. *Well done.*'

She tipped her head modestly. 'Half of it's luck, sir, you know that.'

McKechnie's boss stood up and offered Alex his chair while McKechnie said, 'And the rest of it's four months of good, solid police work. Very, very well done.'

She sat down. McKechnie couldn't stop licking his lips as they talked it over, what charges would be brought against Mullen, where they would hold him during interview. She didn't need to be here for this really but she had to wait for a pause before she said, 'Sir, I've got a different case waiting for me upstairs.'

'Sure.' McKechnie held a hand up. 'OK. PSU will be coming in tomorrow and combing the division. We don't want this failing on appeal because someone got a free ice lolly. You ready for that?'

'We are, sir. PSU need to know that we've already applied for a warrant to search George Wilder's house. We'll pass it on to them. He's still upstairs.'

'Better extend that to Tamsin Leonard as well.'

Morrow felt her stomach tighten. They were gunning for Leonard. They were going to clean out the entire department top to bottom, shave off the redundancies that way, smear her if they had to, all for the kudos of getting Benny Mullen. She'd been wrong to say she was ready for PSU. She wasn't.

'Leonard's out of questioning but she's given us her house keys and we'll have a look there. Also,' she said, 'several officers' phone numbers are known to whoever is attempting these bribes. They definitely have Tamsin Leonard and George Wilder's numbers. Just heard Gobby was contacted on his mobile as well.'

McKechnie didn't get the significance.

'Mobiles aren't like house phones. There's no central register,' she explained. 'We can't know how they got the numbers but it suggests access to information from somewhere, possibly our files.'

'I see.' Though he plainly didn't. 'I'll pass that on. Well, don't let us keep you.'

She left after a round of handshakes and big grins and shut the door behind her, walking back out into the world of George MacLish and Francesca Costello. It was less morally comprising than the world of McKechnie's office.

Back in her office she shut the door carefully and called home.

'Hello?' Brian panted, he'd been running to beat the answerphone.

'Ye OK?'

'Yeah.' She could hear him smiling and caught herself smiling back. 'All good,' said Brian. 'Two poos, one-fifty mills of milk *each*.'

'Ooo, that's good. Did any come back up?'

'Danny a wee bit on a burp but Thomas is getting bigger as I look at him.'

'You must be tired, love.'

'I am.'

'I looked at you this morning and your face was all saggy at the sides. We're getting old.'

'Aye.' They were grinning down the phone and whispering to each other as if they were side by side in bed.

'We got a big break. I might get Christmas Day off.'

Brian knew not to count on it but he said 'lovely' to the possibility. '*Big* break?'

'Massive.' She couldn't talk on the phone and he didn't ask.

'Christmas Day off? Be nice.'

'Yeah.' Morrow felt as if she was melting into the phone. 'Bye.'

'Bye.'

She sat down to the reports on her desk, a dull task after the excitement of the day. They were the usual, dreary dead ends every investigation generated: no lead on the gun, no lead on the ammo shells, no footprints they could use, nothing on the burnt-out car outside the Lyons' – a report showed it was a teenage joyrider and the neighbours' had been reinterviewed about it and all confirmed it. They'd seen the car being towed.

Leonard knocked and came in, looking a little afraid. 'Ma'am? MacLish's lawyer's asking how long.'

'Who is the lawyer?'

'No one I know.'

'OK.' Morrow pushed her chair out from the table.

Leonard looked nervous, blinked rapidly. 'Ma'am, why is George still being held and I'm not?'

'That's none of your business. They're going to search your house, do you understand?'

Leonard nodded.

'No inch will be left unexplored. *Clear?*'

She nodded heavily again. Morrow knew then that Leonard had nothing to hide and she did a reckless thing: 'You're coming upstairs with me.'

'For interview?'

'To speak to MacLish.'

Leonard looked startled. 'Is that a good idea?'

Morrow wasn't sure herself but she knew they wouldn't want a major case overturned because of a technicality over the value of Leonard's corroboration. PSU would be more likely to find in Leonard's favour if they had a reason to. 'Do what you're told.'

She gathered her papers and Leonard trailed after her upstairs to the viewing room, looking in at room two on the remote-view monitor, both aware that room three was still turned off, that Wilder was in there, sweating his bollocks off.

MacLish was tall and thin and wired. Dressed in a blue T-shirt, the 'Superdry JPN' logo in yellow flock on the front. His arms were so muscled he looked as if he was tensing, or dehydrated, staring forwards into blank space, a soldier on parade. Morrow thought it was probably quite easy to stay thin if you had eaten as much prison food as him.

His head was shaved but even on the grainy monitor his

colouring was still obvious: his eyelashes and eyebrows were ginger-white, very distinctive, very Scottish and his skin colour so pale it appeared tinged with blue.

Distractingly, his lawyer was catalogue-model handsome, tousled black hair, a long face. He wore a navy blue suit, too good for this interview. Maybe he was going on somewhere. Morrow watched as he took a pen from an inside pocket and clicked it to write on one of the forms. For some reason this offended George MacLish and he stared at the lawyer until he looked back, flinched and put the pen back. It took a particular type of nutcase to intimidate his own lawyer. It was going to be a cockfight.

'That's why I need you in there,' said Morrow quietly. 'D'you see?'

Tamsin Leonard spoke under her breath. 'Thank you.'

'Just do your job, Leonard.' Morrow sounded rude and meant to.

They opened the door and walked in, taking their seats opposite George MacLish and his bonnie lawyer; Morrow on the inside, Leonard on the outside. Morrow was glad to see that MacLish looked wrong-footed by the two females interviewing him, his eyes flicking between the two of them, taking in Morrow's matronly bust and Leonard's complete lack of sexual projection. Not a friend to women, was Morrow's guess.

Leonard fitted the cassette tapes into the machine and switched them on. Morrow waited until they were recording before telling Georgie MacLish his rights, that he was being filmed, and they'd like to ask him about his whereabouts on Tuesday the twenty-first of December at about twelve o'clock.

MacLish looked enquiringly at his lawyer.

The lawyer sat up, looked both officers in the eye and spoke. 'Hello. I don't think we've met before.' His voice was gruff, his Edinburgh accent lending him an unfamiliar intonation. 'I'm Henry Donaldson. I'm representing Mr MacLish and he has a statement he would like me to read out on his behalf. OK?'

Morrow nodded.

Donaldson turned to a hastily written sheet of paper, scratched-out words, his writing so bad that it was hard to tell if it was in long- or shorthand.

'My client, Mr MacLish, would like to confess to the following: on Tuesday, the twenty-first of December, at midday, he entered the post office premises at number 189 Great Western Road with the intention of robbing said post office of the cash there. He had with him an AK-47 pistol. He proceeded to rob the post office and in the course of that robbery a man was murdered when Mr MacLish's gun accidentally went off. He had no intention of killing anyone. He is aware that carrying the gun with live ammunition means that he will be held liable for the death of the gentleman who died there but he would like to state for the record that he did not go there with the express intention of killing anyone. He just wanted the money.'

Donaldson looked up and delivered his final line like a Christmas kiss: 'And he has instructed me that he fully intends to plead guilty at the arraignment.'

'Does he?' Morrow was addressing MacLish but Donaldson replied for him.

'Yes, he does.'

'Mr MacLish,' she said, leaning over the table to him, meeting his furious eye. 'I've had a read at your record.'

He smirked at that and licked the side of his mouth. He'd been chucked out of the house by his mother when he was fourteen. In the eleven years between then and now he had spent two and three quarter years out of prison. He lived in Greenock and was a known associate of the wild McGregors, a clan known for loan sharking, stolen goods and every half-assed drugs operation in the picturesque villages and towns of the west coast.

'Not a happy story, is it?'

MacLish shrugged a bony shoulder and smirked at her again.

'So what was this about? Did you just want to go home for Christmas?'

He didn't like the implication that prison was his home. 'I've places I can go,' he said.

'Like where?'

'Wha'?' He'd heard her, he was just playing for time. She let him sit with it and finally he snapped and shouted, 'I'VE GOT A FUCKING HOUSE, ANYWAY.'

Morrow looked at her notes. 'Kyleburn Terrace?'

'Aye.'

'Is it nice there?' She'd run a quick search. Kyleburn Terrace was Stab Central.

MacLish stared at her through hooded eyes, his mouth fixed in a threatening smile.

She changed her tone. 'Where did you get the gun?'

He sat back. 'Found it.'

'Oh, really? Where?'

'I can't remember.'

'That's forgetful. Unless it happens to you a lot, finding guns, does it?'

He didn't answer.

'When you found it, was it in a bag or anything?'

'I can't remember.'

'Maybe it was in a box, under a car?'

'I can't remember.'

'Maybe it was in a bag at a bus stop?'

'I can't remember.'

'At a party—'

'I think,' Donaldson interrupted, 'we've established that Mr MacLish doesn't remember where he got the gun.' He meant it kindly and gave a hopeful little eyebrow raise at the end. He wanted a bloodless, routine interview with a cup of tea at the end. He was pleading guilty. They could go home and forget it all over

Christmas. She realised very suddenly that Donaldson was on his way to a party.

'I want you to remember that an old man was shot to death in front of his four-year-old grandson.' Morrow turned back to MacLish. 'Have you ever owned a gun before?'

'Can't remember.'

'You were arrested with a pistol eight years ago, can you remember that?'

'I can't remember.'

'Can you remember how to spell "gun"?'

MacLish ground his teeth at her, livid that she'd implied that he was illiterate.

'Seriously, Mr MacLish, given your patchy school record, can you read and write?'

He leaned forward. *'What makes you think I can't?'*

'Well, you're obviously not keeping a diary.' She examined her notes, making him wait. 'Brendan Lyons. What does that name mean to you?'

He nodded sideways at Donaldson. 'He saying it's the guy that died.'

'The man you killed.'

'If you say so.'

She pretended to read from her notes: 'Brendan Lyons, at the post office with his grandson, aged four, buying stamps for their Christmas cards. You pull him out and shoot him in front of the wean.'

'I never.'

'Oh.' She looked to Donaldson. 'I thought you were pleading guilty?'

'He came out to help me, looking for a cut o' the money. But the gun went off.'

'He was after the money?'

'Yeah.'

'I've looked into his life, he didn't need money.'

'Ever'b'dy needs money.'

'What made him think you'd give him money? Did you have an agreement beforehand?'

'Nut.' But MacLish's gaze skittered across the table top.

'When did you first meet?'

He looked at her, unblinking. 'Never met.'

'Just that once?'

MacLish looked at her and she at him and he told her: his gaze flicked from one of her eyes to the other looking for details, trying to work out what she knew.

'Who told you the alarm was off?'

A flicker of panic.

'That's why you went there, isn't it? Because you knew the alarm was off. Where did you hear that?'

He had to come up with something and he knew it: 'In a bar.'

'Which bar?'

'The Hoops bar.'

It was a Republican bar and MacLish had Loyalist tattoos, time smudged, colour faded. She pointed to his forearm and a UVF tattoo. 'You hanging about in Republican bars, picking up stray gossip, are you? Brave man. What do you think guys in prison will make of you murdering the old guy in front of the granwean?'

Donaldson leaned forward amiably. 'In what way is this relevant?'

'The wean was looking away.'

'He looked back and saw his grandpa cut in half.'

They looked at each other. A prisoner who hurt children was a legitimate target for other prisoners. Most prisoners had a sentimental attachment to children that verged on the Victorian.

But MacLish seemed sure he could make a case for himself: he rolled a careless shoulder at her.

'You ever hear what happened to Francesca Costello after her mother was killed?'

He missed a breath. 'Who?'

'Francesca Costello.'

'Don't know her.'

'She was fourteen when her mum was murdered, over in Battlefield.'

Donaldson leaned in. 'We haven't discussed this—'

'Oh, aye.' MacLish was suddenly animated. 'I heard about the mother, aye. Battlefield. I remember that.'

'Well, Francesca got sent into care. Ended up in St Margaret's.'

'I was there.'

'I know.'

'She'll be out now, probably?' he said, as if that made it all right.

Morrow nodded non-committally.

'What? She's not dead.'

'Still, not everyone's fit for care. Some people never really recover from that.'

She looked at him, thinking about Francesca, about the smell of her and the dirty cuffs, and her face was a mask of sorrow and disgust. MacLish read her and for a moment she saw him know what he had done, that he had caused that. Then she saw the shutters come down.

'When you met Brendan Lyons before, were you alone?'

He didn't answer.

'When was it exactly?'

'Never met him,' he said flatly.

'He knew you.'

Donaldson leaned between them. 'I think we need to stop here. I think I need instruction.'

It was a good point to stop at, before MacLish got the chance to find out she knew nothing.

'OK.' She slapped her file shut and turned off the tape, telling it they were stopping for a comfort break. 'We'll turn the cameras off and you can talk in here, is that acceptable?'

MacLish opened his mouth to object but Donaldson over-ruled him. 'That'll be fine. Thank you.'

Outside, Leonard stopped Morrow in the corridor. 'Ma'am, are you sure about me being in there with you?'

'Go and find me a comprehensive list of his associates. Meet me back here in fifteen minutes.'

Leonard walked away.

Morrow leaned in to find Routher in the viewing room. 'Having a wee sit down?'

'No, ma'am. McKechnie's been in here watching. He wants to talk to you.'

McKechnie was alone, had a stack of files on his desk and seemed to be reading one.

'Sit down.'

Morrow took the seat. 'George MacLish confessed, sir.'

'I know.' He didn't seem that pleased. 'Charge him and shut it down. We need to concentrate on PSU.'

'He's confessed to the robbery, sir, but it's not just a robbery, it's a murder, it deserves—'

'He confessed to the murder, Morrow, I was listening.'

'He said he did it but he didn't say why.'

'Shut it down.'

She knew it was hopeless but she protested anyway, 'Sir, it deserves a proper investigation.'

'Charge him.'

They looked at each other. McKechnie was right, she knew he was, but George MacLish was cutting his interviews short with a guilty plea. He had been told to plead guilty. They'd never find out who told him the alarm was off, how he knew Brendan or why he went there.

McKechnie tried to smile. 'Anyone would think you were reluctant to take Christmas Day off, Alex.'

'Sir, we can't shut down whole departments every time some-one leaves a bag of money at a door. You might as well give them keys to the building. We have to put on a show at least.'

McKechnie understood what she was saying. 'OK. But first thing in the morning we start this.' He tapped his file. 'I'll be here at nine thirty.'

Morrow stood up. 'That's not first thing in the morning, sir, that's two hours after the shift changeover.'

She looked at him and, for reasons she couldn't quite explain, they smiled at each other. 'These are good men, sir.'

'I was *watching*.' He was talking about Leonard and he wasn't happy. 'They've been to Wilder's house and found Sainsbury's bags full of money in his chimney.'

'Oh shit.'

'Quite.'

'Have they been to Leonard's?'

'They're there right now.'

Morrow didn't dare ask if they'd found anything. 'Have they been there long?'

'Thirty minutes.' Evidently they hadn't yet because McKechnie wasn't shouting at her. 'You're all very loyal to each other on this team. That's not always useful, d'you understand? You've been picked over with a toothcomb. She hasn't.'

Morrow heard him: hoping isn't knowing.

'Yes, sir.' Morrow nodded. 'Goodnight, sir.'

'Goodnight, Morrow. Good day today.'

'Yes, sir.'

She swung into the incident room, looking for Leonard and found her sitting in front of a computer screen with a list of names, all from Greenock or Gourock, some family names recurring. More recently MacLish was associated with the McGregors, who were currently chewing their way up the shit pile out there.

Morrow watched Leonard's eyes flicker across the screen.

219

How did she know, really, that Leonard was trustworthy? She might filter out the real associates. She might have already done it. Morrow just didn't know.

'Print them all up and put them on my desk,' she said.

As she turned away she knew she would have to run the check herself, cross-check with Leonard's list, that the search for MacLish's associates would turn into a check on Leonard.

Harris was coming in the door and she nodded him out into the corridor. 'Look, um, I'm a bit stuck. After Christmas, we're having a wee christening do. Would you stand godfather to them?' She was embarrassed suddenly and tempered the compliment with a lie. 'I asked someone and they'd sort of said yes, but they can't make it now and we need someone.'

Harris widened his eyes with delight. 'Be honoured.' Then he pinched his mouth tight. 'Ma'am, you know I'm a Catholic?'

'Yeah.' She waved a hand in front of her face. 'It's, d'you know it's for Brian's mum really.' Another lie. 'So the religious thing isn't that . . . you know. Just don't come in a Celtic top, is the only thing.'

Harris shook his head and smiled. 'Honoured,' he said, and then he shook her hand. She smiled and shook his back.

21

Rosie Lyons smiled and lit a cigarette, took a deep breath and blew a thick stream of smoke into the cold morning air. She had planned this. All along she had been stringing Martin into this, tricking him, and now she was laughing at him. He wanted to put his hands on her neck and squeeze the breath from her. He wanted the unbridled honesty of that chaos back in the post office to come here and shoot her in the guts.

'You're dead angry with me, aren't you?'

'I think you're a fucking bitch.'

She chortled at that and put her hand on his arm. 'Oh come on' – she said it as if they'd both been in on the joke – 'your thumb's awful far up your arse.'

'What does that mean?'

'Don't take everything so serious.'

The door behind them swung open and the janitor came out, lips pursed and angry. 'Miss? Please put that cigarette out. There's no smoking in any of the school grounds.'

Rosie and Martin turned to look at him. Down the brightly lit school corridor, the Academy's deputy head whom Rosie had shouted at, watching them, her arms crossed, furious. A morning bell rang in the distance, sounding like the start of a new round.

Rosie grinned at her. It wasn't that Martin liked the school, or the deputy head, he thought she was a dick, actually, but Rosie had used him, as if he was part of them, part of the enemy, and she made him feel foolish when he had meant nothing but good.

'Put it out, miss.' The janitor was afraid of the deputy and fear made him a little aggressive.

Still watching the woman, Rosie said to him, 'You in a union?'

'Put the cigarette out or leave the grounds, miss.'

'Join a union,' said Rosie, 'because it's going to get worse.' She took a draw on her cigarette and turned away. 'Come on, Martin.'

She dropped off the step into the playground and walked towards the gate.

The school was small and highly selective, a neoclassical villa very near the Lyons' house. The parents' car park was half full for the junior concert. They made their way towards the big cars and Martin saw that smirk on her face.

'The fuck was that for?' he said.

She smiled broadly. 'That was for my dad.'

'You did that for your dad?'

She looked tearful, and nodded. 'Oh my God, he'd have loved that.'

Martin wondered at a senior who daydreamed about inveigling his way into the office of a prim deputy head, sitting quietly for the first ten minutes as the woman introduced the school and explained the selection procedure, before aggressively asking her to explain how she could use the terms 'selection' and 'teaching'. Rosie had spoke loudly, accusing the woman of having no professional integrity. She was just cherry-picking, Rosie said, raising her voice, and she should be ashamed because they were syphoning off parents with resources who could improve local schools if they were made to send their kids to them.

The rant continued with a lot of pointing and Rosie shouting and leaning across the table.

Martin was stunned. He wasn't listening to what she was saying and felt the teacher wasn't either. They were both just sitting there, waiting for Rosie to stop being an asshole.

She was in the middle of some elaborate, old-fashioned point about false consciousness when the deputy head came to life and phoned for the janitor to come and get her out of the office.

Martin raised his voice now. 'She didn't hear anything you said, you know.'

'No, I know.' Rosie was still smiling. 'I just wanted to say it.'

So they walked now, across the playground, through the parents' car park to the side gate. Rosie smiling to herself and smoking, and Martin trailing behind her.

'I was trying to help. You made me look like a dick.'

'I'm sorry, that wasn't what I meant to do.'

'Why did you take me in there?'

Rosie stopped at that and took a draw on her cigarette. 'D'you think I was giving you into trouble as well? I wasn't. You insisted on coming in with me, remember? In the waiting room, I said wait outside and you came in.'

Martin thought back. She had asked him to wait. He was angry because he felt like she'd been shouting at him. 'You know what I was doing in there?' he said. 'I was trying to make Joe safer, get him out of that environment.'

She bumped his arm with her elbow. 'You can't do that, Martin.' She pointed at a white SUV. 'See that car, there? One in ten chance that's a gangster's car. Range Rover there? That's probably a drug dealer's. Car next to it – his lawyer. Joe would be less hidden here than at the local comprehensive. See? They're all moving up. That teacher is part of a revolution she doesn't know anything about. No one knows what's going on in this city . . .' She walked on, dropping the few steps to the street. 'You can't see the pattern until you're part of it. And we're stuck in it.'

'Well,' he said when they were both on the pavement, 'I'm sorry for whatever the fuck it was I did to you. Obviously I'm an asshole too.'

'No, Martin. You're a good guy. That was kind, you meant to be kind.'

He was trying. That's what she didn't get – he was killing himself trying to do the right thing. People he knew spent their days swimming and doing fucking yoga, buying cars and gambling and sailing and burning themselves out on coke and sex and getting married. He moved to shitty places and got involved with filth like her and listened to them. He shouted at her then, 'I'm busting a gut trying to fucking help.'

'But you're not helping. You feel fucking awful because you're not helping. You're picking lottery winners, Martin. You're trying to connect with people. It's no substitute to just give them stuff. You need to invest yourself, not give *stuff.* That,' she touched his forearm, 'those dots, that's like thirty-three runs at a wall.'

He looked at his arm. He felt the dots sting, as if he was impregnated with failure, stained with it, as if she was saying that he was as imperious and as vacuous as his parents.

The warmth of her bare palm on his cheek felt shocking. 'I know what you want.' Rosie slipped her arm through his, tugging him along the road.

And Martin, powerless, beyond angry, followed fat, smoking Rosie in her cheap clothes up the road.

22

Harris was distracted during their drive to Abbi Cabs. He couldn't stop speculating about Bannerman, who did he report to, who would be conducting the investigation, how did they relate to him in the chain of command?

'Give it a rest,' said Morrow.

'He'll prime them to come for me, won't he? He hates me. He's spiteful.'

'You know why Bannerman hates you,' she said. 'He's right to hate you. I'd hate you if you did that to me.'

'I just don't want them to waste this – all their resources. I mean, shit, if there's *bags of cash* floating about I don't want them to get distracted by a petty fight with me. You *know*?' He looked at her. 'You know?'

'Yeah.' It was a bit over the top.

'He's *spiteful*. He's a spiteful man.'

Morrow didn't think Bannerman was especially spiteful and she wasn't enjoying Harris's shift in mood at all; it was damping the triumphant afterglow of getting Hugh Boyle and Benny Mullen. She got a genuine cheer from her squad at the briefing this morning and the search of Leonard's house had found her clean. Morrow didn't want to listen to Harris carp all morning.

Harris parked the car, pulled on the handbrake and looked out of the window at the Abbi Cabs office: a low, free-standing cottage with a slanted tiled roof, one of the incongruous estate workers' cottages in Anniesland, a village on the outskirts of Glasgow which had been swallowed in one Victorian gulp.

Brand new luxury flats and the playing fields of a private school laid siege to streets of miners' bungalows.

The Abbi Cabs cottage stood alone in a sea of red chip gravel, the train line looming behind it presumably the reason it was cheap enough to use as a mini cab HQ. She saw immediately that the alarm system on the building was new and each of the corners had a high-tech CCTV camera perched on it.

Harris coughed. It sounded dangerously like a prelude to another Bannerman salvo. Morrow opened her door quickly and got out, slamming it behind her with eloquent vigour. Harris got out slowly and looked at her over the roof of the car.

She held her hands up at him. 'His dad's the bloody Assistant Chief. He was never going to disappear. Live with it.' She walked away.

Harris stood still. She was almost at the door to the cab firm before she heard his feet crunch slowly after her. She waited for him.

'You wait and see,' he said. 'That PSU investigation'll centre on me.'

There was nothing more to say. Morrow shoved the door open and walked in.

Three orange plastic chairs in a row, next to a coffee table with neatly laid out newspapers. A giant Coke machine hummed in the corner. High on the wall a shelf held a television, right next to another CCTV camera, trained on the door. A man's face appeared through a serving hatch trimmed with red and gold tinsel.

'Where to?' Donald didn't recognise Morrow but she knew him.

'Hiya,' she said, smiling. 'We met at the Southern General the other night.'

He frowned. 'Of course.'

'I was with Rita Lyons, you said I could come and talk to you?'

'Aye.' He disappeared, the hatch slid shut. She heard a scuffling and a door opened in a back corridor. Donald reappeared around a corner and beckoned to them to follow.

Harris was behind her as she walked around the corner, through a metal door and into the office. A modest radio system had a Sudoku book sitting open on it in grey grainy paper with a pen lying in the spine.

'You like those puzzles?' said Morrow.

'Aye, keep the brain working, know?' Donald waved them to an armchair and a high bar stool and retook his own seat. 'Anyone want a coffee?'

'No,' said Harris, 'we're fine, thanks.' He was still a touch huffy but not so much that Donald would notice. Annoyed at him, Morrow took the armchair and left him to climb up on the stool. She waited until he had sat down before saying, 'Harris, can you get the forms out?' making him scramble back down to get the clipboard out of his bag. He climbed back up and took Donald's name, address and contact numbers.

'So, Donald,' she said, 'this is just to give us a better idea about who Brendan was: could you tell us how you met him?'

'As I said, it was a long time ago. We were both in the GMB, we met there.'

'At a meeting?'

'On a picket line.' He warmed at the memory. 'God, that was almost thirty years ago, in the eighties, there were a lot of picket lines then, I can't remember which one.'

'He must have been older than you?'

'Oh, aye, about ten years again. Thirty seems very old when you're twenty.'

'But you got on well?'

'No, not really. I don't think he knew who I was for the first four or five years I knew him, actually. Bren was a bit of a star in the movement; he was a great speaker, he organised study groups for the younger guys. Gave us reading lists and organised discussions, old-fashioned really, taught us debating skills. Fat all use now, I suppose.'

Morrow smiled. 'Not much call for them in the cabs business?'

Donald smiled ruefully. 'Actually, being good at arguing is useful in a Glasgow taxi but it was a way of harnessing all that anger among the young guys, know?' His face clouded over as he remembered. 'We were so angry. The party was in disarray, factions everywhere—'

'Is this the Communist Party?'

'No. He was in the CPU but I was in Labour, well,' he jerked his head to the side, 'I was a member of Militant but we were all in Labour.'

Harris chipped in: 'You caused all sort of hell, didn't you?'

'We were trying to steer Labour to the left. Some of us. Others were there for other reasons.'

'Some people blamed you for making the party unelectable, didn't they?' Harris looked uncomfortable. 'Giving the Tories a straight run in three elections.'

Donald nodded heavily. 'You're from an old Labour family.'

Harris blushed. 'Yeah, so?'

'We didn't make it unelectable.' Donald seemed to have had this discussion many times. He sat back and crossed his arms, slowing it down. 'Even if we'd all voted Labour the Tory majority in England would have cancelled it out.'

Morrow wouldn't normally have allowed a political discussion with a potential witness but Donald was smiling and seemed to be enjoying it. She chipped in, 'If you'd formed a proper alliance with the UK Labour Party you could have presented proper opposition to the Tories.'

He grinned and pointed at her. 'Better. But coming out of a period of consensus politics all the parties were swinging to the right. The Tories shifted and reset the agenda and the party was drifting to the right to catch up.'

'That's a separate point,' she said. 'Answer the first point.'

Donald laughed at that and she smiled back. 'Is that the sort of thing Brendan taught you?'

'That's exactly the sort of thing he did. If you gave a speech he'd give you notes, put a pause in there, three-beat repetitions, stuff like that.'

'"Three-beat repetitions"?'

'"Education, education, education." That sort of thing. Using phrases that make the audience feel part of a movement, stronger than they are individually. Powerful stuff.'

'Why did he give up politics?'

Donald looked a little sad. 'Auch, people move on. Weans come, grandweans. Saps you. You get tired, get old, there isn't the respect there once was.' He looked at his hands as his fingers braided around one another for a moment and then slipped apart.

'Did something happen to sap Brendan?'

Suddenly Donald raised his voice and looked over her shoulder. 'Well, Rosie getting pregnant, being young and that, and then his mum-in-law she got sick and there was a load of doctors and that. Things get on top of you, don't they? Time consuming.' If Morrow had been a Brendan to him she would have told Donald to keep his voice steady, not to change the pattern of his speech, not to keep blinking like that.

'So, nothing particular happened to Brendan?'

Donald shook his head, lips pressed tight.

'But you didn't lose touch?'

'No, I still saw him. I got to tell him what he meant to me. That was, know, an honour, really. I wouldn't have this business if it wasn't for him, I wouldn't have gone to college or got my accountancy diploma. My dad died when I was young, so, he really mattered to me.'

'Father figure?'

'Father figure.'

'And you know Rita?'

'Aye, Rita always calls me if she needs a cab. She knows I'll get straight to her, 'cause it's her.'

Morrow liked his loyalty but wondered if something else lay behind it, maybe a romantic connection: 'Do you know Rosie?'

'Yeah.' Straight answer, no deception. 'And Joseph.'

'Did Brendan have any debts?'

'Not that I know of.'

'Did he have any dealings with criminals?'

'No, no, not at all, no.'

Donald shook his head, shifted in his chair, looked away. He didn't like lying to her, she could tell, because when he spoke again his voice was high and anxious. 'It's not as if Brendan's done *nothing*, you know?' The deception was choking him. 'I mean, there's guys elected who wouldn't even be in politics but for Bren.'

'Right?'

'Like Kenny Gallagher, he was one of Bren's boys.'

'Oo,' said Morrow. 'The "Class traitor" guy.'

Donald sighed. 'Aye, that fanny. He was close to Bren at one time. Even now, there's nine on the city council due to Bren, teachers, union officials got their start with Bren. He really made a difference, ye know?'

Morrow gave him her card and thanked him, left a small pause in case he decided to tell her the truth. He didn't, but had enough conscience to avoid her eye.

She stood up, held out her hand. 'Thank you, Donald.'

He shook it. 'As I said, you know, anytime.' At the door out to the sea of gravel he muttered: 'I feel like my dad died again, know?'

She stood and looked at him. 'Anything you want to tell me, Donald?'

'Like what?'

'What happened to Brendan, why he chucked politics?'

Donald shook his head, a gesture so small it looked like a shiver. She thought suddenly of Rita's cigarette flaring in the dark of his cab outside the hospital.

'I can see you're very loyal,' she said, stepping outside. 'But if you think of anything.'

'Sure.'

She pointed back up to the high-tech cameras on the roof. 'You keep money on the premises?'

'No, but burglars don't know that. The building isn't over-looked. I need it for the insurance.' He raised a hand in a formal wave and slipped back inside, shutting the door after himself.

She didn't distrust Donald, she believed he was sincere, especially about Brendan Lyons, but she gave the building one last look and knew he was lying about the security system. She saw a camera on the roof rotate towards her as she climbed into the car. Motion-sensitive CCTV. It must have cost a packet.

She was back in the car with Harris and his mood and his paranoia.

'Could you do with cheering up?' she said. 'Fancy a wee Christmas jaunt?'

Harris started the engine. 'Where to?'

'Let's go and see Pavel and Kenny Gallagher.'

He grinned. 'Really?'

'Pavel first. That's as much as we've got time for, eh?'

Harris pulled the car out, spraying gravel. She looked back and saw all of the cameras slowly swerve to watch them.

23

Kenny Gallagher stood in the small room behind the platform and watched them come in through a two-way mirror. Pete had hired a room to accommodate fifty journalists. Even on a good day that was optimistic and this wasn't a good day. A department store in town was staging a Santa appearance on a roof. Edinburgh City Council were holding a press conference to explain the grotesque over-spend on the half-built tram system. Pete told him it was a PR disaster: Kenny had insisted that the press release be exclusively about McFall despite Pete's advice that the TV news wouldn't carry two dispute-riven political press conferences in one thirty-minute slot; too samey, too dry.

The STV camerawoman turned on the lights, dazzling Gallagher through the mirror, making him visible, he feared. He stepped back to the shadows in a corner. They were old lights, blindingly bright and on old-fashioned stands. And they were warm too, he could feel the heat already. They had a new set of lights that didn't give off so much heat, he'd seen them, but presumably those ones had been carted off for the Edinburgh statement. The heat of these lights would make you sweat, make you look as shifty as Nixon.

The important thing, he told himself, was to look as if he was telling the truth. He would lose the court case but this was a seed of doubt in the public's mind and it had to be credible, something they could run with, something that could be referred back to when he lost.

I am a good man. I am one man against a giant machine. I am doing this for other people, for Annie's dignity, for the faith they have placed in me.

He could see Pete in the room, standing by the door, welcoming the journalists as they arrived, give this one a joke, that one solemn concern, changing his act to suit the audience, inviting them all to sit at the front of the room. Most of them took his cue, Kenny had heard him do it so often he could almost read Pete's lips – I've saved a seat for you down there, Michael, yeah, front row, go on, down there. It was so that the room looked busy in the frame of the TV camera. A lot of empty seats made a statement look unimportant.

It was almost time and so far they had three unknowns, an old woman with a notebook (a notebook!) Paddy Meehan and Buchan both with DAT machines at the ready, the STV crew and the dolly-bird reporter, wearing a degree of make-up that looked perfectly normal on TV but a bit clownish in real life.

Pete looked at his watch. A young guy appeared at the door. Kenny had never seen him before. He was very young but wore a light brown tweed jacket and his bag was a battered school satchel, old but expensive. Without looking at Pete, ignoring his invite to sit at the front, he took a seat halfway down the room, right in the middle of two empty rows.

Keeping his eye on him, Pete left his place at the door. He walked along to the guy, spoke, and gestured to the front row. The guy held a hand up pleasantly, insisting that he'd stay where he was. Pete spoke again. They looked at each other. The guy stood up, his nose inches from Pete's, taller than Pete, meaner than Pete. Pete's hand contracted to a fist and the guy sneered, brushed past him, knocking chairs over. The front row turned to look as he left, swinging his bag and knocking over another chair on the way out.

Pete turned to them, said something that made them laugh. They turned away, back to the front and Gallagher saw then a snide, pleased look pass between Meehan and Buchan. Nasty. There was no need for it.

It was time. Pete shut the door and walked down the aisle to the front of the room. Kenny watching him through the mirror, walking towards him. Kenny admitted it to himself: he suspected that Pete wanted the press conference to fail, that Pete was scouting for another job.

Pete opened the door and the white TV lights burst into the dim room.

'Time,' he said, shutting it after him.

'Who was that you saw out?'

'Journalist from the *Globe* down south. Here to disrupt proceedings. He'd been briefed as well, sit in an empty row. He must have been the trainee. He was so green he even had his question written out in longhand – "Derek Geller – how know him?"'

Kenny's heart hammered in his throat. Women over beds, over sofas, two men, one man, cocks, hands holding tits, fingering cunts, tits and cunts, fingers in, fingers out and STV lights, Buchan and Meehan, *Globe* journalist taking notes.

Pete's finger was in his face. 'You're sweating.'

Gallagher turned away, lifted a glass of water to his mouth and drank past the lump in his throat. He drank the entire glass and then poured another one and drank half of that. He'd need a piss now, almost immediately he'd need a piss and it would distract him from those thoughts. He couldn't have that swimming around in his head and look honest.

'Who is Derek Geller?'

'I don't know.'

'They've got more on you?'

'They can't print more,' said Kenny, pulling himself up. 'Soon as this becomes subject to a lawsuit they can't print more.'

'Short-term solution—'

'Then I lose and whatever they print just looks vindictive.'

It made sense to him as a strategy, when he said it out loud.

The images were gone from his head and he felt the urgent need to get out there, to get on before they came back.

'Come on,' he said, passing Pete, storming the door and taking the three steps up to the rostrum in a single wide stride. He nodded hello to everyone. 'Meehan?' a nod. 'Buchan, how are you today?'

Buchan was startled. 'Yeah – OK.'

Gallagher reproached himself: he should have been pleasant to Buchan in the first place. That animosity was needless. He smiled up at the STV crew. 'Where do you want me? This seat? Or—'

'We've lit you for that one,' said the camerawoman.

Kenny sat down in the far seat, pulled the mike over to his mouth and adjusted his jacket so that it sat flat at the front. 'OK?'

'Yep,' called the camera.

'Shiny?'

'You're fine, Kenny.'

The TV presenter sat in the front row, on the edge of her chair. She was lit too, and, though he hadn't begun speaking, she had already assumed a listening pose and was being filmed, presumably for cutaway shots.

Pete climbed the stairs and sat down next to him slowly, dropping a set of papers on the table in front of him, setting his iPhone down and flicking it to silent.

'OK, Pete?' Kenny said it as if they'd just met.

Pete gave him a friendly smile, faking it, doing better than Kenny would have expected.

'OK,' said Kenny, talking over their heads as if to a full room. 'Let me start by thanking you all for coming here. I have an important announcement to make today with regard to the allegations against me made by the *Globe*, an attack on me and my family—'

'Will you be suing them, Kenny?' Paddy Meehan pointed her DAT at him like a handgun.

Pete pulled the mike over towards him by the stand. 'There will be time for questions later, Paddy. Just let the man talk.'

Kenny felt picked-on and he needed to pee, but the old fight was returning to him.

'In the past,' he said, 'I have been accused of many things: being a careerist, a factionalist, a fascist, of stealing money from the party, attending orgies, having affairs, encouraging crime, dealing drugs. None of these claims are true.' Gallagher knew he was giving good face, sad but understanding, because the audience was empathising, craning forward slightly in their chairs. He looked up at them for maximum impact. 'Now, in the run-up to this election, I'm accused of having an affair and misusing my expenses to pay for my . . .'

The only word he could think of was bitch. That's what kept coming to him – my bitch, the bitch, bitch bitch.

'*Extramarital partner.*' They smiled at that. Kenny smiled back awkwardly and held his hand out in entreaty: 'I'm so sorry, I don't really know the terms for these things. Whatever you would call someone you were having an affair with—'

'Mistress,' said Buchan, giving a slow blink.

'Oh, of course, thank you. "Mistress." I'm accused now of paying for my *mistress*,' he nodded gratefully at Buchan again, 'to travel with me to Inverness out of parliamentary expenses,' he looked down to check a bit of paper, 'on the tenth of October this year, on a night when I was at a fund-raising party with thirty other people. We were raising money for a sheltered housing project for adults with learning difficulties, to promote independent living.'

He looked down again and changed his mood: sorrowful to angry. 'This cannot go on. Now, I have always been a campaigning politician before I was a party political animal. As some of you may know my younger brother James was killed by a drunk driver and that was what drove me into politics in the first place, and I see here a continued campaign of misinformation, an undermining of the democratic process. Someone has to stand up to these multinational organisations with huge resources. I am prepared to do that. Now, as in disputes before, because I don't lie, I'll admit from the beginning that my chances of winning are very slim. But I simply cannot allow this blatant injustice to go unchallenged.' He looked up, nervous face, half in entreaty. 'My first step will be to sue the *Globe* and Globe Media for defamation of character in regard to these allegations.' Big reactions from all of them and he knew he'd done the right thing. 'I am standing down at this election to fight this fight and if I'm not bankrupt or in prison,' he smiled, they laughed, 'then I hope to stand again at the following election. But I want to apologise to my constituents for stepping down. I hope they can see that I can't represent them properly while pursuing this fight because I have a young family.'

He gulped and dried at that, allowed fear to flicker across his face, knowing it would be picked up by the cameras. 'Are there any questions?'

Three hands shot up. The camera's muzzle panned slowly towards the presenter, sitting pert and ready.

'Jennifer,' said Pete, taking charge and pointing at her.

'Is your wife Annie supporting you in this action?'

Kenny smiled warmly. 'Yes, Jennifer, my wife and three wonderful children are supporting me in this action,' he said, remembering to repeat the question back to her, because they often cut the questions out of the broadcast.

Jennifer smiled warmly back. The camera turned again, a slight shift, to the others in the front row. Jennifer's smile dropped into her lap.

'Paddy Meehan?'

'Jill Bowman was with you in Inverness on the eighth of October. Who paid her expenses then?'

'OK.' He nodded as if this was a new question. 'Right: Jill Bowman is a member of the youth committee. It's my understanding that she comes from an ordinary, decent, but by no means rich family. The question of her expenses being paid would never have come up if she came from a rich family. The implication of this is the exclusion of working-class people from the political process.' He sounded adamant, felt sincerely aggrieved.

'Were you having a sexual affair with her?' continued Meehan.

Here he struggled, looked confused. 'No. I don't know why anyone would think . . . she's . . . she's very young. I'd hate for this to turn into a witch-hunt against her. I mean she's . . .' He shrugged, made the regretful face of a disappointed father. 'She's young.'

'You mean she wishes she had an affair with you, but she didn't?'

'Right, Meehan,' said Pete, 'I think you've had your turn.'

But Meehan wasn't to be put off. 'No offence, Kenny, but it'd have to be an awful dark room for her to look at you and see Justin Bieber.'

Everyone laughed at that. The camerawoman laughed at that. Kenny laughed along with them, waiting until everyone had calmed down before he spoke. 'You know, Paddy, as far as I understand it Jill hasn't said anything about this. Young people are reluctant to participate in the political process precisely because of this sort of gossipy nonsense, so it would be especially regrettable if Jill was victimised by an industry with a proven track record of dirty tricks and illegal behaviour.' Pete was fiddling with his iPhone, the face was alight, distracting Kenny. 'My understanding of it is that McFall and the *Globe* are responsible for these allegations and it's a shame they had to drag a perfectly nice young woman into it.'

'Why not sue McFall then?'

'They printed it.'

'Would you be happy for Jill Bowman to talk to us?'

'It's not for me to say, Paddy.' Pete should have been stopping Meehan, but he was tapping something in his phone. 'I mean, as

I say, I don't know where McFall got this from, whether it was from Jill Bowman or someone else . . .'

'It's not just McFall.' Meehan's eyes flicked to Pete, as if she too was expecting him to stop her. 'Other members of the constituency party have made allegations that you were having an affair with her. What do you say to them?'

Gallagher was sweating now, controlling his breathing to stop himself raising his voice. 'Well, people can say what they like. I think allegations have to be separated from speculation.' A fleck of spit sailed from his mouth over the mike, catching the light. 'And we can't take away their right to do that. That would be just as bad.'

Pete looked at him. He seemed a little stunned. He looked about the room.

'Yes. Buchan?' Pete was in charge again.

'For the record, Kenny' – smug fucker, Gordon Buchan – 'are you saying you "never had sexual relations with that woman"?'

Meehan and the lady with the notebook smiled at each other, the only two apart from Gallagher who got the reference.

Kenny laughed sadly and held his hands up. 'I never had a relationship with Jill Bowman. But, you know, I didn't release her name to the press. You'd need to ask McFall about why he saw fit to do that. And, ah, Jill's a nice young person and she'll be under an enormous amount of pressure right now and I would ask you to be fair to her if, and when, you do interview her.'

The lady with the notebook put her hand up. Pete didn't know her name.

'Yes?'

'What would you like for Christmas?'

'Peace,' he said, and they all laughed together.

Pete wound it up with a thank you and a merry Christmas. Then, unusually abrupt, he just stood up, walked off and through the door at the back. It was rude. The journalists watched him go, surprised and, worse, interested.

239

Making light of it Kenny stood up and got off the platform. He shook all their hands individually, looking them in the eye as he thanked them for coming. He remembered to ask Gordon Buchan about his older brother – Pete had briefed him – before walking casually off through the door himself. He shut it carefully.

'Pete,' he raised his hands, 'what the fuck?'

Pete held the bright face of his phone up. 'Derek fucking Geller?' He'd asked someone who knew Derek, or knew something about Derek, because Pete suddenly seemed to know. 'Derek Geller? You skeezy fucking prick.'

'What are you talking about?'

'D'you know how much previous that prick has?'

A text. He'd got a text during the conference and whatever Pete had heard, it was bad. But it was Kenny's own business, not his. 'There's no need for rudeness—'

'*Rude . . . ?*' Pete slumped against the wall. '*Rude*ness?'

It did sound a bit fey. 'Well, you know, I mean, I told you I don't know him and—'

'A bald-faced lie. He's been your friend for fifteen years. He met you through Brendan Lyons.'

Kenny held his hands up in surrender. 'Pete. I met a lot of people through—'

But Pete was shaking his head and picking up his coat. 'This is not for me, man, I'm—'

'You believe them?'

Pete stood still for a moment.

'You believe Globe Media against me, Pete?'

Pete stood up, a little unsteady as he flattened his jacket over his arm. 'I'm not Annie.'

'What does that mean?'

'I'm not a fucking mug.' He opened the door to the corridor, hurrying to get out before the journalists. 'I resign,' he said, as the door fell shut behind him.

That's when he knew for sure: Pete had another job.

Kenny lingered in the shadows watching through the mirror, trying to gauge the mood of the room as the journalists and crew packed up and wrestled their coats on.

They all smiled at each other, tipped their heads, thumbed back to the seat the *Globe* journalist had sat in, passing disparaging remarks about him.

Kenny had pulled it off.

24

Martin Pavel took a long time to answer the door. When he opened it Morrow and Harris could see why: the house was so big he might well have been a quarter of a mile away when the bell rang. Beyond the fairly grand front door was a hall of mansion proportions. Red granite pillars the colour of fat-mottled steak rose to the fifteen-foot-high ceiling. The doors leading off the hall were monumental Greco-Roman temple doors. And standing in the hall, straight from the shower, was Martin Pavel, wet-haired, wearing nothing but a pair of grey jogging trousers, tattooed like a human crossword.

'Hello, Mr Pavel, do you remember us? We met you at the hospital.'

He blinked. 'Sure.'

'Can we come in? We'd like to talk to you.'

He glanced behind them. 'Sure, come in.' He stepped aside. 'Come on, it's cold, I'll shut the door.'

Both Morrow and Harris hesitated, the contrast between his appearance and his surroundings piquing their interest and making them wary at the same time. They were tying up ends, just wanted to know for the sake of tidiness that the ULF wasn't a gun club that MacLish's defence lawyer would bring up at the trial. They were covering their backs.

'Please, come in.' Pavel opened the door wider, encouraging them to use it.

Morrow took the lead, stepping into the warm hall, her heels clattering on the Victorian tiles. The unexpected grandeur of the house made them move strangely, stiff, sneaking looks around.

'Mr Pavel, we've had a bit of trouble getting hold of you. You're not registered as a student at Glasgow University.'

'I was too late to register.' He frowned and held up a left hand, gesturing down the hall. 'D'you want to come into the kitchen?'

'Thank you.'

Pavel lifted a washed-out T-shirt from a chair and pulled it over his head as they followed him past a set of stairs leading to the upper floors. The paint had been stripped from the elegant banisters, the wood limewashed, as had all the doors. Even the furniture looked as if the owner harboured a more modest domestic aesthetic: a small Arts and Crafty chest of drawers, a pale love seat, and china ornaments depicting shepherds and women swishing their ball gowns hither and thither.

As they passed one of the grand doors Morrow noticed a light mist of dust swirl on the tiles in front of it.

'Do you live here alone?' she asked as they passed through a passage at the back of the grand hall.

'Yeah. Just me.'

Martin led them down a low servants' corridor to a kitchen that might have been lifted whole from a modern house and dropped into the room. The kitchen window was a long rectangle, the ceiling low, pitted with halogen lights, the units cream, the cooker a too-clean Aga.

He opened a hand at a small round pine table with four chairs. 'Please.'

A pine fire surround, carved with apples and leaves, a bunch of fake flowers in the grate. A plaster cupid sat on the mantel, ankles coyly crossed, holding a little bird on its palm. Morrow sat down at the table, feeling simultaneously intimidated and snobby.

'Orange juice or anything?'

'Nothing, thanks,' said Morrow.

Outside the window a whitewashed courtyard had a dry fountain in the middle and some benches. In one corner stood a concrete statute of a fey woman in a long gown smiling vaguely down at a bird that seemed to be pecking her foot.

Pavel sat opposite them, hands on the table. 'What, uh, can I do for you?'

Morrow found herself reading his arms and neck. He was very muscled and slim.

'OK, Mr Pavel.' She took out her notebook and a pen. 'How do you come to be living here?'

Pavel knew exactly what she was asking him but played for time. 'In this house?'

She hardened towards him suddenly. 'Yes. In this house.'

'I rent it.'

'You rent this entire house?'

'Uh hu.'

Uh hu. A Scottish colloquialism. Back to that again.

'OK.' She started again. 'Who are ye and where are you from?'

'All over.'

An American colloquialism, delivered with a twang.

They stared at each other. Morrow chewed her cheek and tapped a finger on the table.

'Martin, who rents this house?'

'I do.'

'Is it from someone you know?'

'No. I rent from an old couple. The wife has cancer so they've gone to Houston for treatment. It's hopeless, he tells me, but they want to "try in style". Kind of sad. Especially if you've ever been to Houston.'

'How much is it a month?'

He looked embarrassed at the mention of money. 'Hm, I'm not that sure . . .' He grimaced at her.

'*Why* are you not sure?'

He cast his eyes down. 'My lawyer pays for it. He picked it.'

Finally she was talking to the real him. 'Your lawyer?'

'Yeah. I, um . . .' He looked a little frightened. 'I have inherited a lot of, um, money.'

'OK.' He seemed so ashamed she wanted to change the subject. 'Why do you think the grandfather stepped out to help the gunman?'

Martin shrugged. 'Well, clearly he was trying to draw his eye away from the boy . . . isn't it?' He looked at them to see if there was any other possible explanation. 'Isn't that it?'

'What makes you think that?'

Martin thought back. 'He said "you". He recognised the man and the gunman knew him. Either, ah, Brendan, is that his name?'

'Yeah.'

'Yeah, either Brendan was going to point him out afterwards or the guy was going to kill him there. And he gave Joseph to me to look after.'

Morrow looked at his neck and read 'Beasts'. 'Not to be rude—'

He blushed and put his hand over his neck. 'No, I know.'

'—but you're not who I'd choose to babysit my kids.'

'I know.' As if distancing himself from it, he held his hand quite far away and pointed back at his neck. 'This means something entirely different in other cultures. Trust me, I'm not, you know.' He nodded. 'Really, I'm not.'

'Why do you think he chose you?'

'I don't think he saw me. I was behind him.'

'OK.' Morrow jotted notes down, leaving a pause for a change of direction herself. 'Are you interested in politics?'

'No.'

'But you're a member of several political organisations.'

He looked from Harris to her and back again. 'Am I?'

'The FEPA and ULF, for example.'

'Oh. That's not political. The Unity of Life Foundation is my own foundation.'

'What's a foundation?'

'It's a way of ring-fencing money to give away. When you put it in there you can't get it back.'

'Are you giving the money away?'

He nodded seriously. 'Fast as I fucking can.'

'Have you ever been poor?'

'No.'

'I have. It's pretty rubbish, Martin.'

'Well, it'll take me a while to get there.'

'So, not really political? Yet you seem to know a lot about guns.'

'Why is that relevant?'

'Why do you know so much about them?'

He shrugged. 'Just do. Done some shooting. For sport, self defence.'

'With real guns?'

'Sure.' He sat back. 'People do. Not here, but they do.'

'Do you keep guns in the house?'

'I actually don't like guns. I came here partly because there's no gun culture here. No kidnap culture. If I was in Mexico I couldn't go out, couldn't go into shops. Same in Moscow or Kiev or some parts of the States. Here, I'm good.'

'Right?' She shut her notebook. 'OK, Martin, I'd like a look around your house.'

He leaned forward over the table slowly, looking out of the window, distracted. 'Why are you asking me all of this?' he said quietly. 'I'm just a witness . . .'

Morrow nodded. 'I'd like to look round.'

He looked at her, suddenly self-possessed, arrogant almost, and when he spoke his accent was solid drawling East Coast aristo: '*Tourist.*'

Then he stood up with his head down and raised a hand to the door.

The tour for the tourists took almost twenty minutes because the house was vast. There were eight bedrooms, all untouched, all ready for occupation and each had a bathroom of its own. As well as five reception rooms performing different functions, the house was attached to the mews cottage and the staff rooms. Everywhere were fake flowers, everywhere were strange dolls and cupids and pictures of ladies in long dresses lurking in gardens, hanging about ballrooms, all done with soupy brush strokes in pastels. Morrow could tell everything was expensive but little of it to her taste.

Pavel expressed surprise at some of the rooms. He seemed to be living in only three of them: the kitchen, his bedroom and the bathroom that ran off it. He hadn't really unpacked: when she asked him what was in a duffel bag at the foot of his bed he said it was all of his clothes. She thought he might be thinking of running, but Harris asked, 'You travelling somewhere?' and Pavel said, 'No,' before turning calmly away and walking back out into the first floor hall.

Morrow followed him out. 'This is enormous for someone who lives in three rooms.'

'It's not *that* big,' he said, holding the banister and taking the first step.

Morrow took the stairs behind Pavel, looking at his neck, at the flawless marzipan skin and downy white hairs sitting on the deep ink blackness of the tattoos.

'Rosie Lyons said she met you.'

'Rosie?'

Morrow watched the tiny hairs on his neck lift from his skin. 'She said you came to see her.'

He turned on the stair, looked alarmed. 'No. I didn't.'

'She met you. Out running.'

'Oh.' He drew a breath. 'Oh. Sure, yeah. We bumped into each other. Just that one time.'

It was the final phrase that caught her attention.

She watched the white hairs rising on the back of his neck, saw his hand tighten on the banister and had a strange feeling that something was troubling Martin Pavel, and Rosie Lyons could tell her what it was.

'We're running late, ma'am,' said Harris as he drove into Lallans Road and parked. 'We might not have time to go and see Gallagher.' He looked a little disappointed.

Morrow checked her watch. Sure enough, they had fifty minutes to get back to the office. 'Ah, we'll make it. We'll just ask the Lyons about Pavel quickly, and then we'll go and see him.'

She opened her door and stepped out at the same time as Harris. The clouds were gathering overhead, threatening rain, darkening the day, as they hurried through the gate and pressed the doorbell. The hall light was off. No one came to the door. Stepping back she could see that no lights were on upstairs.

She put her hand on the glass door. It felt warm. The heating was on. She stepped over to the front window and found the Christmas tree was turned off.

'Maybe they've gone to a panto or shopping or something,' suggested Harris.

'The granny doesn't go out much, does she?' It seemed odd that they were out, slightly troubling, until it occurred to her – 'Nursery Christmas show!'

Harris clicked his fingers and pointed at her. 'Course!'

They took the car, though it was less than three hundred yards away, afraid the rain would come on. The outside gates of the nursery were chained shut but the lights were all on inside. Morrow buzzed the entry buzzer and asked if it was the show or the party today. The nursery nurse said it wasn't.

'Is Joseph Lyons in today?'

'He came in this morning for just half an hour and then his mum came and got him again.'

'Was he sick?'

'She said it was a family emergency.'

After she hung up Harris suggested the granny had been taken ill.

'That'll be it,' said Morrow, less convinced than she sounded. 'We're wasting time anyway. Let's go see Gallagher and phone around on the way.'

25

Morrow and Harris drove along the winding motorway that followed the curve of the river to the Hillhead Constituency Headquarters. She had called every A&E department in the Lyons' local area and found no one by the name of Lyons. Then she remembered that the granny was not Brendan's mother but Rita's mother and rang the office, telling Leonard to get Rita's maiden name and called the hospitals back. The granny hadn't been admitted under that name either.

'It's not that big a deal,' Harris reminded her, leaving the motorway. 'They could still just be at a panto.'

'Aye,' she said, but it felt wrong.

As they came to the narrow alley of warehouses and the constituency office they began passing posters of Kenny Gallagher's face. Handsome for a politician, but not for a celebrity, Gallagher was known as a good guy. Unusually for a career politician he could laugh at himself, made jokes about his privileged background and really seemed to care about the people he represented. He shopped at an unglamorous supermarket near the train station and you could stop him and talk to him about your worries and he'd listen. That's what everyone said about him: he would actually listen.

The posters caught the big scar on his cheek. The injury, Morrow noted with resentment, had been given to him by a provisional officer on his second time doing crowd control. He'd panicked when he saw the crowd surging towards him and lashed out. If the press hadn't been there it would have been a reprimand at worst. The provi, after two years on a waiting list and ten months of training, got the sack. Every year now Gallagher ran the Great North Run to raise money for COPS, a charity that supported the families of police officers who had been killed in the line of duty.

'There it's there,' said Harris, a little excited, as was Morrow.

They didn't need to be here really, they had MacLish but nothing was leading anywhere and they had one hour left before PSU moved in. Harris's sense of dread was almost tangible; she could see him wincing intermittently when he remembered what they were going back to. The most they could hope to get from the interview was background on Brendan Lyons – any grunt could have done it but Harris needed cheered up and they both wanted to meet Gallagher.

Harris parked and looked at the low building with the big party sign over the door. 'Ah, the Reset.'

'Oh my God, is *that* the Reset?'

'Indeed it is. Glasgow folklore, right there.'

Gallagher's party office was in what had once been a famous gangster bar, back when Glasgow was a boom town. It was no coincidence that the Reset, the offence of reselling stolen goods, was in the warehouse district. The bar's actual name was Cain's, and it used to be open all night to accommodate warehousemen coming off their strange shift patterns. For decades the Reset was the night haunt of hardmen and professional resetters. They'd nurse a drink all night and wait for burglars and light-fingered warehousemen to come to them with whispered bills of lading: want a quarter ton of unrefined sugar? Eight ton of lead ingots or a hundred bales of cotton? There was a rumour that the local circus bought their elephant in the Reset, but that rumour may have been started by Cain herself.

'Come on, then.' She opened her car door, aware that she had an uncharacteristic smirk on her face. Harris stepped out and smiled back at her across the roof. 'Just quickly.'

'I'm more interested just to see the old bar, actually,' said Harris, giggling for no reason. 'Because of all the history in there, you know?' It was a fib: he was as excited as she was about meeting someone from the telly.

They walked through the old saloon doors into a deserted reception area hung with noisy campaigning posters, calls for support. The plaster walls were still grey and smeared with the hands of lurching drunks.

'Who are *you*?' A woman stood up from behind a high desk. She wore tracksuit bottoms with pockets so full they made her diamond shaped. Her T-shirt demanded that somebody Make Poverty History.

'Strathclyde Police.' Morrow held up her warrant card. 'Looking for Kenny Gallagher.'

The receptionist spat a tut at Gallagher's name and poked a finger at a door across from the desk. 'Bastard's in there. Emptying his office.'

Harris tittered at her vehemence and followed her finger to the door set deep into the wall.

Morrow knocked. After a pause a man's voice called out, asking who they were. They told him. A shuffle of feet and the door was opened. Gallagher himself peered out at them.

Harris and Morrow gawped, neither of them ready to meet a face so familiar, but Gallagher smiled. 'Can I help you?'

Morrow was the first to get it together. 'Speak to you?'

He looked worried. 'Um, bit busy . . . ?'

'It's about Brendan Lyons.'

'What about Bren?'

'We're the police. Brendan Lyons was killed on Tuesday.' Morrow heard herself saying it, mumbling, informing the man bluntly of an appalling fact. 'We've . . . need to ask about him.'

The door opened wide and there stood Kenny Gallagher.

'Bren's *dead*?'

'I'm afraid he was killed in the course of a post office robbery.

He was there with his grandson. We think he may have recognised the robber.' It was weird, looking at a face so familiar, with so much back story. She couldn't quite take in the fact that he was an actual person. 'Can we ask you a few questions about him?'

He looked behind them, suspiciously catching the eye of the tracksuited woman on the desk. 'All right, Margaret?'

'*Fine*,' snarled Margaret. 'No thanks to you.'

Gallagher smiled awkwardly. 'Well, sorry about that. Officers, could I see your ID?' Morrow and Harris handed them over and he examined them, keeping them standing at the door to the office. 'I'm very sorry to do this but do you have a number I can call to verify your identities?'

They weren't really supposed to be here but Morrow thought McKechnie might even get a kick out of a phone call from Kenny Gallagher. She scribbled his direct number on a scrap of paper from her pocket and gave it to Gallagher.

'Who's this?'

'DI McKechnie. He's our boss.'

Gallagher looked at Margaret again, glanced around the lobby and shut the door on them.

Morrow and Harris smirked at one another.

'That smarmy bastard's let everyone down,' said Margaret, but it sounded second-hand.

'Right?' said Morrow.

'He thinks you're journalists, kidding on you're police . . . people, to get into his office.'

Harris and Morrow turned back to the door just as Gallagher opened it wide. 'Yeah, come in.'

They shuffled into an office full of cardboard boxes and stacks of paper. 'Packing?' asked Morrow.

'I haven't actually started yet.' Gallagher kicked an empty box under a table to let her get to a wooden chair that might well have been left over from the Reset.

'Nice room,' said Harris.

Morrow sat down and watched as Gallagher lifted a matching chair over for Harris to sit next to her. 'This bar was famous,' she said, 'you know, this building.'

'Yeah, we heard about Cain's.' Gallagher took a seat behind the desk, themselves sitting sidelong to him, in a row, as if they were being interviewed by him on a talk show. 'Famous bar. Police officers from the Partick Marine used to raid it all the time.'

She waited for Harris to say something but he was starstruck and not really listening.

'Is that right?' said Morrow.

'Think it was a bit of a den of thieves,' he whispered conspiratorially, and circled a finger in the air. 'Surrounded by warehouses, you know how it used to be.'

'Hmm, we're not really here to talk about that, though.'

He nodded heavily. 'Bren Lyons.'

'Yes, sir, Bren Lyons. You knew him, I understand?'

'A long time ago.'

The door flew open behind them and they turned to find a tall man in a denim shirt, long hair pulled back in a ponytail at the nape of his neck. He stopped when he saw Morrow and Harris sitting there. 'Who are you two?'

Morrow looked to Gallagher.

'Sorry,' smiled Gallagher, 'this is my press secretary, Peter McIlroy . . .' The smile froze as Peter McIlroy came in.

There was a small woman behind him, little more than a girl. She had a puffy face, seemed to have been crying. She didn't look up. Her hair was pulled back in a high ponytail, making her look younger yet, and she was dressed as if she had a day off school: in a silver bomber jacket and jeans worn over silver high-heeled boots.

'Who are they?' McIlroy nodded at them.

'We're DS Alex Morrow and DC Harris from Strathclyde Police.'

'Pete, I think you should go.' All of Gallagher's warmth seemed to have vanished.

But Pete wasn't afraid of him and continued to address Morrow. 'Why are you here?'

'We want to talk to Mr Gallagher. Alone.'

McIlroy looked to Gallagher for an answer. Gallagher sighed. 'Brendan Lyons was killed on Tuesday.'

'*Bren?*'

'He was shot in a post office raid, they said.'

'Did you know Brendan Lyons?'

'Aye.' McIlroy was more shocked than Gallagher had been, staring tearfully into the middle distance, trying to take it in. 'Oh my God ... *Bren* ...? How's Rita? Was Rita with him?'

'No, Mrs Lyons wasn't there.'

'My God, *Bren*? Shot? That's unbelievable.'

'Sit down, Pete.'

Pete slumped into a chair, staring at the floor. The girl hovered uncertainly in the doorway.

Gallagher looked at the sad girl standing there. 'Look, just come in,' he said. 'Shut the door behind you.'

Awkward, she stepped into the office and shut the door, holding her jacket tight around her, nodding a hello to Morrow and Harris.

'This is, ah, Jill.'

'Hello,' said Harris, the only one with manners.

The girl sniffed a hello and stayed by the door, hands behind her as she leaned on the wall.

'We wanted to ask about Brendan Lyons, what sort of man he was, what sort of things he might be involved in.'

Gallagher puffed a laugh at McIlroy. 'You don't seriously think Bren was involved in anything illegal, do you? He was the most honourable person I've ever met.'

'No, we don't, but we do think he knew the gunman and we're wondering where from.'

'And how close are you to finding him?'

Morrow blinked, looking defensive, misdirecting him. 'Pretty close,' she said, thinking of George MacLish sitting in the cells, growling at the wall.

Gallagher nodded. 'Is there anything hampering you in your work?'

'How do you mean?'

'I mean anything I can do to help.' He tipped his head as he spoke, giving little half nods, looking from one to the other. He looked very handsome now, his shoulders down, utterly engaged in their problem. It was like being hypnotised, she realised suddenly, his charisma was like a tractor beam. Morrow nodded a 'Thank you,' wondering if he had learnt to do that or was born with it. She frowned and looked at her hands, remembering a police surgeon telling a story, silly story, about a psychiatrist: whenever he left a prisoner and got to his car and thought 'what a nice a guy' or 'maybe he *is* innocent' it was a signal that he should go back and do a test for psychopathy.

She said, 'What we're after is a sense of who Lyons was and what sort of people he would have contact with now, why he stopped being politically active. Were you in touch with him?'

'Um,' he blinked at the floor, 'no, I haven't seen Bren for a few years now, he sort of fell out of the movement really. The last I heard he was planning to move to Mallorca. Didn't he?'

'No.'

'Well, I haven't seen him for years. Can I ask, how did you get my name?'

'Donald McGlyn.'

'Donald?'

'In the context of Brendan having a lasting influence. I suggested he was a spent force and he mentioned you.'

'Oh, yeah, I can see Donald hating that. He's very loyal, Donald. It's a lovely quality.' Gallagher sat back in his chair and his eyes glazed over a little. 'Bren was a shop steward at McTashan's, the old paperworks?'

'Oh yeah.'

'They were making everyone go part-time, building up to shutting it down, making them all go part-time so that the redundancy package would be far less. The union went along with it. He left and formed his own union. Tiny but we had a strike and marched and we won the dispute.' He smiled at Pete, misty-eyed, as if remembering their honeymoon. 'He'd only been there three months, still on probation. They didn't renew his contract, there was nothing in it for him, you know. He was a really honourable man.'

'What were *you* doing working in a paperworks, no offence?'

He smiled. 'None taken. I had just graduated. Didn't know what I wanted to do. I was drifting.'

'Pete, you knew Brendan Lyons as well?'

'Aye. Annie, Kenny's wife, her parents were in the Communist Party with Bren. So was my gran. Knew him through there.'

'Was he a nice man?'

He shuffled his feet and thought about it. 'Not *nice*. He was *sincere*. Not a careerist like me and him.' He pointed at Gallagher. 'Bren was a good man. He'd a temper though. Got expelled from the party, bet Rita never told you that, did she?' He was smiling, maybe at her, maybe at Kenny, she couldn't quite see his eyes through his glasses.

'What for?'

'Someone called him a liar, said he hadn't pressed people hard enough for their membership fees. Bren lost it and punched him.' He drew a deep, whistling breath through his teeth. '*Quite* a few times, as I recall.'

'Was he prone to violence . . . ?'

'No. Just in his younger days, man-to-man stuff, cowboy honour, that sort of thing.'

'Hey.' Gallagher was looking at her. 'You look exactly like

someone I know . . .' He squinted hard at her. 'I know you. Oh!' He reeled theatrically back in his chair. 'Oh, are you any relation—'

'Danny.'

'To Danny?'

'Yeah. He's my half-brother. Same father. Different mothers.' She pressed her lips tight and nodded, wondering how the hell Glasgow's most famous Labour party politician knew Danny.

'Very different mothers, I suspect.'

She felt strangely smug about that. 'I'm surprised you know Danny – is he a constituent of yours?'

'I don't *know* Danny. Not socially. I bump into him sometimes. I met him through Bren, did you know that?'

'My Danny?'

'Bren sent me to see Danny once, about a boy. Danny helped the boy out.'

'Oh.' No one had ever told her a pleasant story about Danny before, it was nice. Maybe that was why Danny had implied that Brendan had dealt with criminals. Maybe he meant himself.

'Very sadly, that boy died of an overdose six months later.'

'Oh.' Not such a pleasant story. It felt more realistic that it had a sad ending. 'Well, thanks very much. We should go, maybe.'

Gallagher stood up. 'I hope I've been of some help. You should ask at the airport about the politics.'

She looked at him. 'Airport?'

'The taxis.' Gallagher could see that she didn't get it. 'The co-op among the taxis.'

She shook her head.

McIlroy interjected, 'Bren was head of the taxi drivers' co-op until they got taken over. Did you not know that?'

'His wife said he drove buses.'

'Yeah,' said McIlroy, 'after he got ousted from the taxis.'

Morrow found she could hardly breathe in the airless room. 'He was the head of the co-op?'

Pete McIlroy held her eye in a way that she found a little

disconcerting, as if he knew the significance of what he was telling her: 'The taxi drivers all chipped in fifty quid a year to pay the airport for the right to the taxi stand. Then the airport got taken over by a big company. They put it out to tender. They got a massive bid from a bus company – twelve times the co-op's bid. The airport took the cash and Bren was out.'

She looked at Harris. They should have known he was a taxi driver. This far into an investigation they should at least know what the guy did for a living. Rita had lied. Donald McGlyn had lied, but it still should have come up somewhere. Harris looked stunned, he gave a little shrug.

She cleared her throat. 'And then Bren retired?'

McIlroy shrugged.

She gathered her notes and put her pen away, quickly gathering her things to go.

Kenny stood up and walked them to the door. 'Thanks for coming in,' he said, inappropriate and distracted, as if he was already onto the next thing. Morrow nodded back to the girl standing by the wall. 'Bye.'

The girl didn't look up. She seemed terribly young and very sad. Morrow didn't feel right about leaving her there.

Gallagher watched the door shut behind the police officers. He was afraid to look up, but he did, first to Jill, standing against the wall as if she was about to be shot. She didn't look back but felt him looking at her. Her chin buckled and she started to cry.

'Oh, Jill,' he said, a tired warning in his voice.

She covered her face with her hands. 'I don't want this to be me,' she sobbed, her voice muffled. 'I don't want to be . . . this . . . *me.*'

Kenny watched her, wondering if she was a suicide risk. He looked at Pete. Pete shouldn't have brought her here, not in front of other people and today of all days. It wasn't fair to him or to her.

259

'I brought Jill here,' said Pete, 'because I think we need a reality check.' He went over to her then, took her elbow and led her, blind, to a chair. Jill wept quietly behind her hands.

'Jill.' Pete was looking at Kenny. 'Jill, what are you going to say in court?'

She sighed, sat back, clutching the arms as if she was on the stand. 'Well, I'm not going to lie.'

'I don't want you to lie,' said Kenny.

'But you're claiming defamation, Kenny.' Pete spoke so loudly Kenny was a little afraid he could be heard outside. 'If people believe you, that makes her a liar. And she's young, Kenny, that's all she'll ever be to most people: a liar.'

Jill sobbed again. A tress of her blond hair slipped over her hand. She had nice hair, thick, strong hair and not dyed either, natural blond, cuffs and collars. In a good light, with the right expression on her face, it was a bit like fucking Marilyn Monroe.

Pete patted her back. 'You can go now, if you want, pet.'

She looked up at Pete helplessly and he handed her the car key. 'Go sit in the car and I'll be out in a minute. I'll drop you back home.'

She took the key slowly and stood up, turned to sniff at Kenny, to say something but stopped herself. She shuffled over to the door and stopped again with her hand on the handle.

'Jill, I'm so sorry about all of this. It was never my intention ...'

She waited, hoping perhaps that he would say something more, something useful. Kenny couldn't think of anything to say. She dropped her head and opened the door and walked away.

Kenny watched the door shut behind her. She might go and cry on the step of the office, she might be snapped out there. Pete usually took the trouble to think about his well-being and it seemed inconceivable that he hadn't done so this time. He was deliberately trying to fuck him up.

'What did you bring her here for?'

Pete snarled, 'That's what you're doing. You're ruining that girl's life. And all that bollocks about exclusion from the process, you're making it unsafe for girls like that to participate because bastards like you'll get a hold of them and fuck them. Who else is getting dragged into this? You think they won't find everyone? They already know about Derek Geller. Where did this stupid fucking idea come from, anyway?'

'Me.' But that wasn't true. A switch flicked in Kenny's mind: he knew it was Annie's idea but that would sound dumb and reckless and petty so he said again, 'Me. It was my idea. The papers can't say—'

'The paper are completely fucking IRRELEVANT, Kenny. Wake up. People have been tweeting about this for *three days*. It's true now.'

Abruptly Kenny realised that Pete was right. He felt foolish. He'd missed the point entirely. Pete finished with, 'Be a man about it, for fuck's sake.' He stepped over to the door and opened it. 'Apologise to your wife and kids and try not to do it again.'

He slammed the door behind him.

'I can't,' Kenny said quietly, but Pete was gone.

26

Morrow listened to McKechnie harangue her over the phone, her expression stony. He wanted them to come in right now. PSU were here, waiting for her, she was the primary officer and they needed the details from her.

But Morrow had already told him she wasn't coming in and they both knew she wasn't going to change her mind. 'I need to ask the Lyons about his job, sir, it's material.'

'I've given you three hours' grace already.' McKechnie was muttering into the phone; she had a feeling that the PSU officers were in his office or nearby and he was worried they would hear him. 'You've used up all your brownie points for Mullen on keeping Leonard. Do you understand?'

'I understand that, sir.'

'They're used up. You could be looking at a disciplinary here, d'you understand?'

He wouldn't discipline her. They both knew he wouldn't. He liked her and she liked him and she wasn't doing a bad thing or an unreasonable thing. All that could happen now was for their positions to get more and more entrenched. So she hung up on her supervising officer.

Ahead of them, halfway down the Great Western Road, a black cloud of heavy rain billowed along the tree-lined street, following the line of the road, bringing gloom and cold with it.

Harris stopped at the lights and indicated right as Morrow's phone rang. It was McKechnie again. She put her thumb over the speaker, pressed answer and rubbed the mouthpiece before hanging up. Then she waited for ten seconds and pressed answer so that it would be engaged and sound as if she was trying to call McKechnie.

'Harris, what do you know about the airport taxis?'

He shrugged. 'Got taken over by the McGregors out of Greenock, so that makes perfect sense.'

'They're cleaning money through the taxis, Brendan is head of the co-op, maybe they send MacLish to muscle someone and Brendan sees him. They see each other in the post office . . . He must have gotten an awful fright to help him with a robbery though.'

Harris pulled up and parked in the Lyons' street. The house was dark. 'Still out,' he said.

Rain began to wash the windscreen, heavy blinding rain. She found herself reluctant to send him out in it. 'OK, you go around the back of the house, see what you can see.' But she opened her own door to be fair and climbed out into the wet and cold herself.

Harris pulled his collar up, hunched his shoulders and made his way to the gate, disappearing behind the hedge. Her phone rang again.

'Sorry about that, sir, I was calling and you were engaged.'

'No, *you* were engaged, Morrow.'

'Look, sir, before we close it up we need to know not just why Lyons helped MacLish but why we never found out he was a taxi driver.'

'Because witnesses lie, Morrow, mystery solved.'

The rain grew suddenly heavier, bouncing off the pavement, splashing her legs and ankles, drowning out McKechnie's voice. Morrow lowered hers. 'It should have come up that he was a driver. MacLish is with the McGregors out in Greenock, that must be how they met but the fact that he was a driver, some witness would have told us. Someone's been hiding it, sir. If we've got someone in the department messing with evidence on this case, they could have done it with other cases. We can find them. PSU will love us for it.'

He hesitated at that: 'Where are you?'

'I'm at the Lyons' house. They're missing.'

'Which ones?'

'All of them.'

'Get back in thirty minutes.'

'Yes, sir.'

She hung up, considered getting back into the car, out of the rain, but felt it would seem a bit high-handed. She was weighing it up, thinking about getting back to the office and changing into a set of dry clothes, when a car turned off at the top of Lallans Road.

The headlights swept her irises as the car slowly crawled towards the far kerb, the street light catching the driver's face. He was looking at Morrow, smiling as if he knew her. He had a string of red tinsel along the dashboard of his car and a little Santa dolly hanging from his rear-view. She smiled back.

He pulled over, parked outside a cheery, bright house. Inside the living-room window a small tree was smothered in tinsel that was a match for the red stuff on the car dashboard. Beyond the tree a grey flickering light shifted on the living-room ceiling. Moving matinée movies in a warm house two days before Christmas. Morrow hunkered into her wet coat and smiled at the man getting out of his car.

'Hiya,' he said, opening the back door of the car and pulling out a heavy gift bag with cartoon penguins in Santa hats pictured on it. She half expected him to give it her, an early suburban Santa.

'Ye all right, there?'

'Aye.' She had to talk loud to be heard over the rain. 'Yourself?'

'Fan-tastic.' He held his bag up triumphantly. 'Crimbo!'

Morrow found herself grinning. He looked over at the Lyons' house.

'Ye looking for Rita over there?'

Morrow glanced back at the house and saw Harris's head as he came around the side from the back garden.

'They're not in. I'm a bit concerned.'

'Oh, they're away. They went off to Mallorca this morning. At least,' he shrugged, 'I'm assuming it's Mallorca.'

'They had suitcases with them?'

'Oh,' he pondered, 'I don't know really. They shouted over at us, "Have a nice Christmas and New Year" type thing. Like they weren't going to see me before then.'

'Was anyone with them?'

'Just that cabbie guy. They're always getting that cab.'

'Red cab?'

'Aye. Oh, hiya again.' He was looking over her shoulder at Harris. 'Did ye find out who torched Bren's taxi in the end?'

Morrow turned and saw Harris, soaked, cold, standing open-mouthed in the shadow of the burnt-out car. He stood still as the rain hit him.

The neighbour knew he had said something catastrophic. As if to mitigate whatever he had done he called again, ''Member ...? When ye just came yourself?'

Harris was looking at the ground. Rainwater ran down his face, dripped from his nose, from his lip, from his chin. He didn't raise his hands from his sides to swipe it.

Behind Morrow the man said something about Christmas and happy and hurried away. Somewhere in the street they heard him open a door, slam it shut behind him, leaving them alone in the road.

She had been in with MacLish, interviewing him with Leonard, and Harris had come back and asked the neighbours and they told him Brendan Lyons was a taxi driver and his car was firebombed. And he'd come alone, which no straight officer would ever do, because he'd known already what they would tell him. That Brendan was a taxi driver.

The rain ran down his face, dripping from his eyelashes and Harris didn't move. Morrow took three steps over to him, swung her fist as hard as she knew how and punched him in the face.

He shut his eyes as his head reeled to the left. Morrow felt the crunch of cartilage in her fingers, saw the rapid swell on his face as blood flowed to his eyes and nose.

Street lights and rain glinted on the sudden flow of black blood from his nostrils, rushing like a gutter stream onto his left shoulder. Still his hands hung limp by his side.

He turned back to face her, opened his mouth to draw breath and peeled open his already swelling eyes.

Alex Morrow couldn't bear to look at him. She raised her fist and punched him again.

PSU were already looking for Harris when they got to the station. They wanted to know how Harris's face got into that mess and also, from preliminary reports, why he had a bank account with tens of thousands of pounds coming in unrelated to his salary.

She watched him being questioned on the remote view, holding a packet of ice to his face, refusing medical attention and a lawyer.

Harris wouldn't say where the money came from or why it came or how it got in there. He refused to tell them how he came by his car or whether his wife knew about it. He refused to tell them when he first got it. And he also refused to tell them how his face came to be in such a mess.

Morrow watched him on the screen and felt the bruises on her knuckles. She felt the tingling memory of cartilage breaking, felt the crunching sensation of it in her elbow and it made her feel sick.

McCarthy came into the room and stood sadly behind her. He didn't speak. He didn't have to, his sadness was palpable.

Morrow didn't want to watch Harris being dissected in front of other people.

She walked out, downstairs, to the dark of her office and picked up the phone for Abbi Cabs.

'Abbi Cabs, where to?'

'Donny, is that you?'

'Aye, who's this?'

'DS Alex Morrow.'

'Figured you'd be calling.'

'Where are they away to?'

'Mallorca. 137 Carrer d'Alliande, near Puerto Andratx.'

'Won't they mind you telling us this?'

'You're not who they're running from.'

She heard the reproach in his voice. 'You never told me Brendan was a taxi driver.'

'Aye, I did.'

She shut her eyes tight, afraid to ask. 'When?' But her voice was too tense for him to hear her.

'Sorry?'

She cleared her throat. 'When did you tell us that?'

'To your pal, the guy that came the first time.'

'DC Harris?'

'Aye. First time.'

'Did he just come himself?'

'Aye. Said you were busy.'

She stood in the dark and swallowed hard. When she finally found her voice she thanked him for all his help and hung up.

Moving suddenly fast, she took out her mobile and Danny picked up immediately, 'All right?'

'Aye,' she said, listening to her own voice to see if it sounded normal. 'You OK?'

'Aye. What's happening?'

'Ah.' She knew why she'd called but thought it would sound strange if she blurted it out. 'Just, eh, thinking about you. I met Kenny Gallagher today. He recognised me from you.'

'What d'you mean?'

'Squinting at me and said was I your sister. Told me a nice story about you helping some wee guy out.'

She could hear Danny grinning. 'Did he, now?'

'He did, aye.'

'Aye, I seen him at a charity do the other night. Good guy, Kenny.'

'Is he?'

Danny chortled. 'D'ye not think?'

'I don't know. Seems a bit smarmy.'

'But he mentioned that he knew me, did he?'

She wanted to say something nice to someone. 'Aye, he spoke of you very highly.'

'Ah, well, he can't be all bad.'

She smiled. 'Aye, so, Danny, anyway, I meant to say to you the other day, at the christening after Christmas: Brian and I wondered if you'd be godfather.'

There was a pause on the phone. She didn't know quite what it meant until Danny spoke quietly into the receiver. 'Aye, Alex. I will be.' His voice was thick, his lips brushing the receiver. 'I will.'

She sat at her desk in her quiet office and listened to the scurry outside, heard whispered conversations and exclamations as the word about Harris spread through the division.

27

Jill Bowman got Pete McIlroy to drop her in the town. He had wanted to pick her up at her house and drop her back but she wasn't sure she wanted him to know where she lived, exactly. Jill didn't like Pete. He'd tricked her into going into the office today: he said she should come and help Kenny, talk to Kenny. Then he wouldn't even let her speak, just barked at Kenny that he was hurting Jill. It wasn't for Pete to do that, stand up for her. She could stand up for herself.

So she got him to drop her at traffic lights in town so that their goodbye was quick. She didn't want Pete near her house. Then she spent two hours wandering around the Christmas shops. She had used all the Christmas money from her dad already but she knew her aunties would give her cash as a present and lost herself in Zara, trying on things that might end up in the sale, sequined minidresses she could wear as a top over trousers, trying on boots. When her legs got tired and she ran out of patience with the crowds she caught the bus home, sitting at a window on the top deck, watching all the poor people outside ploughing their way through the blinding rainstorm. She was lucky because the bus stopped just outside her house. She didn't even have to cross the road.

She ran though, the fifty yards to the door, because the rain was coming down so heavy and it was so cold. Her fingers were numb as she worked the key into the lock.

A fug of cigarette smoke hit her nose as she opened the door. Her dad was in.

'Dad?'

'Aye. Here.' He was sitting in his 'office', a space under the stairs, surfing the internet for the *real* story behind major world events, none of them current. The assassination of the Archduke Ferdinand, 9/11, AIDS, Nigerian oil workers, anything irrelevant to his own life commanded his obsessive attention. He distrusted everything but the internet.

She walked over to him. 'What ye looking at?'

'Just some stuff about the riots. I'm going out for fags, want anything?'

Jill thought her way through the petrol station shelves. 'Nah.' What she really wanted was a cup of tea and her jim-jams on and a watch at some shite on the telly.

'OK.' He stood up, his eyes still on the screen. 'Don't touch that because it takes me to a link I want.' He looked at her. 'Where were you today?'

'Just in the town.'

'With Shelly?'

'Aye, with Shelly.'

'Righto.' He pulled on his coat and a heavy woolly hat. 'Not be long.' He slammed the door behind him.

Jill took off her jacket and hung it on a hanger so it would dry in the right shape. She sat on the bottom step and pulled off her silver high heels. She'd worn them because she knew she was going to see Kenny but he hadn't even looked at her, not properly. She remembered when he did look at her properly. She remembered when he couldn't stop looking at her, touching her. She remembered the thrill of that first time, when he came to her room in Inverness and said he'd never met anyone like her and did she feel it too and she felt faint that he'd noticed her, him, Kenny Gallagher.

As they lay on the bed, him devouring her, kissing her, loving her without even taking his trousers off properly because he was in such a hurry, she felt so special, so extraordinary, because she'd seen pictures of his wife, she knew she was gorgeous and yet he was with Jill. She was even better than his wife.

She was thinking about Annie Gallagher when the doorbell rang, making her jump. Her dad would have his key. He wouldn't ring, not unless he knew she was still just inside the door. Jill stood still, looking at the door, waiting for another clue. The bell rang again, followed immediately by an urgent rap on the door. Not her dad. A journalist. They had found her address. Or worse, it was Pete.

Cringing, she tiptoed over to the door and heard a sing-song voice, a man: 'I know you're in there!'

He said it as if it was a joke and he was a friend but she didn't know the voice. Not Pete.

She looked out through the peephole. A young guy, quite handsome, she didn't know him. He wore jeans and a green jacket, quite cool and had a bag, the strap slung across his chest, a brass buckle on it. It was raining but he didn't look that wet. He'd been in a car. He looked back at her through the peephole and smiled softly. 'Gonnae open the door? It's battering down out here.'

'Are you a journalist?'

'No.'

Jill dropped back onto her heels. 'Who are you then?'

'God, honestly, I'm about as far from a journalist as you can get.'

He was good-looking, about her age and he wasn't a journalist.

Jill brushed her hair off her face, pulled her top straight and her jeans up before she opened the front door, just a bit, and peeped out. 'Who are you then?'

He looked her up and down, seemed to like what he saw because a broad, warm smile broke out over his face. He looked so handsome that it took her a moment to notice the other man swinging around from the right. He'd been standing flush to the outside wall and this was a different kind of man: scruffy, sunken cheeks and eyes, a snarling man. He stuck his foot in the space at the open door as if he was stamping on a spider.

Jill glanced back at the handsome man and his knee was raised to his chest, like a dance.

The foot flew forward, the sole of it kicked the flat of the door, smashing it open, throwing her back into the hallway, ripping her top at the shoulder. Blood on her shoulder, actually running down her arm, and she shouted, 'For fuck's sake!' at them and 'You've cut my fucking arm!'

As if they couldn't even hear her the men walked casually into the hall and Jill held her arm and realised that this was a different order of things. They didn't care that they had cut her or ripped her top.

They looked around, the scruffy one bent backwards as he looked into all the rooms, making sure no one else was there.

'Get out,' she said weakly. 'You can't . . .'

The scruffy one, the nasty-looking one, looked at her then and licked the side of his mouth. Behind them a key scratched at the lock and Jill shouted for him. 'Dad!' she screamed, 'Help me!'

The handsome man turned swiftly, twisted the lock and yanked the door open revealing her father on the step, holding his little front door key like a tiny gun. 'Who's—'

'They've broke in,' Jill shouted. 'Dad!'

Her dad looked to the men for an explanation but the scruffy one reached up, knocked her dad's woolly hat off his head and grabbed a fist full of his hair, pulling down, making her dad double over as he was dragged into the hallway and the hand-some one slammed the door shut.

The scruffy man swung her dad around in a circle, pulled and pulled, faster and faster, smiling, letting off a little squeal at one point, making her dad stumble over his own feet. Then the scruffy man's face fell straight, as if he had lost interest in the game and he slammed her dad, crown first, into the wall by the living room. Her father slid down the wall.

The scruffy man leaned over him and shouted, *'He's,'* spit flecked on her father's face, 'wanting to talk to his girlfriend. You gonnae fucking shut up?'

She watched as her father curled up tight, eyes clenched, knees contracting to his chest as the scruffy man shouted, "Cause it's none-of-your-fucking-business.'

'Dad,' shouted Jill, sobbing now. 'That's not my boyfriend.'

But she didn't know if her father could hear her because he didn't open his eyes.

'Well.' The scruffy man had dropped his voice. 'Mibbi he will be in a minute.'

Her dad kept his eyes shut but tried to move then still clutching his head, pushing himself up the wall. They watched him for a minute, his long legs scrabbling against the carpet, like a foal trying to stand for the first time. Then the scruffy man raised his hand slow and slammed a fist down on his crown again. Jill's dad dropped heavily onto his side. He didn't move.

'Dad!'

The handsome one put his hand on Jill's shoulder, spun her round to face the stairs and shoved her, making her walk up them, punching her on the back when she stumbled.

Jill turned on the half landing, saw her father's feet twitching. She heard a cough, wet, a rattle.

He punched her to her bedroom door and she stood, trembling, the pink sign *Jill's Room* blurred by tears. Jill knew that she should not go in there but a thump on her back made her lurch heavy, slump against the door and he opened it so that she fell into the dark, on to the floor.

Jill Bowman was a messy person. She didn't open the curtains in her bedroom because the neighbours across the road could see in. It was always twilight in there.

He kicked her soles, getting her feet out of the way, as if she was a bag blocking an aisle, and shut the door behind them.

He flicked on the light. 'Sit,' he said, looking at the messy bed.

Jill scrambled up to her feet. She looked at her books, at her desk with her college work open on it, at her bag by the chair. She looked at the photos on her wall, her in Madrid with the school, her in fancy dress, her in Inverness, and she began to cry, hands limp at her sides. She had no idea what to do.

'Fucking . . .' Exasperated, he punched her on the side of the head, a sharp hard blow, and she twisted as she fell face first onto the bed, her own little bed, bouncing on her face, still crying, her mouth frozen open.

Twisting around to free her mouth she looked up at him. He was a different person from down here. He looked furious, disgusted and bared his teeth.

'*Why do you make me do this to you?*'

He waited for an answer. Jill didn't know what he was talking about and she couldn't think of anything to say that wouldn't make it worse. She was crying, panting and he looked terrifying. She shut her eyes then, felt the bed bounce beneath her as he dropped a heavy knee next to her hip. She smelled crisps, cheese and onion crisps, on his breath. He leaned in and whined low, 'You do it, when *ye know* what I'll do?'

She was glad she couldn't see him. He jabbed a punch into her back, on the kidney, and she arched reflexively but it wasn't that sore. As if correcting his mistake he punched her in the same place with the knuckle of his middle finger sticking out and a web of pain made her back spasm into a sharp arc. Then he went for her stomach. Not a punch, worse than a punch: his hands grabbed the waistband of her jeans and he climbed off the bed, trying to yank them down, the other hand grabbing her knickers and pulling at them too. But Jill stayed on her side, scissoring her legs until she felt the weight of him shift back off the bed. He was over her, holding her jeans front and back and pulled them off until they were dangling from her ankles.

Then his mouth was by her ear, sour cheese, his hand was on

her thigh and he slapped and punched her legs open and shoved his fingers into her.

'See: this is what happens to bitches that fucking clipe.' He shoved his hand hard into her again. 'Say Kenny Gallagher never touched ye or I'll come back and I'll cut the cunt out of ye.'

Her eyes were open now. They were wide open, staring at the wall, taking in everything in her peripheral vision. He got off her, stood up, wiped his finger clean on the leg of her dangling jeans and adjusted the strap on his messenger bag.

'See, hen? This is what happens when ye play with big boys. Big boys play big-boy games. Not nice, is it?'

Jill kept staring at the wall, at the pink wall, as the bedroom door opened. A green smudge left the room.

She heard the sound of her dad groaning very far away. Then the front door opened. Then it shut. And then they were gone.

28

Hot rain, a damp wind blowing in off the Mediterranean and the effort of climbing the deceptively steep hills around Puerto Andratx made Morrow sweat deep into her coat. The holiday town seemed deserted in the pause between Christmas and New Year, or maybe the locals knew better than to try and walk around at lunchtime. McCarthy, walking next to her, seemed to find it exhilarating, smiling and panting as they took the steep road, reading the numbers on the walls shoring small houses up on the hillside for a peek at the sea.

They found themselves beyond the Lyons' house number, doubled back, checked their notes before finding a small break that led to a tall narrow alleyway around the back of one of the bigger houses. The ground was worn bare through the dark green undergrowth, the chalky soil beneath damp and grey.

Morrow, uncertain, kept her wits about her, watching the end of the alley for clues, aware that McCarthy was behind her and had her back.

At the end, the space opened up to reveal a modest house, more of a shack than a home. It was squat and shuttered, painted faded-rose plaster with a sloping shingle roof and a plain chimney. To the side of the yard, against a wall, stood a big blue sign 'Se Vende'.

Hot and angry, thinking about Harris, Morrow hurried along the uneven paving to the splintered green front door and knocked hard.

They could hear a radio inside, pop music, bouncing off the

low stone rooms and a woman shouting in the high, dissonant voice mothers use to be heard over traffic.

Rita opened the door. 'Oh, you didn't walk, did you?'

McCarthy answered, 'The taxi driver dropped us down the hill, he couldn't find the address.'

But Rita wasn't listening, she was reading Morrow's face. 'You better come in.'

Rita, Morrow and McCarthy sat on a stone bench under the lemon trees in the small garden, the scent of the lemon flowers sweet and pungent when the light breeze shook the tree. Rosie, looking happy and content, brought them out a big bottle of 7Up, three plastic beakers and a bag of salty crisps on a tray.

Morrow and McCarthy wore heavy, dark clothes, thick material, completely wrong for the climate. Rita wore sandals and a loose dress with a green print.

She apologised for leaving Scotland without informing the police. They had to get out, she said, it wasn't safe.

'What makes you sure you're any safer here?' asked Morrow, wondering at the tinge of spite in her own voice.

Rita waved a hand dismissively. 'These are not international people,' she said. 'They want us out of the way, so we're out of the way. They could find us but why bother? It's a different matter if we're just down the hill.'

Morrow asked her what she really wanted to know: 'How did you get the money to buy this place?'

'Martin Pavel gave it to us.'

'He just gave it to you?'

'He sent us ahead on a private plane. Rosie said we need to get out of here and within two hours we were in the air.'

'He sent you "ahead"?'

'He's moved in over there.' She pointed vaguely up the hill.

'Martin Pavel's here too?'

'Yes.' Rita blinked disapprovingly. 'He's not my sort of person at all but . . .'

'Oh, are Rosie and he . . . ?'

'No.' Rita looked hard at Morrow and gave a hopeless little shrug. 'Not even that. Who the hell knows? He's doing our gardening.' She took a crisp and ate it indignantly. 'He's building a vegetable garden.'

'Are they just pals then?'

She shrugged and chewed. 'Who the hell knows. I hate young people. They confuse me.'

Morrow looked up the hill. Villas jostled with each other for a view of the sea. None of them looked very fancy.

'Rita, you lied to me about Brendan's job.'

'I did.' Rita lifted the bottle of 7Up and poured them each a glass. 'We don't trust the police. We've been to the police about all of this and nothing happened.'

'I understand that,' said Morrow.

Rita poured and looked up at her. 'Are you going to explain to me how that happened?'

Morrow watched the bubbles pop on the surface. She didn't know what to say. People I trusted were lying shits. 'It's part of an ongoing investigation—'

'Into *what?*'

She wanted Morrow to say 'police corruption'.

'The operation of various gangs in Glasgow and the outlying areas . . .'

'Bribes,' said Rita, mocking.

Morrow looked at Rita's smug face and recalled the sickening crunch in her elbow. 'OK, Rita, we're here two days before New Year to try and find out what actually happened to your husband.'

'In Mallorca with your work. How awful for you.'

'Well, it is awful for me. I had twin boys four months ago and I want to be at home. But I'm not home. I got up at three thirty this morning to come here because I don't want it to happen to anyone else. Will you help me?'

Rita held Morrow's eye as she lifted her lemonade to her mouth, her tongue darting out to meet the edge of the plastic cup and guide it in. She drank and put the cup down on the tray. 'Well,' she said, enjoying the power differential between them, 'You'll have to tell me what you don't know—'

'Greenock.'

Rita took her cigarette holder out of her pocket, broke it apart and put in a fresh plastic filter. Then she took out a cigarette and fitted it to the end and lit it. 'Brendan was taken to Greenock.'

'The gunman came from Greenock.'

Rita nodded. 'I heard that.'

'Tell me what happened in Greenock.'

Rita drew hard on her cigarette. 'Bren went to work.' She got lost in the memory for a while, and brought herself back. 'He went to work, arrived at the taxi rank, at the back. Two guys got in. Bren said to them, 'No, sorry, you have to go to the front cab' but then he looked back and they had a big gun. They said we're from the McGregors, drive us to Greenock. The boss wants to talk to you. So he drove them to Greenock. You've heard of the McGregors? They're never out of the papers.'

'I've heard about them. Whereabouts in Greenock did they get Brendan to drive them to?'

'Some club, he didn't know it, they had to direct him. Said it was a pit. An old bar painted black on the outside and they took him down to the cellar and through some big metal doors. No windows, and just two chairs, like old office chairs. And they sat him down in one. In the other chair was a man and his face was beaten so badly Bren couldn't tell if he was a young man or an old man. He was tied into the chair and just sort of sagged there, groaning, while they talked to Bren. There was blood on the floor around him . . .'

'What did they say to Bren?'

279

'"Be reasonable."' Tears trembled in her eyes. 'It sounded ridiculous but that's what they said, "Be reasonable."'

'They did all this for control of the taxis? It's a lot of trouble for a money-laundering outlet. Couldn't they just open nail bars?'

'No, no it's much more than that. Bren used to say that taxis are the arteries of the city. They use them to clean money, sure, but they can move packages, pick people up, kidnap people with them, they know where everyone is and where they're going. Bren used to say that if you own the taxis you own the city.'

'Who was the other guy in the cellar?'

She shrugged. 'They never mentioned him. Bren said it was like he wasn't there. He was just there to scare Bren, show him what they'd do. Then they said they knew Rosie and Joe and me and Mum, they knew the nursery and to back off. And they let him go.'

'What happened then?'

'He was so scared he cried all the way home. He had to pull over on the motorway. He wasn't a man to cry.'

'Did he give up politics then?'

'No. Next day he got up and went to work and carried on talking to guys about a counter-bid and organising themselves. Then the taxi was firebombed outside the house, so that was it. He reported it to your mob, told them everything and they never contacted him again. He phoned and phoned but they never had any information.'

'Do you know who he spoke to?'

'No. He didn't want me to know. Said it would be safer that way.'

Morrow thought of Leonard, how she was right, that they would ask one cop to lose a file, one cop to drop a caution, all tiny infringements building to something as big as this: a good man like Brendan Lyons having to leave the country for his own safety.

'He gave up then?'

Rita hesitated. 'You know, all through the seventies and eight-ies nothing could stop him. In the end I said to him, Bren, you've tried, let's just go to Mallorca. This isn't our fight any more.'

'Was that the plan?'

'Aye.'

'What about Rosie and Joe?'

'They were going to stay there, for school. That's why we were keeping the house. We thought, she can have the house and we'll come and stay and it'll be fine.' She looked down. 'They probably can't go back now. Joe certainly can't go back to nursery. There was a spotter outside the day after Bren died.'

'Did Brendan mention any names? Of the guys in Greenock?'

Rita looked at her as if she was stupid. 'How do I know you're any better?'

They caught the evening flight back and Morrow was glad that McCarthy was seated four rows away from her. She watched out of the aeroplane window, following the flight path in the in-flight magazine. She glimpsed Spain through the broken cloud and saw the cloud-capped peaks of the snowy Pyrenees. As she watched she thought about Harris and Francesca Costello and MacLish and dapper, honourable Brendan Lyons pulling his car over on the road back from Greenock to cry about what he had seen.

She thought herself into his place, waiting in a queue at the post office, in a Christmas list reverie, pushing her twins in their double buggy. And then MacLish coming in, someone coming in, with a gun. She looked at him and knew him, and he looked back and knew her. She felt their eyes meeting and the spongy handle of the buggy as she squeezed it hard. He wouldn't be able to let her pick him out of a line-up: his bosses would kill him for going out on his own. From the moment their eyes locked MacLish was going to kill Brendan Lyons.

In the noisy cabin, looking down in the dark at the snow-capped

Pyrenees, Morrow saw the dirty floor, felt herself move away from the double buggy, encourage a bystander to step closer, to claim the boys for their own. She saw herself walk over to the gunman and help him. She felt the sting on her palm as she slapped an innocent woman and the cold draught on her ankles from the door as he stood in front of her and lowered his gun to her belly. She looked up at a sun setting over a wide, flat prairie of soft white cloud and knew that she would have been half glad as the barrel was lowered because she had got him to the door and her boys were safe.

In the newspaper stands inside the airport every national and local paper carried the same story: Jill Bowman was denying that she had an affair with Kenny Gallagher. It was a bitter slur against a brave man.

'He's going to get a fortune for that,' said McCarthy.

They didn't have any luggage and so were the first out to the cab rank.

A man dressed for an arctic winter asked them where they were going.

'Glasgow,' said McCarthy, fooled by his short spell in warmer weather into standing tall in the rain.

The man waved them to the front cab.

They got in, sliding the door shut after them and the taxi took off.

'Is that the London flight in?' asked the cabbie, glancing at them in the mirror.

Morrow was lost in her own thoughts. 'No.'

He swerved around two roundabouts and took the slip road onto the motorway. His eyes kept flicking back to them in the mirror, as if he was guessing who they were, where they'd been.

'We're police officers,' she said finally. 'We're investigating Brendan Lyons' murder.'

'Brendan?' He shifted upright in his seat. 'Is that right? I heard about that.'

'Did you know him?'

'No, before my time, I only got my licence eight months ago. Heard about him though.'

'Did you hear about the McGregors?'

'Oh, aye.'

'Aren't you afraid to work here?'

'What other option have I? I'm not working the city, that's for sure, it's worse there. My cousin worked the city taxis, weekends only. Weekend nights, it's a parallel universe, all drugs business, but you know that.'

McCarthy nodded amiably. Morrow didn't.

'I mean, my cousin, yeah? He had no idea when he started, you know, he only did it for two years and it was good money right enough, but he had no idea how extensive the problem was in Glasgow, just no clue. You don't unless you're on a rough scheme, do you?'

'Hm.'

'The stories he told us, honest to God . . .'

'Like what?'

'Oh, drunks, lap dancers, stab victims going to hospital. Chaos. City's in chaos.'

The driver didn't understand that they heard the stories as a reproach to them, to the job they were doing, so he ploughed on, warming to his story.

'One guy was famous for hailing a taxi and spending the night getting dropped off at various places, nipping in and getting the taxi to wait. Did that all night. Big tipper too. My cousin got paid three hundred pounds by him one night. He hated it. He said he felt like a drug dealer.'

Morrow couldn't take it any more. 'What can we do if people like you take their money?'

He heard the anger in her voice, and answered her quietly,

'Well, in his defence, he never took that call again, left it to the others to rush over to get him.'

They were approaching the Kingston Bridge, normally a slow area of traffic, but the roads were almost deserted because of the holidays and they sped along the dip and up and over the river.

'What do you mean "took the call"? How could your cousin know the call was from him?' asked Morrow. 'Did he always come from the same address?'

'No, no, from his phone number. If you call once your number is stored on the system. Where you go, where you're coming from. All that.'

They had Leonard's number and Gobby's. They had all their numbers. They had the address of the post office. They knew where everyone was going, where they came from, who was going to the airport with suitcases and it was all stored in the computers of a taxi firm owned by the McGregors.

'Is that true for all the taxi firms?'

'Oh, aye,' he said, 'any taxi firm with a switchboard.'

29

Kenny Gallagher sat at a table enjoying the warmth of the New Year's Eve sun on his face, the company of his beautiful wife and the luxury of wearing shades in winter. Annie had shades on too. They suited her. Her heavy coat was open to accommodate the winter sun and she was wearing a tight white dress. He loved her. He was glad they were back to normal. He'd chanced his career to keep her and won.

It was a good restaurant, right in a pedestrian precinct with a lot of nice shops, walled in by plastic hedges, warmed by overhead heaters. It was space for the smokers, really, but on a crisp day it was a lovely place to eat.

In front of him lay the rubble of an excellent meal; lemon sole on a bed of steamed spinach, served with warm bread. Full but not too full. Warm but not too warm. And now, unexpectedly, rich but not too rich. Globe Media had settled out of court before the ink was dry on Jill Bowman's interview.

Kenny was content for the first time in a long time. They had been to the bank this morning, to pay the cheque in, and he suggested lunch. When they left here today, when Kenny dropped her home, he'd pop in to the house on the pretext of seeing the kids, hang about for supper maybe. He'd wait and get the kids to bed and then when the bells came, he'd broach the subject of moving back in. Annie hadn't brought it up, but she was here with him, having lunch, and it was nice.

Passing shoppers in Buchanan Street looked at them, their eye drawn by Kenny Gallagher, Gallant Gallagher, and his fine wife.

The waiter came over, lifted their plates and cleared the table, using a little brush to clean the linen cloth of crumbs.

'Anything else for you, sir?'

He looked at Kenny, face twitching, recognising him.

'I'd like a coffee and a cognac. Do you have Delamaine?'

'Extra de Grande Champagne, sir?'

'How much is that? Per glass?'

'I believe it's twenty-three pounds.'

Kenny raised his eyebrows at Annie.

'No,' she said, 'that's crazy money . . .'

'Come on, it's New Year's Eve.' He held two fingers up to the waiter.

'Two coffee cognac, sir?'

'Yes, please.'

She looked at him reproachfully as the waiter left. 'We didn't get that much money out of them, Kenny. You have to remember that you won't be working this year.'

He took her hand and squeezed it. 'This once.'

Annie pulled her hand away. 'On the subject of that, Kenny, you not standing again: I was, um, approached.'

He grinned. 'Oh, really? Who approached you?'

She spoke quietly. 'Alison Collins.'

The Assassin. He was surprised by that. 'God, I thought she hated me. Never imagined she would want me back.'

'No.' Annie reached halfway across the table to his hand and then drew back, as if she couldn't bring herself to touch him. 'No, Kenny, Alison approached me to see if *I* would stand.'

'*You?*'

The coffee arrived. The waiter set the table with great ceremony: the cafetière, the milk, coffee sugar, petits fours and two enormous crystal balloons with radiant, caramel brandy.

He gave them a little talk about the brandy, a history of it, delivered in a sonorous voice. Annie busied herself pouring just her own coffee, putting the milk in, leaving Kenny to listen.

The waiter ordered them to enjoy and left them alone.

Kenny leaned across to her. '*You*, stand for election?'

'Why not?'

'Well.' He gave a little laugh. 'For a start, you don't have any experience.'

'Neither did you when you first stood. And I've been in the party for as long as you have.'

It was nonsense. The Assassin was shit-stirring, that was all. It was nonsense. Who'd look after the kids all day? She hadn't thought it through properly. Kenny smiled and lifted his glass and toasted her. 'Well.' He tried to keep it light. 'That's a turn up.'

But Annie didn't reciprocate the tone. She said heavily, 'Not to me, it isn't, Kenny. You know I've always had ambitions.'

Kenny thought she'd given that up. She hadn't mentioned it in a long time. But he didn't want to argue with her, not today, not if he was hoping to move back. He smiled noncommittally and swirled his brandy glass, sniffed the sweet woody nose, raised the rich brandy to his mouth and sipped. Warm and deep, the cognac slid into him, radiated warmth and goodwill from his gut to his finger tips. That was a cheap shot by the Assassin. She was a cow.

Annie lifted her glass. 'God, twenty-three pounds ...'

They each took a chocolate and bit them. The conjoined flavours of coffee and cognac and chocolates were delicious, rich, and they calmed him, made him feel as if everything would be all right. He'd stay for supper. They could talk about it then. He thought about her pissing at him and his hand strayed to his hairline, to the little bump left by the scab she had made.

The door of the restaurant opened behind them. A drunk woman in a very expensive fur coat was helped down the narrow path to the street, tittering to herself as she leaned on the arm of a cross man, possibly her husband.

She turned to the audience as her embarrassed husband manhandled her out of the hedged corral. 'Hippy New Year, everyone!'

Everyone raised their glasses and cheered back 'Happy New Year!' and even her husband smiled and said 'And you' back. By the time the couple reached the end of the street they were hugging and laughing.

'Hiya.' Danny McGrath stood beyond the hedge, grinning at them. He wasn't wearing a coat, just a washed-out black jumper, as if he had just gotten out of a car.

'Danny,' Annie called over to him playfully, 'd'you never wear a coat?'

Danny grinned at that. 'I do sometimes . . .'

'Shouldn't this be one of those times? It's so cold.'

'Hey, Danny,' said Kenny, 'come and join us. Let's have a New Year drink together.'

Danny didn't drink, everyone knew that about him. He never lost control. He grinned. 'Do they do Irn-Bru there?'

'They do everything here,' said Kenny, not certain that they did serve Irn-Bru.

Danny obviously didn't want to sit with them. He hesitated by the hedge, but then changed his mind. 'Auch, why not?'

Grinning, he came around to the entrance and looked around for a chair. He found one at another table and pulled it over, scraping the feet of the chair across the concrete, soiling the mellow mood of the place.

'Where's the waiter?' Annie sat up and looked around.

'I think he's inside,' Kenny said, watching Danny sit the chair nearer to her than him.

'I'll get him.' Annie took her napkin from her lap and put it on the table, stood up, wobbled daintily on an ankle but caught herself. 'Gheesh,' she said. 'I never drink during the day and this is why.' And she went indoors.

'So,' said Danny sitting back, 'you won, man.'

Kenny toasted Danny with twenty-three quid cognac. 'I won.'

'Congratulations.'

'Thanks. Thanks,' Kenny said. 'I appreciated what you were

saying that night, Danny, about being a big fish in a wee pond.'

Danny drew a breath through his teeth. 'Aye,' he hissed. 'They'll go for you.'

'Make stuff up,' said Kenny.

'So they will,' nodded Danny. 'Whatever would really hurt you, they'll make it up.'

'Pull you back down to their level.'

'That's right, man.'

They nodded together, keeping time, brotherly metronomes.

'What you doing for the bells?' asked Danny.

'Probably just home with the wife and the kids.'

He seemed surprised by that. 'Really?' He grinned then and took a chocolate without asking, throwing the whole thing in his mouth, though there were two or three bites in each.

Kenny watched him, thinking about Annie and the Assassin, and was struck by the sense that everything seemed vaguely sinister, suddenly.

'Well,' grinned Danny, his teeth smeared brown, 'wish I could. Got a do I have to go to. Full of wee fish. Big yins and wee yins.' He leaned over to the side, into Kenny, and whispered softly, 'I run the taxis.'

'To the do?' said Kenny, thinking it was a charity for wheelchair users or their families or something.

'No. *I run the taxis.*'

Kenny smiled. It sounded like a punchline or a code, but Danny didn't smile back. Kenny felt he should say something. 'Yeah?'

'Yeah,' Danny echoed back, telling him it was OK. 'Legitimate. It's all legitimate. You didn't know that about me, did you?'

'Um, no.'

'No one does. I can't get a licence, I have to run it under someone else's name.'

The conversation was going in an odd direction; Kenny wished Annie would come back.

''S a shame, you know?' continued Danny. 'Because you can't get the credit for it, know?'

'Sure.'

'People don't really know who ye are . . .' Danny was looking at him intently. 'And legit businesses are a pain, you know? Have to keep records of everything. In taxis you need to keep a record of where they went, when they went, so the taxman knows you're not skimming. Pain in the arse.'

'That's the modern world,' said Kenny, wondering if Annie had gone to the toilet, and if she had, whether she would have gone to the one upstairs or, further away, downstairs.

Danny was on a roll: 'They make you keep records for tax purposes. When you're picked up or dropped off they keep records.' He looked at Kenny. '*For years.*'

Kenny realised suddenly that Danny wasn't just chatting, enjoying the sun and chatting, that Danny was telling him something significant.

'Changed her story, didn't she?' Danny smiled. '*Bowman.*'

Kenny shrugged. He didn't like this.

'Can I . . . ?' Danny's big hand was over the plate of petits fours, a slim porcelain dish with a row of six exquisite chocolates on it.

'Please.'

He picked up the dark cocoa truffle and threw it into his mouth like a pill. Kenny heard the hard chocolate coating snap between his teeth.

Danny said, 'Sent some of my guys to see that lassie, have a word.'

'. . . Guys?'

A woman brushed past Kenny, squeezing between him and the chair next to his, casting a deep shadow of chill over him. Even after she had passed by Kenny felt colder.

'Got records of you going to her house, man. There and back. Fifteen times in one month. Dropping her home after late nights in the office. Taxis from trains and hotels. You and her. Dates, times, everything.'

Kenny saw Danny clearly now, a thug in a cheap jumper, cold, scary, and how he had been waiting all these years for a flaw to exploit.

'See, I want a licence for the taxis,' said Danny quietly. 'I want to move up a stair.'

'Danny, I can't do that. That's a local council matter and I'm a member of the parliament. I won't even be that soon.'

Danny was leaning towards him and he spoke very quietly, 'You find a way. Or I'll fuck you up.'

Annie appeared at the door to the restaurant, shades still on, and sashayed towards them. With a slender hand she stroked her right buttock, flatting her skirt behind her knee as she sat down. 'Waiter's coming. What have you two been talking about?'

Kenny left it to Danny to answer. 'Resolutions.'

Annie looked sceptical and Danny gave her a languorous smile. 'Nah, OK, ye caught me in a lie. Business.'

'Not today. Let's have ten minutes off. It's boring.'

'It's not boring to us, is it, Kenny?'

Kenny raised his balloon glass and emptied it, holding the brandy in his mouth so long that he scalded his tongue. He put the glass down on the crisp white linen. Twenty-three quid. He couldn't taste the good in it now, just the burn, and he saw then, clinging to the inside of the glass, an oily smear, iridescent amber in the bright New Year sun.